# THE GLASS CHAMELEON

*Too many people with secrets. Morgan Lee knew who they were and what they wanted to hide. That's probably why he's dead.*

Ageing Indianapolis private detective Deets Shanahan is asked by an old enemy to investigate a murder – one to which his old adversary could be linked. He says no, but Howie Cross, Shanahan's sometime partner, takes the case and finds links to the crime in lush and decadent New Orleans, where he looks for something – anything – that will shed light on the case.

# THE GLASS CHAMELEON

Ronald Tierney

**Severn House Large Print**
London & New York

This first large print edition published 2010
in Great Britain and the USA by
SEVERN HOUSE PUBLISHERS LTD of
9-15 High Street, Sutton, Surrey, SM1 1DF.
First world regular print edition published 2006 by
Severn House Publishers Ltd., London and New York.

British Library Cataloguing in Publication Data

Tierney, Ronald.
    Glass chameleon. -- (The Deets Shanahan mysteries)
    1. Shanahan, Deets (Fictitious character)--Fiction.
    2. Private investigators--Louisiana--New Orleans--
    Fiction. 3. Detective and mystery stories. 4. Large type
    books.
    I. Title II. Series
    813.5'4-dc22

    ISBN-13: 978-0-7278-7828-1

Printed and bound in Great Britain by
MPG Books Ltd, Bodmin, Cornwall.

# One

Drifting out of sleep, Shanahan thought he heard a dog barking. It sounded as if it came from somewhere else in the neighborhood. Then, as his brain lost all traces of whatever cinematic images flashed on the inside of his sleeping skull, the seventy-year-old gained a bit of clarity. He realized that the whir of the air-conditioner and the closed bedroom door made a near sound seem distant.

The sound came again. It was Casey, Shanahan's sixty-pound hound, barking up against the bedroom door. Whatever it was that caused his dog to bark wasn't serious. Shanahan could tell the difference between kinds of barks. There was a serious growling bark for wild animals – raccoons, possums. Another was a short yip just to get attention, often playful. There was a standard simple, but repetitive, bark for unfamiliar sounds or people. This one was just a mild alarm: 'Wake up. Something's going on.'

Shanahan sat up carefully, so he wouldn't disturb Maureen. She slept on her side, face away from him and towards the door. He could make that out in the light from the digits on the clock radio. The numbers cast a dim blue light, just enough illumination for the eye to discern shapes in the room – and in a harsher way tell the time: 3:10 a.m.

He slipped out of bed barefoot, grabbed the robe hanging on the hook on the bedroom door. He ventured against the rush of heavy August heat into the small hallway that separated the two bedrooms. Casey walked beside him through the living room to the door. Shanahan preferred to walk the distance in the dark so he could see before he was seen.

He peered out of the single pane of glass of the front door, reached to his right and flicked on the porch light.

The man outside was looking down. Sad. Or patiently waiting. Shanahan waited. The man looked up, giving Shanahan a full, bearded face. It was Max Rafferty, a lieutenant, last Shanahan heard, usually devoted to public relations for the Indianapolis Police Department. Not an on-duty kind of cop. Also, not a friend, so this wasn't likely a friendly call. It could only be trouble.

Shanahan opened the door.

'Sorry,' Rafferty said, barely above a whisper.

'What's going on?' Shanahan asked, his voice conveying more annoyance than he felt.

6

'I want to talk.'

'At three in the morning?'

'Yes, I'm afraid so.'

Shanahan had a moment of panic. Was Rafferty here to give him some bad news? Had someone he loved died? He tried to imagine who that could be.

'What's wrong?'

'Can I come in, please?'

Shanahan stepped back, switched on a lamp by the sofa. Rafferty came in.

'Hotter in here than outside,' Rafferty said, forcing a smile. He sat on the edge of the sofa, far forward, uneasy, not committing to stay. He wore an expensive black linen sports coat, a loose-fitting black silk T-shirt and black pants.

'Looking pretty slim there, all in black,' Shanahan said, almost adding something snide and mean. But there was something wrong with Rafferty. Really wrong.

'I need your help,' Rafferty said hoarsely, looking down, leaning forward and hunched into himself. He cleared his throat. 'I know, given what we've been through, it's pretty weird that I'm coming to you. I have no one else.'

'Go on.' Shanahan pulled his robe tighter.

'This isn't easy,' Rafferty said. 'If you wouldn't mind, could you sit down? This might take a while.'

'Maybe I should put on some coffee.'

'Yeah.' Rafferty buried his head in his hands. 'Yeah. Maybe.'

Shanahan, in the kitchen, flicked on the light. He wasn't ready for that much light. He put beans in the electric grinder, smothered it with a towel before pressing the button so the sound wouldn't waken Maureen. He poured water in the automatic coffee maker, put the coffee in a filter and set the machine to its task. When he came back in, it appeared that Rafferty hadn't moved at all.

Shanahan sat across from him in an upholstered chair. He thought Rafferty looked totally exhausted, drained. Something was definitely wrong.

'It'll be a few minutes, so why don't you tell me what you're here to tell me.'

'How ... how do you feel about homosexuals?'

That came out of left field. It took Shanahan a moment to gather his thoughts.

'I don't know. I don't think about it.' He didn't like questions like this. 'Makes no difference to me. I don't try to run other people's lives. Only people I have problems with are bullies.' The last sentence was meant to sting. 'Why?'

'I'll get to it. Tonight, I visited someone. Someone I visit regularly. We're close.' Rafferty looked at Shanahan squarely, then went on. 'Got there at midnight. Not unusual. It's the way things are.'

Rafferty was speaking slowly. It was clear to Shanahan that the cop was trying hard to keep his words or his emotion under control.

'OK,' Shanahan said.

'Shanahan...' Rafferty struggled with his voice. 'He was dead.' Rafferty's voice broke at 'dead'. He turned away, body twisted. His shoulders shook.

'I'll check the coffee,' Shanahan said, on his feet and heading toward the kitchen. He didn't know what to do when people cried, let alone when a man wept. It was even more problematical when it was someone he disliked. He stood in the kitchen, just staring at the coffee maker. He counted to ten slowly. He went to the cabinet and plucked from the shelf a bottle of J.W. Dant and two glasses and returned to the living room.

Rafferty was composed. 'Sorry.'

Shanahan nodded, set the glasses down on the coffee table and poured what would be a couple of shots into each glass. He took one with him back to the chair.

'You're probably a Scotch man, but all I have is bourbon.'

'It'll do the trick, thanks.' Rafferty took a sip.

'How did he die?'

'Bullet to the head.'

'Suicide?'

'No, I thought so at first, but there was no gun.'

'What do the police say?'

'I called. Anonymously.'

This was trouble, real trouble, Shanahan thought. 'Why anonymously?' he asked, though he was pretty sure he wasn't going to like the answer.

'I need some time,' Rafferty said. 'I need some help.'

'You just made me an accomplice,' Shanahan said.

'I know. Worse, you don't owe me one. You owe me nothing.'

'Why me?'

'I don't think this will come as much of a surprise to you, but I don't have many friends.'

'You had one,' Shanahan said.

Rafferty laughed the way some people do when the cosmic joke is on them, and there's nothing else to do.

Shanahan hadn't meant it that way. He'd spent his lifetime keeping his emotions under wraps and had always hoped others would do the same. Tending raw emotions wasn't his strong suit.

'I'm sorry,' Shanahan said. He could count on one hand how many times he had uttered that phrase.

'I didn't deserve him, but he sure as hell didn't deserve to die, Shanahan.'

'How long did you know him?'

'Five years.'

'What do you think happened? What was it, a burglary?'

'Nothing missing that I could tell. Money still in his wallet. He could have had something that somebody wanted that I didn't know about. But everything looked normal, except...' Rafferty stopped. It was apparent he didn't like what his mind was revisiting.

'Defensive wounds?'

'Shot in his sleep. In his bed. No sign of a struggle. He didn't see it coming. It looked like he was asleep. You got the picture now,' Rafferty said, 'about him and me.'

Shanahan nodded. 'You want me to look into this?'

'They're going to make their way to me at some point,' Rafferty said. 'We were pretty discreet, but we had a few dinners out. I think, but I'm not sure, but he might have had a friend who knew about us. The moment the police make the connection to me, I'm likely to be the only person they look at.'

'What makes you say that?'

'That's what I'd think. A closeted cop? Lover is going to out him and ruin his career. He would never do that...' Rafferty's eyes filled with tears and he went silent to keep it in. 'But that's what people will think.'

There was a long silence. Shanahan sipped some bourbon. He didn't want to ask him a question until Rafferty felt like he could talk without falling apart.

'What I need is time,' Rafferty said finally. 'There's no question my career is done. No matter what happens now. And I know I have to be very careful how I look into this. That's why I need you.'

'So you're going to investigate?'

'Not officially, of course.'

'And me? What am I doing for you?'

'I see what you mean,' Rafferty said. 'Won't work, will it?' He laughed that same laugh as before. 'You think I did it.'

'Lover's quarrel. Jealousy. Access to guns. You were in homicide. You know how it works. You know how a criminal thinks and how a detective works. And with me following your lead, you can take me where you want me to go.' Shanahan watched Rafferty. He wasn't getting angry. He wasn't taking it personally.

'I'd have to stay out of it,' Rafferty said.

'Yes.'

'How could I?'

'I understand. In your shoes, I couldn't either.'

Rafferty stood, downed the rest of the bourbon. 'I've talked too much.' He went to the door. 'So, where do I stand?'

'I'll wake up in the morning, thinking this was just a strange dream.'

'You considered it, didn't you? Helping me?'

12

'I did.'

'You're a good man.' He smiled. 'I'm not. Never have been. But I've never murdered anyone, and I certainly wouldn't have murdered Morgan. He was the only thing in my life of value.'

Shanahan switched off the lights and crept back into bed, allowing Casey to share the cool, conditioned air of the bedroom.

'You know, if you'd take off your coat, old boy...'

Shanahan hated to leave the bed, knowing he would have to face the heat. Maureen had beaten him out of bed, though her scent remained on the pillow next to him. What was it? Something citrus and nutty.

As he moved toward the hall, a piece of the dream was still lodged in his brain. His younger brother Fritz. They were in a long, narrow hallway, dimly lit. Shanahan could barely make out Fritz at the other end. Somehow Shanahan knew that Fritz wanted him to come with him. But just as Shanahan started, Fritz disappeared around the corner.

And that's how it went, from hallway to hallway, up strange and dark stairways to other hallways, Fritz always just ahead. If there was a story that preceded this seemingly endless pursuit, or one that followed, Shanahan couldn't recollect it. It was just a dream; he tried to convince himself. But

Fritz. It had been so long since Fritz was in his consciousness. Why now?

The thermostat in the hall said ninety-four. It was nine in the morning and ninety-four degrees.

In the kitchen, Maureen was squeezing oranges for fresh juice. She wore only her nightgown, loose and flowing, salmon-colored with a low neckline. She was weathering her forties quite well. Shanahan acknowledged his good fortune frequently.

'There are some benefits to heat waves,' Shanahan said.

'Mmmnnn,' she said. 'You're not very good at covering your tracks.'

'I'm not?'

'Who was here last night?'

'Whatever do you mean?' Shanahan asked.

'Two glasses. If you'd slipped out of bed to sneak a sip, you wouldn't have used two glasses.'

'Who said it was me?'

'You suggesting I did a little sleep drinking?'

'Now that's a possibility. Also, Casey. There's Casey.'

She grinned. 'I suppose so.'

'Yes. I've caught him a couple of times. When we're asleep he invites some folks over. I've taken to marking the bottle.'

'I didn't hear you get up,' Maureen said.

'A mariachi band could play through the

bedroom and you would snore away.'

'I don't snore.'

'Rafferty.'

'What?'

'Rafferty stopped by.'

'In the middle of the night?' she asked.

'He did,' Shanahan said, going to the coffee maker.

'Last night's coffee. Undrunk.'

He poured himself a cup and put it in the microwave. 'I'll make some fresh in a minute.'

'What did he want?' she asked.

Shanahan kept nothing from her. He had no secrets. But this wasn't his secret to tell.

'He thought I could help him. I couldn't.'

'With what?'

'Aren't you talkative this morning.' He found the morning *Star* on the small kitchen table. The story was below the fold. Short. No pictures.

'Had to be something. In the middle of the night.'

'Just very early.'

'You're not going to tell me, are you?'

Shanahan remained quiet. Anything he said now would make it worse.

'All right. There will be a time when you want something. I don't know what and I don't know when.' She handed him a glass of orange juice.

'At least it's not the juice.'

15

'Oh no, pal, it's not the juice.'

Shanahan sat at the table, glanced at the article, a news flash really. It was news the paper obviously squeezed in at the last minute.

A thirty-three-year-old male was found dead early this morning in his Northside home. Police, who would not identify the victim pending the notification of next of kin, say they are investigating the possibility of foul play. Though few details were available at press time, police said that a tip came from an anonymous phone call.

The story would be filled in a bit by the noon news on TV. He would follow the story. He followed most murders. This one was special. He and Rafferty had a history.

Maureen sat down across from him.

'You and Rafferty got along all right,' she said. 'You'd tell me if he was up to his old tricks.'

'We had a drink and a conversation that I think I promised to keep secret.'

She touched his hand. 'You know I don't need to know everything about your life, what goes on. I just don't trust Rafferty any farther than I could throw him.'

'And you could throw farther than I can,' he said.

Einstein, the ancient and bony cat, crossed

the kitchen slowly, having emerged from wherever he chose to spend the night. He stopped, looked at Shanahan, giving him the long, tough stare. 'It's time for food. Where in the hell is my food!'

'You should have named him Clint Eastwood,' Maureen said.

There were other things Shanahan didn't tell Maureen. He didn't tell her about his diminishing peripheral vision or how occasionally his brain would short circuit and he'd spend some time in an arbitrary piece of his past – in cold Korea waiting to be shot at, on his father's small farm in Wisconsin. He had slipped back to Paris once for who knew how long in a kind of pleasant melancholy.

She finished her glass of juice and headed to the bathroom to get ready for an early-morning realtor meeting. He read the story again.

He wondered how the police department would handle it if the investigation led to Rafferty. Usually, the police protect their own. But there were two problems with that theory. One was that Rafferty wasn't well liked among his own. Too much politicking, too much kiss ass with the higher-ups, and way too much time preening in the media spotlight. The other problem was that Rafferty was romantically involved with a guy. They wouldn't mind letting the public know that this was what happens when you put a 'queer' on the force.

Rafferty needed a friend. Did he have any?

Maureen appeared in the doorway.

'What are you doing today?'

'I have no idea,' he said, knowing full well if there was enough on the news at noon, he might nose around a little.

'You sure Rafferty's hooks aren't into you?'

'I'm fine. Rafferty isn't.'

# Two

It was nearing noon, not that it mattered to Howie Cross. He sat sweating in a lounge chair by the pool, a stone's throw from the beach and the Atlantic Ocean.

Miami in August wasn't any more comfortable than Indianapolis in August; but there was a pool. There was an ocean. In landlocked Indy you had to belong to a club to swim or be wealthy enough to have a pool for the four months of the year you could use it. And there was no beach, no nearly naked women walking the sand in his hometown. Women were fully dressed and traipsing about air-conditioned malls.

In his early forties, Howie appeared more

fit than he was. His body seemed to thrive on deprivation of key nutrients found in vegetables and fruits and benefited from his perhaps too frequent pleasures with what came in bottles – tequila, rum, vodka, wine and beer.

August was low season in Florida, and Howie was in the midst of other bargain hunters. There would be no celebrities, and perhaps the coolest of the glitterati would be somewhere else this time of year. Howie cared as much about celebrities and the glitterati as they did about him. Even so, South Beach, where he'd visited on business not all that long ago, seemed like a bustling place.

Howie almost went to the beach rather than the pool on this last day of his stay. Because it was his last he didn't give much of a damn about yesterday's embarrassment. He had walked down the steps from one of the decks that overlooked the ocean to cool off in the pool. On his way down, he saw a man and a kid, most likely a father and son, tossing a football round in the shallower of the two pools. What caught Howie off guard was that the man – the size of a polar bear – had rolled down his all-too-small Speedos, revealing the full cheeks of his ass. Cross hadn't realized he was staring, caught up as he was with figuring out why a man would do this at a public pool, when he heard the child scream loudly and clearly for all the poolside visitors to hear.

'Dad, that man is staring at your butt.'

Howie picked up stride slightly, pretending none of this was happening; hoping beyond any realistic expectation that the audience would think the boy was talking about someone else.

That was yesterday. As far as Cross was concerned this wasn't the kind of butt anyone could care about, yet its ugliness lingered in his mind.

Fortunately the exhibitionist wasn't at the pool. Howie went to the deeper of the two pools, slipped over the side and swam the length of it several times. Though he slept alone each night, at odds with his intent, he had been able to relax. Each day he swam in the morning in the pool before lunch. He napped, then took his towel to the beach and read under an umbrella, breaking occasionally when he was too hot to swim broad laps, parallel to the beach, in the ocean. He napped again and lounged around his air-conditioned hotel room until dinner.

At night he'd have a few drinks, ogle the crowd, and perhaps more telling of his age, he was in bed by eleven, the time when the revelry began. Thing was, he never felt so calm, so rested.

He dried himself off, picked up the small canvas bag that held his sunscreen, his book, and sunglasses. He stopped off at the poolside bar, ordered a margarita. He took it with him to the stairs and up to his room. In the small but complete kitchen, he put the drink in the freezer and went to the bathroom. He looked at himself in the mirror before stepping into the steamy shower. He didn't look that bad. Of course the lights and the mirrors here were kinder than the ones at home. And despite the fine dinners, he may have peeled off five pounds of bloat.

This was nice. He didn't mind being alone. With the exception of a few intermittent, short-term lovers, he'd spent most of his life alone. And it was fine. But he wished he could have shared the days with someone, if for no other reason than to witness and therefore confirm that he was having a nice time.

After the shower, he dressed in clean, loose clothes and retrieved his margarita from the freezer. He flicked on the television set and scanned the seemingly endless choice of channels. There were Hispanic channels, fashion channels, sports channels ... Bored, he went to the phone and dialed his own number, pushing the right buttons to get him into his voice mail.

He didn't expect much; but there was always a chance that someone wanted to hire him or – and he didn't like to think about it – a call about one of his ageing parents. There were two calls. One was from the mortgage company. He had sent them a check where the written amount contradicted the number of dollars he indicated numerically. Could he get back to them?

They're lucky to get a check at all, he thought.

The second call was surprising. It wasn't just that it was somebody who might want to hire him, but that it was who it was.

'This is Max Rafferty,' came the voice. 'I can't seem to find you at home, so I hope you are checking your messages. I need to talk to you. About taking on a project. It's important that we keep this confidential. The phone number I'm about to give you is my cell phone. Do not call the IPD. Call my cell.'

Rafferty provided, then repeated the number.

'I know you and I haven't hit it off in the past, but we can work something out. Maybe I should have come to you first, being an ex-cop and all. This is all in the strictest confidence. I talked to your pal Shanahan. He said no, but he's keeping what I told him quiet. Call me as soon as you can.'

Cross didn't know what to think of the message. Was it a prank? Rafferty hated Shanahan more than he did Cross. Why would a cop want to hire a private eye? This wasn't kosher. He took a sip of his margarita and glanced at the TV screen. A long, lanky model in a sheer gown paraded toward the camera, revealing one bare breast. Cross liked long and lanky and definitely liked breasts.

He debated with himself until a new and less interesting fashion show took over the screen. He picked up the hotel phone, dialed the number.

'Hello, Rafferty.'

'Rafferty. Cross returning your call.'

'Where are you calling from?' Rafferty asked.

Immediately suspicious, Cross responded, 'Does it matter?' Maybe this was some trick to arrest him for something.

'No. I need to talk to you.'

'Why?'

'Now's not a good time. When can I come over?'

Cross laughed.

'I'm not in Indianapolis.'

'Where are you?'

'Too far away for you to drop over. What little game are you playing?'

It was Rafferty's turn to laugh.

'If you committed some heinous crime somewhere, I don't know about it. This isn't about you, Cross.' Rafferty's voice went softer. 'This is about me.'

Cross decided to trust him. 'I'm flying in tomorrow at six.'

'Evening?'

'Yes.'

'I'll pick you up at the airport. What airline?'

Cross sensed that the impatience and irritation he heard in Rafferty's voice was, in fact, more like desperation.

'I'll meet you at my place. Give me at least an hour.'

'No, the airport.' There was a long silence as Cross took an inventory of second thoughts.

Cross gave him the airline and the time.

'Thanks,' Rafferty said, sealing the deal.

Now was the time to take a nap. He finished his margarita, went to the bedroom, sank on the fresh sheets in a bed that was far more comfortable than his own. Every afternoon of every day of his little vacation, he did this. He drifted off slowly, easily, pleasantly and awoke just as gently, rested and full of energy. This particular afternoon it was not going to happen.

Maybe he'd go to the main stretch of beach. For days he'd gone to the beach just a few feet from the hotel, generally seeing the same people. He put the usual stuff in his bag and walked out of the front door of the hotel and walked on the Ocean Drive sidewalk to a more central beach location. Walking on the sidewalk was easier, faster than trudging through the sand.

The restaurants and hotels on the other

side of the street, on his left, had the late lunchers and early drinkers. There was music. It was a lively stretch, that grew more lively and more colorful later, when the sun went down and the art deco neon went up.

Howie worked up a sweat even though his gait was leisurely. On his right there were no more hotels. The ocean was visible past several yards of sand dunes. At what he considered about the middle of the beach, he cut in toward the water. Once at the beach, he scanned the area for the best spot. More important than finding an area with the most attractive women, was an area devoid of screaming children. He walked through part of the beach that appeared reserved for men with men.

It was a bit of a hike, retreating back in the direction of his hotel, but he found a spot that provided views that most interested him. Not too long ago, he would have just tossed his towel on the sand and settled in, but no longer. With sunscreen, his body seemed to be a sand magnet; and no matter how he rearranged the sand below him, it was rarely comfortable. So he paid the exorbitant rent and settled under an umbrella and on a comfortable, cushioned chaise.

There was an empty chaise only a few feet from his. On it lay a pair of expensive sunglasses, most likely belonging to a woman.

There was a Louis Vuitton bag, half covered by a thick and no doubt expensive towel. A hardback book – *Dangerous Women* – was open, spread on the chaise cushion like an inverted v, pages down to keep her place.

He looked out toward the water. A huge tanker was on the far horizon. A cruise ship was closer, moving like a cheerful glacier into dock. Dozens of people played in the water near the shore. There were a few brave souls farther out. Somewhere out there was his neighbor.

What he couldn't do in his bed, he did almost immediately on the beach. Howie napped. When he awoke he found his neighbor had returned. Her long hair was wet. She was slender and tan. She wore only a bikini bottom and a pair of sunglasses. He guessed she was in her mid-thirties. He had a chance.

'Hi,' he said. 'I hope I didn't snore.'

'No,' she smiled, and went back to her book.

She turned to look at him. She'd caught him looking at her.

'I'm sorry, I'll work on not looking,' Cross said.

'Don't work too hard.'

'You from around here? Sorry,' he said, 'I'm a little rusty when it comes to conversation. And of course, you may not even want conversation.'

26

'If you're trying to pick me up, I should let you know that I'm a working girl.' She pulled off her sunglasses. 'You know what that means, right?'

'Figures,' Cross said, then realizing this might have been insulting, he added, 'just once I'd like to be attracted to a woman who didn't want something.'

She smiled. 'Such a woman exists?'

Cross picked up his book, tried hard to concentrate. He just wasn't going to do it. In some ways, going with a 'working girl' was easier. No fuss. A good time, sometimes, and no baggage.

'So you're not going to talk,' she said. 'Now that you know I'm a loose woman.'

'I like loose women. I just thought that was your way of saying "put up or shut up". I'm not buying love these days.'

'I'm not selling love,' she said.

'No, of course not.'

'We can talk if you find me worthy.'

She knew that he did.

'Sitting in judgment of other people's lives is not part of my personal philosophy.'

'Which is what?' She was teasing him.

'Oh ... it's a mix. You know, do unto others. Add in a little live and let live and an eye for an eye and maybe...'

'A rolling stone gathers no moss,' she suggested.

'That's not my philosophy. That's my fate.'

27

'Why don't you buy me a drink? You can do that, right?'

Cross looked around.

'Not here,' she said. 'Your place.'

'Taking me on as a charity case?' Now it was his turn to smile.

'No. Actually, it's kind of nice when I get to choose who I sleep with. I'm bored out here and I wouldn't mind a little company.'

They walked back by way of the beach, came in through the back gate of the hotel, walked around the pool, picked up drinks at the bar, and went inside, instantly feeling the cool air-conditioned interior.

As Shanahan's car traversed Emerson Parkway to Kessler Boulevard, he was trying to convince himself that he wasn't on the case. This was just curiosity at work. He had the time. Maureen was off showing a house to potential buyers and he was comfortable enough for awhile. The last case paid more than he expected and his Army pension check and a modest social security check kept him afloat.

But the noon news revealed more facts on the murder. The victim's name was Morgan Lee. He lived just off West 71st Street in a neighborhood near Eagle Creek reservoir. All three reservoirs – Morse and Geist being the other two – provided expensive new homes with dramatic water views. For a city with just a small natural waterway, it was exotic and highly desirable.

This was just a pleasant drive, he told himself, as he pulled on to Meridian Street with its stately homes, then soon west on to 71st, which would eventually get him to Eagle Creek.

He tried to imagine Rafferty in an intimate relationship. Not in a sexual way, but interacting with another human being in a way that wasn't sleazily solicitous or maliciously arrogant. He tried to imagine Rafferty and friend on a walk down the canal, or having a quiet dinner together, or laughing at some joint observation of humanity. Who could love him? He shook his head. Eva Braun loved Hitler.

Where did Rafferty and his lover first meet?

Shanahan came to the 71st Street causeway that stretched across Eagle Creek and immediately on the other side he saw the Bay Colony sign. Instead of turning left and coming to halt at the gate, he pulled off to the right on the paved shoulder. He stopped the car. He had a perfect view of the gate. He got out of his 1976 Chevy Malibu and went to the front, lifted the hood.

What he wanted to do was figure out how people entered and left the gated community. The gate was guardless, no doubt operated electronically. There was a wooden panel on the right, which housed a telephone. No doubt delivery people could stop, call their party and be buzzed in. He looked around, spotted a camera on a pole. There was surveillance, but was it really on? What and when did it record?

In a few moments, the gate opened and a silver BMW appeared from the other side. The car went right. The gate behind the car closed slowly, more than ample time for the car to exit and perhaps enough time for another car to enter.

Shanahan pulled a handkerchief from his pocket, wiped his forehead. A big black Chevrolet Impala pulled in behind Shanahan. Unmarked police car, Shanahan thought. Why are unmarked cars so easy to spot? They should really drive Porches or Mini Coopers. The driver got out. It was Lieutenant Swann, one of IPD's homicide detectives.

'What are you doing here, Shanahan?'

Swann looked younger and more innocent than he was. He had to be fifty now. He still wore his dishwater-blond hair in a flat top. He was a decent cop and Shanahan liked and respected him.

'I think my car overheated,' Shanahan said. 'It might be all right now.'

Swann never smiled, but there was a glimmer of humour in his eyes.

'Where were you going?'

'So hot at home,' Shanahan said, 'just out for a drive. Cool off.'

'Who are you working for?'

'I'm not working for anyone.'

Swann continued to stare at him.

'Just curious, Lieutenant. I didn't have anything to do.'

'You've never told me a serious untruth. I hope you're not starting now.'

'I've got a lot of time on my hands.' Shanahan waited a moment, seeing if their past relationship would get him more information. 'What do you think?' Shanahan asked, nodding in the direction of the gate and meaning all that was behind it.

'Execution,' Swann said. 'Gay guy.'

'You know that? How?'

'Things around the house. Magazines. Photographs. Nothing all that compromising, but you can tell.'

'Any sign of a break-in?'

'Not that we can tell. Listen, I'm starting to get a little uncomfortable. I know you're an upright guy and you were on my side when I needed it. Maybe I owe you, but I really shouldn't be talking like this.'

Swann gave Shanahan that sideways look that suggested he didn't quite buy Shanahan's explanation.

'Do me a favor,' Swann said as kindly as he could. 'Stay out of it.'

'Stick with crossword puzzles, right?'

31

Shanahan asked.

'Or get a client.'

'One more thing,' Shanahan said, moving to the front of the car and pulling the hood down. 'Anything missing?'

'Can't say for sure. Nothing obvious. The wallet had some money in it, some credit cards. Not sure what might be missing because we don't know what was there. We haven't ruled out suicide, but bullet entered in the back of the head. Pretty difficult. Then of course, he would have to have disposed of the gun before crawling back in bed to die.'

'Could have been a different kind of burglary,' Shanahan said. 'Art object, jewellery.'

'If that's what happened, whoever it was that did it probably had something particular in mind. Everything was pretty neat. OK?'

'Maybe a gambling debt. Double-cross of some kind.'

'Jilted lover.' Swann said. He waited for Shanahan to say something.

Shanahan shrugged, finally said, 'Pretty cold.'

'You know, if you are on the clock, you got quite a bit of information for your time.'

'I'm not. You going in?'

'To the house? Yes. You? No way.'

'C'mon,' Shanahan said. 'What harm could it do?'

'It's a crime scene.'

'You've already had the coroner through,

right? You've taken the photographs, the prints, all that. Why are you going in?'

'I wasn't there this morning. Just a look around to get familiar with the layout.'

'Me too.'

'Yes, but murder isn't a hobby with me.'

'It isn't with me either.'

'What's your interest in this? Last chance to level with me and maybe we can make a deal.'

'Let's make that deal.'

'So, you were working me?'

'I know someone who knows the victim.'

'Who?'

'Had nothing to do with the crime,' Shanahan said, hoping like hell he was right. 'Just wants some reassurance that things are what they're being reported to be.'

'The body's gone.'

'I know.'

'OK. I'm only going to be there a few minutes. And you leave when I leave.'

Shanahan nodded.

'Are we pretty close to being even?' Swann asked.

Shanahan didn't answer.

# Three

Howie was an ex-vice cop. He was 'ex' primarily because he had trouble arresting people like Elena. In most places, the prostitutes do time, but the john doesn't. The laws against prostitution forced the otherwise commercial enterprise underground where it couldn't be regulated and the girls – in most cases girls, guys sometimes – couldn't be protected, and were therefore especially vulnerable to genuine criminal behavior.

Cross poured the drinks from the plastic cups into real glasses and they moved into the small living room.

'Doing well, I see,' she said. She meant the room.

'Bargain. Internet best buy. Look out the window.' She pulled the drapery aside. 'They call that the "city view",' Cross said. 'Spectacular angle on the parking lot. But I'm happy. This is luxury for me.'

'What do you do ... for a living?' She sat on the sofa, sipped her drink, attentive, amused.

'Private investigator.'

'This is a fantasy thing, right? This is role play.'

'No, it's true.' He pulled out his wallet. Showed his license.

'Used to be a cop, right?'

'Right. Vice.'

'God,' she said, putting the drink down on the coffee table.

'I wasn't very good at it, if that helps.'

She smiled. She was at home with herself. In the course of his vice experience, Cross had seen all kinds of prostitutes from the duped and exploited to the enthusiastically willing, eager to earn in an hour what she would make in two days waiting tables. Elena looked to be one who made the decision without coercion. She was smart, in charge. Her arms were free of track marks and her eyes were clear. She had time to lounge on the beach and read a book.

'I'm going to take a shower,' she said. 'Join me?'

The bedroom was neat. Police had taken the sheets and blankets from the bed, leaving what appeared to be a new mattress. There was a stack of books by an Ian McEwan by the bed. The jacket blurbs suggested the books were of a high-minded nature.

Swann handed Shanahan a plastic glove. 'If you need to touch anything,' he said.

Shanahan put it on his right hand just in case. It was a nice room, walls up to a pitched roof. There was a skylight. At night the light would come from little spotlights mounted on the high ceiling. It would take a ladder to put the pottery on the shelves above the closet. Under the window were several pieces of matching luggage. Two big suitcases, a suit bag, a carry-on. Shanahan knew the luggage was expensive by the pattern, but he couldn't recollect the name. He lifted each one. Empty. All of them empty.

The closet had two sliding doors. The clothes were hung meticulously, shirts all together, sorted by color. Jackets were the same. So were the slacks. Some names he hadn't heard of – Zegna, for example, and Joseph Aboud. But he had heard of Gucci, Burberry, and Armani. The boy had expensive taste. Shoes were lined up below. All of them polished and looking good.

Inside the bedroom was a bathroom. Spotless. There were various bottles of expensive soap and body lotions in the shower. There were no combs or brushes. Shanahan thought the police had taken them, along with whatever device the victim used to shave.

The medicine cabinet above the sink held no prescription drugs. The usual and predictable – pain relievers, a bottle of Tums, band aids, dental floss – occupied the shelves. There was another shelf near the shower. On it was bottle after bottle of body washes, body lotions, body oils, shampoos and conditioners.

Shanahan got down on his knees and scanned the floor. Between the back of the commode and the wall was a piece of brown plastic. It had a partial label.

There was a prescription number and a phone number. The rest of the label was missing along with the plastic. The police had missed it. Shanahan palmed the little brown piece, slipping it into his pants pocket. He'd deal with it later.

The towels were expensive. There was an orchid in a simple pot. White flowers with some buds yet to open. Seemed poetic.

Shanahan walked back through the hall. There was another bathroom, one without much in the way of personal effects. No doubt the guest bathroom. Beyond it was a second bedroom, very attractively done, but without the personal mementos. It had been used primarily as an office. Desk drawers were empty. The desktop had no computer though there was a surge protector connected to a floor plug below it. One doesn't use one of these to protect table lamps. A filing cabinet was empty. The tape was missing from the answering machine.

Not surprising. The police would have taken bills, financial records, correspondence, computer data first thing. Or had Rafferty taken away anything incriminating?

He had the time. He had the knowledge. He knew what the police would look for and how they would make connections.

The living room was spacious. Essentially, there was no ceiling. Or, the ceiling was the underside of the roof. Painted wood, applied like a wash. The grain of the wood was visible. A big comfortable sofa dominated the room and looked surprisingly comfortable. So far, the house was elegant, just this side of ostentatious. For Shanahan, the mark of a good home was comfort first, looks second. This place looked like it did both pretty well.

Shanahan looked around for photographs. None.

There was a step up to a dining area where a modern white-wood table sat, a vase of calla lilies dramatically setting it off. Beyond the table was the kitchen. Spotless. The cabinets revealed various sets of wine glasses, some modern china. In the food department, there were few canned goods. A dozen or so cooking oils, three or four of them different kinds of olive oil. There were three different vinegars. Food was important. There was a wine rack with a couple of dozen red wines and in the refrigerator, there were a couple of white wines, fresh asparagus, a couple of salmon steaks.

The victim and Rafferty had some things in common. Good food and fine apparel.

Maybe there was something to the relationship.

The victim had probably planned a dinner for today. Maybe with Rafferty.

Then he noticed it. A bowl of water on the floor. It was a good size, probably not a cat's. Shanahan opened the lower cabinets and found a twenty-five-pound bag of dry dog food. The expensive kind.

Two glass doors opened to the patio. Hitting the hot air outside was rude. There were plants scattered around the deck, and the deck went around a small lap pool. The water was clear.

Back inside, he found the door to the garage. A black, two-year-old BMW sat, clean as a whistle in the spotless garage.

It was unlocked. Shanahan, using his rubber-gloved hand, opened the passenger side. He reached in, opened the glove compartment. There, in a leather packet, was all the info. Registration, insurance, and the lease agreement. Morgan Lee.

'You have it figured out yet?' Swann asked, stepping into the garage. 'You think maybe he was run over?' The officer nearly smiled.

'Somebody taking care of the dog?'

Swann looked puzzled.

'There was a dog.'

'I'll check on it. Right now, I don't know if there's a next of kin. Haven't got much on the guy. Time to go.'

Swann drove Shanahan out the front gate and over to his car.

'When are you going to get a new car?' Swann asked. 'With that old wreck, I knew it was you before I saw your face.'

Sleep tugged at him. And he would have given in to it had he not felt Elena leave the bed. Slowly and carefully. Was she so thoughtful as to not want to wake him? Cross was cynical by nature. She was a total stranger. He was extremely vulnerable at the moment. She lived on the edges of the law.

He allowed his eyelids to open to mere slits. He could see the reflection of her slender naked body in the mirror. She was looking at him all too intensely. He watched her go to his bag and dig through it. She pulled out his wallet. He wasn't entirely sure what she took, but she took something. Then she grabbed her bag and slipped into the hallway.

Elena wasn't leaving. She hadn't taken her clothing. They might be minimal, but he doubted she would leave naked. He heard the shower. He heard the sound of the shower curtain open then close.

Howie got out of bed, retrieved his wallet. She had taken his credit cards. Not his money. There wasn't much, but it was all there. He put it back, went into the hallway. The bathroom door was open slightly. He peeked in. Her bag was near enough. He got down on his knees. He reached in and slowly pulled the bag out.

He rummaged through it, retrieving his credit cards and finding her wallet. He opened it. A couple of twenties and a fifty. He made mental note of the name and address on her driver's license. He looked into the various little sleeves and pockets and found nothing. He saw a little diary-type book with a clasp. Inside was a list of addresses, phone numbers, and email addresses, but nothing else. He hoped she liked to spend time in the shower. He continued his search, finding a bag full of makeup. The lipstick tube felt light. He opened it. There, rolled up, was money. He pulled the roll out. There were several hundreds. Ten of them. He took two, put the rest back. He nudged the bag back into the bathroom just as he heard the shower stop. He moved quickly and quietly back into the bedroom. He climbed into bed and waited.

She came in, dressed, came over to the bed, kissed his cheek.

'Thanks for a good time,' she said.

'I enjoyed it,' he whispered.

'Don't get up,' she said. 'I know the way out.'

Shanahan, at the small kitchen table, thumbed through the telephone book, the brown piece of plastic of the prescription bottle in his hand.

Area code 504 was New Orleans. Shanahan thought about calling Dr Craig, but didn't. It dawned on him how far in front of himself he was. He wasn't on the case. He would never be on the case. He wasn't getting paid. And Rafferty wasn't the kind of guy Shanahan felt all that charitable toward.

He had to take his mind off of it. Casey wouldn't cooperate. The hound refused the invitation to go outside and play ball. The heat. He could cook dinner. Maureen would probably be home soon. She had a couple of showings and had a meeting with other realtors at the firm. But Shanahan couldn't talk himself into cooking anything, and he was not one to consider a cool salad a meal.

They'd go out. Nothing too expensive, in an air-conditioned restaurant. They would turn on the air-conditioning in the bedroom and shut the door so that it would be cool when they got back. TV. A book. Life wasn't bad, was it?

Cross felt playful. After a shower, a nap, a late afternoon swim, and another shower, he was ready for a little fun. Outside at seven, the sun was still up, the temperature hot, and the air thick. The consolation was that back in Indianapolis it would be just as bad.

Would she be home? As he walked west, he

walked by the China Grill. He imagined it to be a fast food take-out joint similar to those in airport food courts. He glanced in. Didn't seem to be the case. He checked the menu. Not food court food. Lamb Spare Ribs with Plum Sauce and Sesame Glaze. Grilled Szechwan Beef with Sake and Soy. Grilled Garlic Shrimp with Black Fettuccine. Black fettuccine? What was that? Entrees ranged from roughly twenty-five to fifty dollars.

He was at Washington Street and 5th. A few blocks later, he found the building. He also found her name on the rows of buzzers that announced visitors to residents.

The name read: E. Thorson. He pushed the buzzer. Would she be there? Did she live alone?

'What is it?' came the tinny voice.

'Elena?'

'Who is it?'

'Howie Cross.'

There was a long pause, then a response: 'You got your cards back. Why don't you just keep on walking?'

'I came to see if you wanted to go to dinner?'

'You're crazy as a loon,' she said. 'Look, you got a freebie. So don't get greedy.'

It was strange having a conversation with a wall. 'This isn't greed. I want to take you to dinner,' Cross said, unable to contain the laughter in his voice.

'What's going on?'

'I'm amused.' Amused? He'd never said 'amused' before. That was for other people. Then again, that was amusing. Also, her responses suggested that while she may have checked to see if there was cash in her emergency cache, she probably didn't count it.

'Where?'

'China Grill.'

'I thought you were a bargain hunter,' she said.

'It's my last night in Miami.'

There was a long pause.

'Anything more than dinner, and it's billable time.'

'Deal.'

'I'll be down in ... fifteen minutes.'

'Hey, it's hot down here.'

'Meet me at the bar,' she said.

'You're quiet,' Maureen said, sipping a glass of Asahi Dry beer.

'I'm always quiet,' Shanahan said. Their favorite Japanese Restaurant, Sakura, was busy as usual, loud as usual, and the food great as usual.

'Yes, but you are a different quiet.'

'I see.' He took a bite of his Fish Teriyaki. He was told that no self-respecting Japanese would eat anything teriyaki; but he didn't care, the white fish, slightly sweet, melted in

44

his mouth and made his beer taste better.

'It's Rafferty,' she said.

It was true. He couldn't get the Rafferty problem off his mind. Not even for a moment. Maybe somebody else should know about the visit, what Rafferty wanted.

'I went out to Eagle Creek today.'

'Did you have a nice time?' she smiled.

'Yes. I went through the murder victim's house.'

In mid-motion, she abandoned her chopsticks. 'Who are we talking about?'

Shanahan leaned into the table. 'A young man, Rafferty's lover.'

It took her a little while to process the information.

'You're trying to shock me, right?'

'Yes, I was. I'm sorry.'

'Why?'

'I don't know. Maybe I'm a little uncomfortable knowing that you can read me like a book.'

'So you made something up?'

'No. It's true.'

'Don't play with me,' she said, grinning.

'What if I want to play with you?'

'All right,' she said, picking up her chopsticks, pinching a piece of sushi between them. 'All right. Either tell me or don't.'

'You can't tell anyone. I know I don't have to say that, but I have to say that,' Shanahan said, wincing. It was similar to Maureen's 'you're different quiet'.

'OK. I can't believe he'd hire you to find the murderer.'

'He didn't. He tried though. I said no.'

'Then what are you doing?'

'Trying to find the murderer.'

'Oh, I see,' she said, 'it's the idea that you'd get paid that you don't like.'

'No. I've been trying to figure out why. And I know now. He implicated me.'

'What?' she asked. Worry crossed her face.

'I know something about the murder and I'm not telling the police. I have to know whether he did it or not.'

'You think he did.'

'Statistics say that the victim knew his murderer. It's often domestic. Often a lover.'

'Why would he want to hire you?'

'Who could he go to? He hasn't many friends. He can't tell the people he works with. He couldn't trust some investigator out of the phone book.'

'You're going to risk not telling the police?'

'For now, anyway.'

She was gorgeous. Low-cut black dress, long neck, long flowing hair that seemed to sweep back as she walked. She exchanged words with the bartender. It was obvious they knew each other.

'What are you drinking?' Cross asked her.

'He knows,' Elena said, as the bartender

delivered something white with a lime.

'You look beautiful,' he said.

'You need a tailor,' she said, but her smile said she was telling the truth in a fun-loving way.

'I didn't bring anything real dressy.'

'You have me now,' she said, 'for a couple of hours.'

'Unbillable, right?'

The restaurant was huge. Three dining areas, one raised, were visible from the bar. When the hostess guided them to their table, he discovered a fourth. A smaller room that seemed to cater to couples. In the center was a huge, iced sushi bar. They were seated at the far end in the most private space available, and Cross wondered if they did this regularly for Elena. Quiet, intimate, away from prying eyes.

'Not a very nice trick you played. We had an agreement.'

'It's the slow season. What do you care, you got your cards back.'

'How about a little autobiography?' he asked.

'You first.'

'Cop ten years. Married when I was eighteen. Divorced at nineteen. No kids. Drink too much, fall in love with women who aren't good for my sanity...'

'Sanity is something you possess? Something so neat that they can mess it up?'

He sipped his drink. 'Well, maybe that's the problem.'

'What do you want in a woman?'

'I ... guess I don't know. You?'

'I don't want a woman.' She smiled.

'Your past, present, and future.'

'We're done with you already?'

'Uneventful life. Don't play golf, don't perform delicate surgeries, not clever with investments, and don't like Republicans or Democrats. What am I supposed to talk about?' Cross asked. 'You?'

'Born in Flint, Michigan. Went to school in Ann Arbor. Art major. Did some modelling, branched out. Oh, and I know what I want.'

'What is that?'

'A rich old man who has a taste for fine things and the only thing he wants from me is marriage and for me to look pretty and be happy.'

'And sex?'

'Over-rated.'

They ordered the Crackling Calamari Salad, the lobster pancake, and the Barbequed Salmon in Chinese Mustard Sauce.

'OK, what should we talk about?' he asked.

'I am open to anything but lectures about making wise investments and questions about what I'm going to do when my looks go.'

Their conversation, a bantering, teasing interaction for a while, dwindled even before

48

the dessert menu arrived. When the bill came, Cross paid for it with two one-hundred-dollar bills.

'It was very nice of you to take me to dinner after what I tried to do to you,' she said.

'No, thank you, Elena.'

'What for?'

'For dinner. You paid for it,' Cross said, standing. 'I figured it was your way of apologizing.'

She looked down at her purse.

'You didn't count your hundreds. I just took two.'

She grinned, shook her head.

'You all that smart back there in Indianapolis?' she asked.

'If I was smart, I would have kept all ten of them.'

'Then I would have had your knees broken,' she said with a look that suggested she was still considering it.

# Four

'I'm going to have to buy a new car,' Shanahan said to Maureen as he opened the kitchen door to let Casey out into the back yard for the hound's morning constitutional.

Maureen grinned, said nothing.

'That's very sweet of you,' he said.

'What?'

'Not shouting with glee.'

'I was being respectful,' she said, grinning.

'You were overacting.'

'Well, I do think this is serious,' she said. 'You've had that car longer than you've had anything in your life. There has to be a little trauma even from an unsentimental...'

'...old fool.'

'No,' she said thoughtfully. 'Old works, yes. But fool? There is a word,' she said, 'and I think it is much like fool, but fool, no. You're not a fool.'

'Just much like a fool,' he said.

'Give me a little time to think about it,' she said.

He took the plastic remnant of the pill bottle from his pocket, and went to the wall phone. He dialed the number that appeared on the label. A recorded message said that the Royal Pharmacy would open at nine a.m., and provided an address. He looked at his watch. It was just past nine, then he remembered that unlike the rest of America, Indianapolis was not on Daylight Savings Time. That put him an hour off. It would be too early to track down the doctor.

The big, black Ford Crown Victoria awaited curbside.

'Thanks for the limousine service,' Cross said, crawling inside. He wondered if Rafferty had gained weight. The driver's seat was all the way back, and the bearded, corpulent cop looked like he was pinned in by the steering wheel.

Rafferty put the car in gear and accelerated.

'You're late.'

'Tell the pilot,' Cross said.

'Northside, right?' Rafferty asked.

'Butler Tarkington,' Cross said, identifying the neighborhood. Now there was silence. And the silence kept going even after Rafferty negotiated the airport stops and turns and was on the expressway.

'I'm not going through town,' Rafferty said finally.

'OK,' Cross said. What did he care?

'You have a case?'

'No.'

'Want one?' Rafferty asked.

'Tell me about it.'

There was another long silence. Expressway to Interstate 70. The skyline was up ahead to the left.

'I think it's shorter to go through town,' Rafferty said.

'OK.'

Still another silence.

'There's something you're trying awful hard not to tell me.'

'God damn, this is harder than trying to tell Shanahan.'

'You haven't told me anything,' Cross said. 'You tried to hire Shanahan?'

Quiet. After miles of silence, Rafferty spoke. 'I think maybe it's because you used to be a cop. I guess. That's why it's hard.' He looked at Cross. 'I'm homosexual.'

'And you want me to find out why?'

'No, smartass.' Rafferty pulled off on to the shoulder, slowed down, then came to a stop. He put the blinker lights on. 'I need your help. That's very hard for me to say. There's no place for me to go.' He didn't look at Cross. Instead, he stared straight ahead. 'A guy I knew was murdered. I need help finding the person who did it.'

'Don't you tell everybody that this kind of thing is police business?' Cops and private investigators weren't exactly a natural partnership.

Rafferty stared straight ahead. He was either trying to hold back anger or tears.

Cross got it. 'You're afraid that in the course of the investigation you'll be outed. Not a fun thing in a police department.'

'My dear Mr Private Eye, figure it all out. It's worse than that.' He cleared his throat. The beginning of the next sentence was strong and faded quickly to silence. 'The victim was my lover. Get those little wheels and gears working in your mind, Howie.'

'Rule number one. You don't call me Howie. You can call me Cross or asshole or whatever you want, but not Howie. And the wheels went to work pretty quick. You're not only going to get outed, you're going to get arrested.'

'Bingo. And I need some answers before the trail leads to me. At this point, I'm less worried about being found out. I want the bastard who did it. You interested or not?'

'Why didn't Shanahan take it?'

'Talk to him.'

'I will. Then I'll talk to you.'

'The clock is ticking,' Rafferty said.

'I'll call right away.'

Rafferty handed him a cell phone, put on the left turn signal, and checked the side mirror. As the phone rang at Shanahan's place, the big black car pulled back out on to the highway. The light on the high rises gave the city a silver look.

When the rings stopped, a recorded message told him no one was home.

Cross convinced Rafferty to come inside. Up the narrow rock stairs, across a small lawn to a rickety gate.

'Where in the hell do you live? I didn't even know this place existed.'

It was a small Mediterranean-styled building. Red tile roof, smooth gray stucco walls, round-topped wooden door.

'Used to be chauffeur's quarters and garage to a house that isn't anywhere around.'

'Jeeezus.'

Inside, they climbed a few steps, walked across a small room where Cross had his desk and computer, and then down a few steps into a large room.

'This was the garage,' Cross said. 'One of the previous owners put some glass doors in so I have this big room.'

'Figures. You're nuts,' Rafferty said. 'Let's get through this quick.'

'Have a seat,' Cross said, gesturing toward a big brown vinyl-covered sofa.

Rafferty looked at it, then investigated it.

'It's clean,' Cross said.

Rafferty sat, though his face suggested it was against his better judgment. 'His name is Morgan Lee. Early thirties. Shot in the head. I found him, called it in anonymously. Left.'

'You two were ... uh ... committed to each

other?'

'Let's get this settled early. I'm not turning myself inside out for you.'

'You know,' Cross said, 'you are about the last person on the planet that I want to know anything about. Believe me, it's on a need to know, not a want to know, basis. And I need to know.'

'I'll tell you what you need to know,' Rafferty said. His eyes made it clear: don't cross the line.

'Look, I'm a lot easier than Shanahan. I'll even get pushed around up to a point if it keeps the peace; but it won't work the way you're going at it. You're a little rusty with this homicide thing and this one is real personal. So, leave a little room for creativity. Where did you meet him?'

Rafferty looked even more pissed.

'If a question like this upsets you, what do you think of needles? That lethal injection is a killer.'

'That Chinese place. Keystone at the Crossing.'

'Nice place,' Cross said. 'On a cop's salary?'

'He was sitting at the table next to mine. We started talking about food and then travel ... and ... one thing led to another.'

'I need to know. That thing and the other.'

'He invited me to dinner at his place.'

'You knew he was gay?'

'Yes.'

'How?'

'I don't know.'

'He know you were?'

'When I accepted the invite, I'm sure he figured it out. Guys don't invite guys to dinner like that.'

'Did he know you were a cop?'

'Yeah.'

'Right away?'

'It came up,' Rafferty said.

'What did he do?'

'I don't know.'

'He knows you're a cop right off and you still don't know what he did for a living after you knew him for how long?'

'Six months.'

'And you think you should be in charge of a murder investigation?'

'Cut it out, Cross. Do cute on your own time. Investments. He did things with money markets or the stock market. He didn't go into an office. He worked at home.'

'You have a picture of him?'

'No.'

'How did you let yourself become so vulnerable? You're a cop and this is your city. You'd have to know you'd be seen, especially you, face all over the TV all the time.'

'He had a Southern accent. I thought he was from somewhere else. Passing through. That would be perfect.' Rafferty shook his head. 'This is like bleeding to death.'

'But he was going to cook for you. You had to know he lived here.'

'Yeah, that was after. Anyway, I wasn't thinking straight.' He gave a sheepish grin. 'Don't go there.'

'I won't.'

'It's been a long time, Cross, since anyone like that paid attention to me.'

'Like what?'

'Young, good-looking, smart, educated. Didn't want anything.'

'You got along? No heated arguments?'

Rafferty hesitated. Then shrugged, shook his head no. 'We got along all right. Now are we done here?'

'Not yet. Did he visit you at your place, wherever the hell that is?'

'It is where it is,' Rafferty said.

'You're going to have to learn to trust,' Cross said.

'Yeah? Well, Dr Phil, trusting hasn't worked so far.'

'All this fine food, fine clothes ... listen, you probably live in Meridian Hills. Cops didn't make that kind of money when I was on the force.'

'You'll never make that kind of money,' Rafferty said, 'doing repos and wayward husbands.'

'How often did you go to his place?'

'Two, three times a week.'

'Overnight?'

'I can't do this,' Rafferty said. He went up the steps. Cross could hear the door slam.

'What would this cost me?' Shanahan asked the man who came out from the little hut on the used car lot.

It was a '99 Infiniti G20, silver, moon roof. Leather seats. It seemed small compared to his old Malibu, but he liked it. He'd already sat inside. Closer to the windshield than his old car. The hood was shorter. But the door shut with solid sound. The whole car seemed more solid than his old Malibu.

'Make an offer,' said the man, cheerfully. He was in his shirtsleeves, with a tie, loose at the neck.

'No, what you want for it?'

'Power windows, leather seats,' the guy said, nodding. 'Good choice. 63,000 miles. Should go for another 60,000 easy. Cassette deck. Air-conditioning.'

'And that means you are going to sell it for...?'

He named a price.

'That's the best you can do, right?' Shanahan asked. 'I mean this is like a baby Infiniti, right?'

The guy was starting to perspire. The office was probably air-conditioned. Outside wasn't. There wasn't another soul on the lot. The multi-colored plastic flags that were strung around the perimeter of the lot were as still as a photograph.

'Like I said, make an offer.' He tugged at his collar. He was struggling to keep up his enthusiasm.

Shanahan gave him a number.

The guy nodded, but it wasn't one of agreement. It was a nod of 'OK, I am considering what I'm going to say because I don't know just exactly what that will be'. When finally he spoke, he said he'd have to talk to his manager.

'Is that true?' Shanahan said.

The man smiled. Like the nod, the smile didn't mean what it's supposed to mean. It meant 'Please don't play with me. It's too fuckin' hot'. The man said nothing; but that's what his face said when he smiled.

The guy started back to the office.

'Is there anybody even in there?' Shanahan asked.

'I have to make a call.'

'Look, I like the car. This is what it's worth to me. If you need to get more out of it, fine. But don't play games and go inside and have an imaginary conversation with an imaginary manager and come back with a counter-offer. If I don't get this car, it's not a crisis. I'll find another.'

'OK,' the guy said.

'OK what?' Shanahan said. 'You'll agree to that price?'

'That's the OK I was thinking about,' the

59

guy said, somewhere between bored and tortured.

'Now I need to take it for a little drive to a mechanic. What do you think? Is that OK with you?'

'Right now ... yes. We can arrange that.'

# Five

Cross heard the front door open and footsteps approaching. Since Rafferty's storming out, he had meanwhile seated himself on the sofa and was watching a commercial for an exercise machine.

'Yes, Goddammit, I stayed there overnight,' Rafferty said, coming back down into the living room, anger boiling up inside him.

'Rafferty, I don't care if you sleep with elephants, let's get past this strange prudery of yours or whatever it is. I worked vice, remember?'

'If you think I'm going to give you the intimate details...'

'If you think I want them and have those mental images inside my brain, you're too dumb to live.'

Rafferty laughed. 'Look, you have me. I have no place to go. I just need you to tell me if you're in or out.'

'The biggest problem I have with all of this is that you went to Shanahan and then to me,' Cross said.

'Feelings hurt?'

'You missed my point. You hate both of us.'

'Actually,' Rafferty said, calming considerably, 'the reason I don't like you, or him, is that you guys work hard for your clients, and that's usually contrary to what I'm trying to do. You keep a confidence and you're like dogs on the scent. You never give up. That's what I need.'

'Then trust me,' Cross said.

'So are we done with the questions?'

'You have to be kidding? You a real cop?'

'Doctors make lousy patients, so I guess cops make lousy clients. I'm sorry.'

'What did you two talk about when you were together, you and your friend?'

'What's that got to do with anything?' Anger was building again, at least serious impatience.

'C'mon Rafferty, sit down. I'm not trying to get to know your sensitive side. I'm trying to know your friend.'

Truth was, unlike what the cop shows on TV suggested, crimes aren't solved – at least not initially – by a strand of hair, fingerprints, blood-splatter problems, or other trace evidence. You may have to narrow the field that way, but you have to find the field

61

first. If Rafferty didn't kill his lover, then Cross had a big old universe in which to find the doer.

'Music, film and, as I said, food. He is … was an excellent cook.' Rafferty sat on the upholstered chair opposite Cross.

'What did he like?'

'Which area?'

'Any. All. Give me everything you can.'

'Classical, foreign, and shellfish.'

'You are a man of few words only when many would be better,' Cross said. 'Southern accent. You know where he was from?'

'The South.'

'Great. We ought to be able to solve this before the next Ice Age.'

'I don't know,' Rafferty said, sitting down. 'He was uncomfortable talking about his past, about anything personal.'

'You didn't find that suspicious?'

'Actually, I liked that about him. The last thing I want is to spend a whole lot of time talking about our mothers and high-school crushes.' Rafferty stood up again. 'Listen, I need you to agree to take the case or not. I can't keep going through all of this. If you are going to back out…'

'I won't,' Cross said. He stood. He extended his hand. He wasn't going to get much more now. He explained his rates.

Rafferty didn't flinch.

'You got a photograph?'

'You asked that already. No. Neither one of us wanted our picture taken. Know what I mean?'

'I need something. I really do.'

'I'll get you something,' Rafferty said. He stared at Cross. 'You won't ditch me? No matter what?'

'As long as you tell me the truth and don't withhold anything.'

Rafferty laughed. 'You and Shanahan. You're quite a pair. I might as well have gone with him.'

'You still can, if you want.'

'No,' Rafferty said. 'You're easier on the eyes.' He laughed as he moved back up the steps.

It was a fifteen-minute drive back into town from the lot just off the interstate that circled the periphery of the city. It was as if one drove the architectural timeline. Houses built in the eighties gave way to the seventies, until finally they had reached inside the city to about the thirties. The bar was in a deteriorating neighborhood, less and less blue-collar folks as customers and more and more down-on-their-luck people. Harry had half a dozen customers in his rundown but cozy bar on East 10th. The customers were regulars. Couldn't be any more regular, Shanahan thought.

'You could charge these guys property tax,'

Shanahan said.

'Yeah?' Harry said. 'If that's the case you are in arrears yourself.'

Harry was a small man, silver-haired, with thick glasses. He was the only person Shanahan talked to on any frequent basis over the last few decades, his only friend – that is until Maureen came along and changed everything. That's when Shanahan gave up full-time possession of his stool.

The place was barely lit, mostly from neon beer signs. The woman in the comic painting of a Rubenesque nude that hung over the row of booths was the only one who seemed comfortable in the heat. A floor fan re-circulated hot stale air and ensured that second-hand smoke made the rounds of the entire bar. The television, mounted above the bar, was on. The recently installed cable allowed Harry to play sports all day and all night. Baseball was on the screen now, with the announcer's words scrolling below; but it wasn't the Cubs. So, for Shanahan and Harry, it might as well have been a French cooking show.

Harry poured a shot glass full of J.W. Dant bourbon, slid it across the bar to Shanahan, pulled the cap off a Miller High Life and did the same.

'I need some advice,' Shanahan said.

'From me?' Harry said. 'You give advice, remember. I'm supposed to take it.'

'You never do,' Shanahan said.

'Why would I?'

'I'm buying a car,' Shanahan said, downing the shot, feeling the pleasant sting, knowing that was it for the day.

'What? You can't squeeze another ten years out of that '76 Malibu of yours?'

'It's getting in the way of business. Causes people to notice when I'm trying hard not to get noticed.'

'And you're doing something where you don't want to be noticed?' Harry asked, interested.

'I'm trying not to.'

'You don't make any sense,' Harry said.

'I just need you to take a look at the car, listen to it, tell me what you think.'

'It's out there?'

'Yeah. Can you take a minute?'

Shanahan knew the words Harry would use when he saw the car.

He did. 'Hoity toity.'

'A man your age should be driving around in a Buick or a used Lincoln,' Harry said.

'Too sporty for me?'

'Too young for you.'

'It's a sedan, Harry, a four-door sedan, not some little Porsche convertible.'

Harry finally gave in. He also thought the car sounded good, looked good, but confessed that with the increasing use of computers in car systems, he was less and less confident in his ability to determine an automobile's health. Shanahan decided he'd gamble on it despite Harry's thin recommendation.

Shanahan knew he didn't need a car as nice as this; but he also knew this was the kind of car that wouldn't stand out. It was only hoity toity in Harry's eyes. Being a couple of years old and hardly the top of the Infiniti line, it would blend in with all the other silver compacts on the road. All the cars looked alike anyway.

He bid his old Malibu farewell. As he drove back to his little bungalow on the East Side, he felt conspicuous and pretentious in even this slight bit of luxury. Maybe it was hoity toity.

Maureen was still not home when Shanahan arrived. During the length of the drive, the pleasure of air-conditioning, the solidness of the car and the buyer's remorse was dwindling. He was warming to a bit of creature comfort. Now he was eager to show it to the woman in his life.

Cross had tried several times to reach Shanahan. Nothing but a taped message. He'd already committed to Rafferty, but he was still curious about why Shanahan hadn't. Maybe it was just that the elder detective didn't want to work with someone he held in such low esteem.

At six, Cross finally connected.

'Where have you been?' Cross asked.

'Out and about,' Shanahan said, sounding uncharacteristically cavalier.

Cross laughed, then got down to business. 'Why did you beg off Rafferty?'

'He wanted to call the shots,' Shanahan said.

'What do you mean? He's the one doing the hiring.'

'No, he wanted to direct the investigation in very specific ways. You accept?'

'Yep. That all right with you?'

'Sure. I'm not partnering with you on this,' Shanahan said, 'but I know some things you may want to know.'

'Shoot.'

'Morgan Lee has New Orleans connections.'

'Hmmnh, how do you know that?'

'I found a piece of a prescription bottle on the floor in the bathroom. I called the number. It's a pharmacy in New Orleans. The prescription number belonged to Michael LaSalle.'

'Morgan Lee. Michael LaSalle.'

'Comes in handy when you're dealing with initials on luggage, monogrammed shirts, towels, bathrobes.'

'Pretty amateurish though,' Cross said.

'Well, maybe he didn't figure his crimes, if he committed any, were serious enough to get him killed.'

'Could be, and all of this is very interesting, but how in the hell do you know all of this?'

'I got in the house,' Shanahan said.

'How did you do that?' Cross asked, shaking his head.

'Got lucky.'

'Thank you for your full disclosure. You want the case? It's yours. He asked you first, anyway.'

'Are you pouting?'

Cross laughed. 'Maybe. A little.'

'Don't. I don't want the case.'

'Your friend Swann tell you all of this?'

'He didn't tell me a thing. And he's not a friend, Cross. But he is a good cop, unlike Rafferty.'

'You figure working with Rafferty could turn around and bite you in the butt?' Cross exhaled. He thought that Shanahan was probably right. Rafferty did seem to have the talent of turning diamonds into coal.

'But I'm interested,' Shanahan said. 'Unofficially and off the clock, let me watch your back. I need something to do while Maureen is out selling houses.'

'What else do you know?'

'The prescription was for Viagra. I told the pharmacist that the police were interested because there had been a murder and that I was a detective. I just didn't mention I was private, that maybe we could keep the New Orleans police out of it, if we could settle all of this in Indianapolis.'

'You get an address too?' Cross asked.

'No. It wasn't on the file. And the file was old. Three years give or take.'

'The victim was young, right. In his thirties?'

'Early thirties,' Shanahan said. 'My question exactly. Why does some kid need Viagra?'

'Maybe he had high blood pressure and was on some pills that caused problems. Maybe it was recreational? You know, just add to the experience.'

'Maybe whoever he was with wasn't desirable enough to get things going on their own,' Shanahan said.

'Or maybe it was for someone else who couldn't get it up.' Cross smiled.

'Rafferty?' Shanahan said. 'No, the prescription wasn't local.'

'Or someone. Maybe there is a Michael LaSalle somewhere.'

'Michael LaSalle, whoever that is, is connected to New Orleans. I have the prescribing doctor's name.'

'All in a day's work. And you can tell me who did it, right?'

Shanahan gave him the doctor's name.

'He's the murderer?' Cross said. 'You are good.'

'The good doctor might be able to get you to Michael LaSalle and then ... who knows?'

'Maybe. You think Rafferty will spring for a trip to New Orleans?'

'He will if he's smart. Then again...'

'Then again, maybe I'm just window dressing. You know, where he tells the jury that he hired a private eye to find the real killer.'

'One can learn from the O.J. Simpson trial. Thing is, Simpson wasn't thinking right. He waited until after he was arrested.'

'Rafferty said he loved the guy,' Cross said. 'O.J.?'

'OK, two can play the game. Morgan Lee. The victim, remember?'

'All the more reason, I guess. You only kill the ones you love. Still, odd thinking of Rafferty in love.'

'Everybody loves somebody sometime,' Shanahan said.

'Everybody loves somebody somehow,' Cross replied. 'That Dean Martin. One helluva smart guy.'

Maureen called Shanahan the 'Pasta King.' It wasn't true, of course, but after a couple of decades of living alone, he had developed some cooking skills beyond a steak and a baked potato. Though he fell short when it came to sauces and gravies, some vermicelli or penne pasta with any one of a variety of added ingredients could get him through the evening.

So there he was in the kitchen, a deep pan of spaghetti boiling on the stove and a chopping board ready for some garlic and orange peppers. A dozen small scallops and a bowl of butter sat off to the side. In ten minutes, he'd have dinner ready for Maureen, who was getting into something more casual. He had already poured her a glass of chilled Chardonnay, a bottle recommended by a clerk at the store. He had a beer open for himself.

As he smashed the garlic, he realized that he was enjoying his investigating so much more now he was doing it for free. This wasn't the old Shanahan. This was the Shanahan who just got back from a trip to Italy with his girlfriend. This was the man who just bought a new old car. This was the man who no longer spent the better part of the day sitting on a stool in a dark bar, anaesthetizing his brain – though there were certainly still days he spent a few hours there passing the time. Who was this man?

Maureen came in. She wore an over-sized white T-shirt and khaki shorts. Her auburn hair was down and the minimal makeup she usually wore was gone. She looked around the kitchen, found her wine and took a sip.

'Mmmnn, thanks,' she said. 'Where are the greens?'

71

'I'll sprinkle a little parsley in the pasta if that will make you happy,' Shanahan said.

'I'll make a salad,' she said, moving to the refrigerator. 'There's a silver car parked in our driveway. Is this something you want to tell me?' She smiled.

'You like it?'

'Leather seats, moon roof. I like it. You want to trade it in for my Toyota?'

'No, I have to look out after my image,' Shanahan said.

'What image is that?' Maureen said.

'Hoity toity. I'm hoity toity now.'

'Harry said that, right?' It was more a statement than a question. Shanahan didn't answer. 'So Harry thinks you've sold out. Is that it?'

'No, he gets jealous sometimes. It used to be you. Now it's my car.'

'And you?' she asked. 'Which one do you like most.'

'Ask me in a few weeks, when the newness wears off.'

'You mean my newness has already worn off?'

'But your oldness is damned fine.'

'That wasn't good at all,' she said. 'My oldness?'

'Your something or otherness. Incidentally, I think Cross is going on a little trip to New Orleans.'

'Incidentally, how nice for him. Incidentally, how nice for you to change the subject. That was a little clumsy too.'

'Good food there in New Orleans,' Shanahan said, putting the scallops into a skillet with melted butter.

'Yes. Cajun. Creole. Mmmmnn. Blackened redfish.'

'I could blacken the scallops if you'd like.'

'Please no. Take me for a drive tonight? Park someplace romantic,' she smiled, cutting into the romaine.

Ah, he thought to himself. Finally, he had successfully changed the subject. Food. Food was the trick.

# Six

For Cross, it was a matter of determining the next step. There was a murder victim and a client who may or may not be telling all he knows. Still relaxed from all the sun and fun in Miami, Cross was content to let the evening pass without progress on the case. But he did need to think about how he would proceed tomorrow. Before settling into a Shirley Horne CD and a glass of cheap Sangiovese, he booted his computer.

He Googled the victim's two aliases. Nothing he could use. He entered each name with New Orleans and Indianapolis. He got nothing worthwhile.

There was a knock at the door. By the time he navigated the steps and crossed the small room, there was no one at the door. But there was an envelope. In it was a stack of hundreds and a photograph. A dead guy. The dead guy. Frontal. Cross could guess what the backside of the guy's face looked like.

Dark, full head of hair. Small nose. Thick lips. Long eyelashes. On the pretty side, maybe. Blood on the pillow.

How painful was it, Cross wondered, for Rafferty to visit the medical examiner? More importantly, how dangerous was it for Rafferty poking around in a case that wasn't his, but that might lead back to him?

That was a point in Rafferty's favor. He was interested in finding out something.

Cross had some jack cheese in the refrigerator. He wasn't up to fixing dinner for himself. Too lazy. He opened the cheese, cut off a few slices and took them back into the living room.

Horne was singing 'In the Dark'. He almost wished it were Fall, so he could put a fire in the fireplace. A bite of cheese, a sip of wine. The cheese lasted him through two songs. He went back for more, missing a few bars of 'Kiss and Run'.

He wondered if Elena was still smiling.

'Where are you taking me?' Maureen asked.

The air-conditioning was on, the windows were open, the moon roof lived up to its name.

'Out to a romantic spot.'

'The House of Blue Lights?' she asked.

Shanahan wasn't sure it was there anymore. There were many versions of an old tale about a house on a deserted road. One was that a man killed his wife, got away with it, but was filled with such remorse that he built a glass casket illumined by blue lights that lit the sky just above his old mansion. High-school kids would park nearby, tell the story, and hope to scare their dates into their arms. This was well before movies like *Friday the 13th* and *Halloween*. He wondered if such tactics would work today.

'Not scary enough,' Shanahan said.

It took almost half an hour to get to West 71st Street, where Shanahan drove across the narrow causeway and parked just where it ended, across from the entrance to Bay Colony. Light from a three-quarter moon shimmered in the sky above the water as they crossed the causeway.

'Hmmn, aren't we a little old for this?' Maureen asked, as he leaned across to kiss her.

'Not too old. Or maybe I'm just going through my second childhood.'

They kissed.

'I'll be back,' he said, opening the door and stepping out on to the pavement. There were no cars going by.

There was a light above the entrance that spilled illumination on both sides of the gate. A camera, if it worked, would catch the comings and goings, but he wondered how well it would capture cars in the darkness. And if it did, it would have caught Rafferty's car. And the killer's? Presuming, of course, this wasn't the same person.

'You're casing the joint,' Maureen said, getting out.

'Kill two birds,' Shanahan said.

'I'm one of the birds?'

'No, no, no. Getting some fresh air, if you want to call it that, and satisfy my curiosity.'

A pool of light from a streetlamp also illumined the car and the two of them.

'This is about Rafferty?' she asked.

'Sadly, I think it's more about me than him. But yes.'

'What's this about?'

'Secrets. All sorts of secrets.'

'What do you think you're doing?'

'OK, I thought I'd give you my class ring,' he said. There was a bit of haze around the moon. If he remembered right, that meant it might well rain tomorrow. A good sign.

Maybe cool things off.

They half stood, half sat on the side of the car as Shanahan explained more about the case – the suspicions, the possibilities. He kept his eyes on the gate. It was quiet. A few cars passed by. One stopped to see if Shanahan was having car trouble. Finally, he got what he wanted. One of the residents pulled in. The gate opened slowly. The car passed through and disappeared around a curve before the gate began to close. Plenty of time, Shanahan thought, for a second car, lights out, to go in undetected. He had noticed when riding back out earlier with Lt Swann, that one didn't have to do anything for the gate to open from the other side. Not a lot of security, he thought.

'Over here,' Maureen said.

Shanahan walked over to the other side of the car. A little light spilled on what was no doubt a path. At the moment the path only led to darkness.

Maureen was quiet most of the way home, except to say, 'There's really no way to tell if someone's gay, is there? I mean for sure.'

Shanahan didn't answer. He didn't know the answer.

Judging from the time it was and the time he set the radio to go off, Cross figured he'd pressed the snooze button seventeen times. He had planned to get an early start. As it was, he'd get started before noon. That was early. He walked naked into the kitchen, ground some coffee, poured water into the Krups and pushed the button.

Santana suddenly blared from his bedroom. He had awakened between snooze alarms and had forgotten to click the radio off. As much as he loved Santana, he wasn't ready for 'Evil Ways' this early in the day.

The fact that his home was made from thick clay tiles, had a tile roof, and had the branches of a huge maple tree shield his house from the hot rays of the sun, meant that his place was cool despite the temperature outside. But several days of unrelenting heat and humidity meant that the outside was creeping in. And it had. Even so, he slipped on some boxer shorts and a T-shirt. He didn't want his bare butt to stick to the vinyl on the sofa.

In the kitchen he poured Cheerios into a bowl, dowsed them with milk, and munched on them while staring at the coffee machine. He waited for the contraption to sigh its last gasps before he poured himself a cup.

He took his coffee into the living room and settled, clicking on the TV. Too late for the morning news. Too early for the noon news. He gave Regis and Kelly a chance, but Cross wasn't ready for baby week and the cutest baby contest. Dogs, yes. Babies, no. He clicked the screen dark and silent, and was instantly bored.

He found the phone and punched in Rafferty's number. Rafferty answered, but he didn't want to talk. Instead they were to meet at the Lutheran Church on Pennsylvania across the street from the national headquarters of the American Legion.

Cross had some questions. What time had Rafferty arrived at Mr Lee's and what time had he departed? More important, what did he do between those times?

The small brick church was on the corner of Pennsylvania and Walnut. Cross imagined that it was built in the 1800s. It was a Lutheran church so it might have been for the German immigrants. The town was made up of Germans and Scots-Irish, initially. That is, if you don't count the native Americans. Then again, the place was a swamp, so there might not have been too many two-legged inhabitants.

There was parking behind the church, a gravel lot that could hold half a dozen cars. Rafferty's heavy-duty unmarked sedan was already there.

Cross went in the side door on Walnut. As his eyes got used to the dimness, he saw a kind of simple sternness to the interior. Aside from the huge stained-glass windows that let in some light, there was little fuss. Cross maneuvred to the center and down the aisle between rows of pews. He could see Rafferty waiting in the entry, which was better lit. As he approached, he noticed the huge pipes – a real and no doubt ancient organ dominated one corner.

Rafferty looked up.

'Why here?' Cross asked.

'You don't expect to run into too many cops in a place like this,' Rafferty said, looking around. 'I haven't been in here since I was eleven.'

'Last time you were in a church?'

'Back of the altar, there's a stairway. Upstairs, we used to get Bible lessons.'

'You learn any of them?'

Rafferty smiled. 'Didn't take, I don't think. I didn't like all that goody-goody stuff. Even then.'

'Judging by the headlines, there was a lot more going on here than met the eye, and it wasn't the goody-goody stuff.'

'Oh, that's the Catholics. They have all the fun.'

'When did you get to Morgan's house?'

Rafferty went quiet. He closed his eyes. 'Not quite midnight,' he said.

'Why so late?'

'It's the way it was, sometimes. Some Brie. Some pâté. Quiet time.'

Same kind of thing Cross had eaten last night, he thought, but he doubted Rafferty went for jack cheese and seven-dollar wine.

'When did you leave?'

'I don't know. Two thirty maybe. I stopped by to see Shanahan. He'll probably know when I got there.'

'So, two and a half hours? What did you do to pass the time?'

'What I had to do to protect myself.'

'Computer?'

'I checked it just to see if I was on it somewhere. We didn't email so it would have to be something he put in for some reason. I also found some notes he'd saved. That's about it. I pretty much sanitized the place with regard to my presence in his life.'

'With regard to your presence in his life?' Cross repeated.

'Yes,' replied Rafferty, not catching on.

Just as well, Cross thought. 'Anything I need to see?'

'No.'

'Won't there be a phone call record?'

'Maybe. It would show him calling the police department. It doesn't record where the call ends up.'

'You were holding the cards close to your chest.'

'You're implying what?' Rafferty asked.

'You were both awfully careful.'

'That's the way it has to be sometimes. I'm a year away from becoming fully vested in my pension. He seemed to want to keep his life under wraps as well. That's another reason why we got along so well.'

'You were hiding the fact that you were gay in a macho profession. What was he hiding?'

'That's for us to find out, isn't it?'

'You know anything about his life in New Orleans?' Cross was fishing a little.

'No, you know something?'

'New Orleans means nothing to you?'

'Nice place. What does it mean to you?'

'I don't know yet. You know anything about a Michael LaSalle?'

'No. Should I?' Rafferty snapped.

'Maybe. There's some connection. Initials are the same.'

'What are you saying? Where are you going?' Rafferty went to the front door, opened it. He looked out, over the skyline. 'None of this makes any sense to me.'

'Just running some ideas...'

'How in the hell do you know anything yet? You still have friends in the department?'

'Probably not.'

'Level with me, Cross.'

'You don't know anything about this guy before he met you. He had to have had a life. Maybe it was in New Orleans.'

'Maybe it was in Biloxi. Maybe it was Memphis.' Rafferty came back toward Cross. 'Why are you focusing on New Orleans? You know something, don't you?'

'Why don't you run a Michael LaSalle through the system ... however you guys do that now? Let me know what you find.' Cross went back to the front double doors to leave.

'You're not talking this around, are you? I mean, about me?'

'Is this all about your pension?'

Rafferty hit Cross on the shoulder in a not quite friendly way. It was the tough kid in the neighborhood's way of saying 'Back off'.

'Listen, Cross...'

Cross stepped in the cop's face. 'You don't want to do that.'

'I'm sorry. I mean it.' Rafferty backed up a step. 'You know, I'd make it all public in a heartbeat if it would do one of two things. If it would find the killer, or if it would bring Morgan back. Otherwise, there's no point. In the end, Cross, I'm a very practical person. And I'll do whatever I have to do to protect myself.'

'I take your words seriously,' Cross said. 'You willing to put your money where your mouth is?'

Rafferty's face suggested he was listening.

'I need to go to New Orleans,' Cross said. He waited for the reaction.

Rafferty took a deep breath. Nodded. 'No five-star hotels and this isn't a two-week vacation. But yes.'

'You sure you want to know what I find out?'

'Yes.'

'No matter what it is.'

Rafferty suddenly looked tearful.

Cross wanted to be out of there.

The sun had been out when Cross went into the old building. It was gone when he left, something like his mood. Churches did that to him. Depressed him. Up in the sky, even darker clouds were in the distance. They were coming his way.

Shanahan sat in the upholstered chair, rereading the morning *Star* to see if there was anything else on the Morgan Lee murder. The cat was on his lap. Einstein's frail body barely registered weight. Shanahan heard the shower stop. Maureen had slept in – a serious sleep-in. She had no morning appointments and she stayed awake, nursed another glass of the Chardonnay and a very thick book.

She came into the living room wearing a white terrycloth robe and wet hair. She was beautiful, he thought, no matter what.

'You interested in moving into a new place?' she asked.

'What?'

'I've got the listing. It's a really a nice place,' she said. 'Trees, a fireplace. Up an incline away from traffic.'

Shanahan didn't know what to say. His first thought was to dismiss the thought. What did he need with a new place? This one was fine. He was glad he waited around for a second thought. What about her? She had dealt with this place for a few years now. Aside from a little fresh paint, this was Elaine's house and this was his history – Elaine's and his – not hers. And the history wasn't altogether that pleasant for him either.

'I think we can swing it,' she said. 'Not by myself. You'd have to like it. You'd have to want to.'

'Can I sleep on it?'

'Yeah, but don't sleep too long. It's a nice house and it could go at any time.'

'Could one room be mine? I mean ... you know what I mean.' He felt uneasy. He felt uneasy about the car, about having to think about the car and what it meant.

'I do. And yes. Definitely, yes. It won't be *my* house. It will be ours.'

'Sell this one, you mean?' A flash of lightning brightened the room in a surreal fashion.

'Yes, or did you want a *pied-à-terre*?'

Suddenly, the light in the house was sucked out. Thunder cracked so loud, Einstein shot off Shanahan's lap, launched by digging his paws into the old detective's thighs.

'Damn.'

Lightning flashed again, casting quickly changing shadows on the walls.

'All right, all right,' Maureen said smiling. 'You don't want to move, just say so and leave out the drama.'

# Seven

The rain didn't bother Howie Cross. He was escaping it anyway. It might have been better to schedule a trip to New Orleans in March or April when it wasn't so hot and humid, but then he was hot and humid in Indianapolis and before that in Miami. He was getting used to living in a steam room.

The man sitting uncomfortably close to him in the plane wore an Army uniform. Staff Sergeant, Cross noted, seeing just one rocker beneath the stripes. He was a big man and his body seemed to ooze out of the tiny space allotted him. He also seemed to spill out of his uniform. His name sounded French. Unfortunately, with the thick Southern drawl, Cross couldn't quite lock the sound of it in his sleep-deprived brain. Finding out that Cross was to be a first-time visitor to the crescent city, the soldier set about informing him of New Orleans' characteristics and its many eccentricities.

New Orleans, for the most part, lies between the Mississippi River and Lake Pontchartrain, the man told him. It is one of the few cities in the world that is below sea level – that is, of one so close to the sea. Cross remembered movies that showed the eerie, above-ground tombs in the cemeteries.

'You see,' the man said, 'if a big wave'd come in and come over the levee, the water'd be trapped in there, wouldn't be no place to leave. The whole city would be underwater for a long, long time.'

'I should get a hotel room on the twenty-second floor. Is that what you're telling me?'

'N'Awlins,' the man continued, 'is the most un-American city in the US of A. Now, I don't mean that in a bad way, not like San Francisco where they got all of them left-wing weirdoes. I mean, we got our faggots, but faggots down here know to keep it in the Quarter and nowhere else.'

Cross thought that one man's weirdoes were another man's peer group, but said nothing. He didn't want to encourage the discourse.

'But the people in my hometown,' the man continued without encouragement, 'are just from a different place altogether – not a bad place, mind you. Just a bunch of people that look at life a whole lot different than, say, the people where you come from.'

Cross just wanted to lean up against the window, close his eyes and go to sleep. Unfortunately, the sergeant was intent upon educating him, taking no notice of Cross's turning away or leafing through the flight magazine.

'Now where you come from there's lots of people believe in the Bible,' he said. 'Isn't that right?'

'That's what I read in the papers,' Cross said.

'And they sin and they hide it and they feel all guilty. The people down my way feel the same way in as much as we all believe in the Bible too. Difference is, we take a whole lot of joy in our sinnin'...'

'I see,' Cross said. The guy wasn't going to look away until he got a response.

'And in our evil, too!' His smile was greasy.

Now he was done ... for a while.

Shanahan could hear the rain hit the metal hatch. He was in the coal room, in the basement. A gas furnace was installed decades ago, so there was no more need for the black bricks. The walls had been painted long ago and the room was now used for storage. But he remembered shovelling the coal into the furnace one chilly night and his son, Ty, looking into the flames.

'What are you doing?' Shanahan asked.

'I want to see if Shadrach, Meshach and Abednego are dancing in there.'

'And why would they be dancing?'

'Because they refused to worship gold,' Ty said. 'So some bad people threw them into the furnace to burn them up, only they

88

didn't. They danced instead.'

'Good choice. This is Bible school stuff, huh?'

'Yeah,' Ty said cheerily, peering in.

'You see them?' Shanahan asked.

'I think so. They're very small and they jump around a lot.'

'I imagine they're dancing pretty quick,' Shanahan told him.

People see what they want to see, Shanahan thought, as the memory faded and he sat on a box of old books once belonging to Elaine before she set out on her own with the hairdresser. Shanahan opened a large cardboard box filled with photographs, some framed, some in special foldout paper frames, and some loose, some frayed, creased or missing a corner.

Strange, old photographs now. The older ones were sepia toned on thick, hard paper. There was his father – all stiff and stern. His mother, worn, sad and sober. He pulled them out of the box one at a time. Some faces, especially on the old tintypes, he didn't remember or perhaps never knew. Could have been someone from Elaine's side or great-grandparents of his own. His grandmother. He respected her. Quiet. She didn't talk about other people. 'Think your share and say nothing,' she often said, or 'Wait until you've walked a mile in their shoes.'

There was a photograph of a young

Dietrich Shanahan, poker-faced, leaning against the side of a barn, staring back. What was he thinking? What thoughts were in this young boy's head? He had a sober view of the world even then. But there was so much he hadn't anticipated. War. The killing. The long, sad marriage. The longer separation.

There was another, this one of a much younger Dietrich. He was looking at someone off camera. In the lower right-hand side of the photograph was part of a leg, the body out of the frame. Who was that? He remembered. He'd dreamt about Fritz. Out of the blue. Now there was the photograph – a photograph that showed Fritz barely there. How strange for all of this to come up now. More than strange. The only thing left of Fritz was of him nearly escaping the frame of the photograph.

He remembered how sometimes his mother and father would be in Fritz's room. They shushed young Dietrich, shut the door to the room. Shanahan could hear mumbling. Sometimes a doctor would come. The three of them would talk on the front porch, grave faces under the porch light. Shanahan would ask them what was going on. But they wouldn't tell him.

He had stopped thinking of his brother, who disappeared suddenly, without explanations when he was six and his younger brother was four. Father, cold-stone silent as

90

always, would say nothing. And when he asked his mother, as he did many times, she would shake her head, lips as if sewn together. It was as if she had to talk herself out of talking.

Eventually he stopped asking. He stopped thinking of his brother. Dead? Kidnapped? Ran away? Put away? There were no answers and he'd nearly driven himself crazy trying to figure it out. So he stopped thinking about it. It seemed, sometimes, to still haunt him in shadowy ways. It was haunting him now.

He continued shuffling through the photographs.

There was a photo of Shanahan with Harry in their Army uniforms. On leave, sitting at a table in a nightclub with two women whose names Shanahan didn't remember or perhaps never knew. There was Elaine in another. So beautiful, arranging irises in a vase, and another of her standing on a dock, waiting to board a small boat; but it was as if it were another Shanahan who knew her. Not this one.

There was the birth photo of Baby Tyrone, who quickly became only 'Ty'. Ty at five in a cowboy hat on a Shetland pony. There was Ty at ten, right before he too disappeared mysteriously, though, Shanahan knew even then, safely in the care of Elaine and her new lover. That's when the photographs stopped. That's pretty much when Shanahan's life stopped, only to have started again a short time ago.

Maybe, Shanahan thought, he shouldn't have gone looking into the box, dredging up parts of life better lived unexamined. What would he do with these old images? He didn't want to take them with him to the new house. They had to go. What would he do with them? Would he want to weigh down his son with these little pieces of near meaningless history? Yes. Ty could decide. In fact, it was up to him to decide. These were photographs of his relatives, of his mother, of himself. He'd get the box off to California as soon as he could.

Sometimes he acted before he knew why he was doing it, he thought. It just now occurred to him that he was revisiting the past because he was about to leave it. He was ready now to make the move, to give up any remaining resentment and hurt. It was Maureen's time and he was with her.

Cross, in the heavenly silence that descended when the sergeant went to the john, thought about what life must have been like for Rafferty. Cops, as Cross knew from his time on the force, no longer used the 'n' word or any other racial slur in any public way, though they still did in private conversations with those who shared their views. But 'fag' and 'faggot' were still used freely and loudly to denigrate someone, anyone, regardless of their orientation, as it was in schools and in the playgrounds. It is the last allowable slur. Rafferty had to have heard it nearly every working day of his life, had to have ignored it, or laughed along with them.

No wonder he was such an asshole, Cross thought. Pissed and frustrated.

Cross could feel the weather creep into the walkway that connected the plane to Louis Armstrong International Airport. But he couldn't have anticipated the suffocating heat he felt when he went outside to find a taxi. If Miami was walking into an oven, New Orleans was a pressure cooker, temperature pushed up all the way. He thought he could almost swim in it.

The taxi, a van with Venetian blinds and big comfortable seats, was a relief. The driver, a plump young woman, ratcheted up the air-conditioning. She didn't say anything after asking where he was going. The city, at least on the trip from the airport, wasn't particularly different than any other until they crossed big, wide Canal Street and slid into the narrow streets of the French Quarter.

He didn't know what street he was on but it was a good thing it was one-way. There was only room for one car. People walked casually on the sidewalks as if they had all day to get where they were going. Several streets in, the driver turned right, pulled over. There was his hotel, named after a saint, and Cross again was immersed in hot and wet.

Shanahan stood on the porch. He stared at his new car, wondering why he'd bought it. He liked it, but felt odd about having it. Seemed to him pretentious. He felt self-conscious behind the wheel. He knew better, but he felt like people were looking at him. Of course, that was crazy. And even if they did, why did he care? It was better than his old car. This one was solid, tight. It made the Malibu seem like a big hollow tank. The old car was hindering his work. At one time it was just an ordinary Chevy. Now, because of its advanced age and rarity, it was an eye-catcher as well as an eye-sore. One day, it would just die. Why in the hell was he having these thoughts? He didn't care what people thought. Maybe it was just the change. You go along for decades with everything staying the same...

'What are you doing?' Maureen asked, coming to the door.

'Thinking about the rain,' he said.

'You're not either. You're thinking about the car. Buyer's remorse?'

He shook his head no.

'You like it?'

He came back inside.

'I do.'

'Something's wrong,' she said.

'Nah,' he said. The thunder was reduced to distant grumbling. 'You talking about a new house. I deserted that old car that was with me for years. I'm drinking wine.' He almost smiled. 'I'm not sure I know who I am anymore.'

'We don't have to get a new house,' she said.

'No. It's good. This isn't our house, anyway. It was hers. I stayed too long. Time for a change. When can we look at this place you have your eye on?'

The New Orleans weather had already exhausted him, and he was in no hurry to venture from his air-conditioned hotel room. But he had work to do and not a lot of time to do it.

First stop the drug store. Cross consulted the map he received at check-in. Royal Drugs would be only a few blocks away. He'd walked only one block before he could feel his lightweight T-shirt begin to stick to his back. He crossed Bourbon – busy already and night had not fallen. Mid-afternoon and already drunk men walking, music blaring, young, black tap-dancers dancing. The streets were awash with football team T-shirts and baseball caps. Men and women drinking beer and daiquiris and something, judging by the signs in street-side vendors, called 'hurricanes'.

The pharmacy was out of the fifties or forties. Tiled floor, small soda fountain. The only thing that gave away the decade was the rack of Hollywood DVDs.

What Cross got from showing the photograph to the pharmacist was that the dead man wasn't known there as Morgan Lee. The response was more enigmatically silent when asked if the dead man was Michael LaSalle.

Back in the hotel room, with a cold margarita in a large plastic glass that he picked up at a bar downstairs, Cross checked the phone book. The doctor was listed, but when Cross called, he was with a patient. Call after five and before six, the Southern voice told Cross. As far as the Lees and the LaSalles were concerned, there were plenty of them, but no Morgan Lee or Michael LaSalle. The M. LaSalle belonged to a woman, Mary, according to the answering machine.

He could call them all. And he did at a buck a call. Unfortunately, most of the responses were recorded, not human. He noted the ones he'd missed.

He was curious about the French doors almost hidden behind a table chair. He slipped through and opened the doors to find a large balcony. Why had they hidden it? It didn't matter now as he rearranged the table and chair to allow easy passage, noticing that an electrical cord stretched across the passageway. That was the reason. They didn't want him to trip and weren't industrious enough to find another plug. He'd have to be careful. There were only two chairs on the balcony and no table. Another reason to disguise the balcony.

A wave of heat and he nearly retreated, but he had a balcony, dammit. He took what was left of his drink out and sat in the wrought-iron chair. His view wasn't one of the main streets. Residences as far as the eye could see. Most of them with balconies and ferns and flowers. But no people. He moved the chair back toward the door, feeling the air-conditioning seep out on to his sweaty body. A third reason to hide the balcony. People like him would leave the doors open and boost the energy bill. Tough, he thought. He sipped his drink, tried to come up with a plan.

The plan he came up with was go get another margarita.

Cross never napped. When he woke up he was rested and hungry. The room was dim at dusk. He'd missed his call to the doctor. He would try again in the morning. All right, he told himself. Shower, shave, dinner and then out to the bars – unfortunately it would be the gay bars, not the ones that held any promise for him.

Yes, he had a plan.

By the time he was ready he was starved, but clean. He walked the streets, trying hard to avoid Bourbon Street. Unfortunately, there were only two kinds of places to eat. There was the po' boy variety and the expensive variety. Even in the evening he was working up a sweat just meandering. The back streets were quiet and you could hear bats clicking somewhere invisibly up above.

It was more a matter of hunger and impatience that he settled on one of the most expensive places he passed by. The menu posted in front of what appeared to be a small cottage was exotic: Crispy Smoked Quail Salad. Sauteed Sweetbreads. Rabbit. And the one he decided upon – a less adventurous Salmon in Gewurztraminer sauce.

He was done walking. He wanted to eat. He wanted to be pampered. He would, maybe, go half with Rafferty on the dinner tab. The restaurant was Bayona on the Rue Dauphine. There were umbrella tables outside and white tablecloths inside, where he was seated inside at a 'special table', one reserved for stray singles who hadn't the presence of mind to call ahead. This was, after all, a swanky place.

The crowd was rich; you could tell by the clothing, the haircuts and the confidence. Cross would hold his head up high, though he thought it likely that the eight-year-old girl dining with her mother and grandmother had a higher annual income.

As Cross expected, he was treated well – finished plates discreetly removed, wine glass filled in a way that was nearly unnoticeable, and more than one inquiry about how things were going at his little table of one. Cross wasn't about to show anyone at the restaurant the photo of the victim. It was a little too morbid. But he did ask one of the waiters – the one who seemed to be in charge – if he knew of a man in New Orleans by the name of Michael LaSalle.

The waiter's face froze. Eyes widened for a second. There was a slight shake of the head, indicating 'no'. Next a cool smile and a question. 'Is there anything else I can get you?'

Cross was sure the man knew him or knew of him; but it would be pointless to push him. Perhaps Michael LaSalle was known in the French Quarter. New Orleans wasn't a small town, so this could be a stroke of luck.

Dinner and coffee had taken Cross to nine. Probably too early for the bars, but he'd give it a shot. According to the list he took off a website before he left Indianapolis, there were a seven or eight bars in the Quarter and a couple within blocks of Bayona.

The Corner Pocket was empty and the bartender didn't recognize the photo. He was just standing in for an hour before the regular bartender got there and he hadn't been in town very long.

'The place gets lively at ten when the boys dance,' he said.

Cross nodded. He kind of hoped he didn't have to come back, that something would break beforehand.

At the other end of the block was the Double Play. It was busier. At this hour it certainly wasn't rowdy. A few guys, mostly older, drank beer and chatted. Nobody knew anything about Michael LaSalle and their responses seemed sincere. They said the bars on Bourbon were probably already 'cookin'.

Cross tried to find the flow on the street. No cars now, just a sea of people. Most of them looked like conventioneers struggling to get a little New Orleans wildness out of their systems. The street smelled of beer. As he walked, occasional blasts of the blues, then hard rock, then Dixieland bellowed out of the bars. People screamed and whooped, peeking into doorways to see what band was playing, or what girl was stripping. There was even a 'live sex' club. Cross might have looked upon all of that more compassionately had he consumed a little more wine.

The biggest gay bars on Bourbon – both of them – faced each other from across the street itself. Lots of noise. People were beginning to rev up for an evening of debauchery here, as they were all along Bourbon Street. The bartenders at both places worked hard and fast, but they tried to be polite when Cross asked them about LaSalle. They didn't know him. And they didn't recognize the picture. At one bar Cross asked the bartender if he should come back later.

'You won't be able to hear yourself ask the question, let alone hear the answer.'

Cross grabbed a beer, sipped it slowly, trying to kill a little time until ten. He looked around, trying to find something. He wasn't sure he'd know it if he saw it. It was all pretty tame. Then again, it was still early in the party town.

# Eight

Shanahan prepared for bed. He'd watch a little TV while Maureen read. He'd drift off. That was the routine. He wasn't so sure it would be that easy this evening. There was a lot eating at his brain. The old photographs. Memories. The idea of leaving the house he'd lived in for decades. He had no particular attachment to it. It wasn't full of happy times. In fact, his mind had recorded very little of what went on there. Yet, it was something to think about.

Then too, he hadn't divorced himself from

the murder case. It was more than being an old man with time on his hands. There was something important about its resolution. He didn't like the idea of Rafferty getting away with it if, in fact, Rafferty did it. He also didn't like the idea that Rafferty had come to him for help and that Shanahan booted him away. What if he were innocent? And worse, either way, Shanahan was an accomplice to murder or had obstructed an investigation.

Maureen was deeply engaged in one of her mystery novels. This one took place in Paris and no doubt involved food. That would make it a three in one for her. He wasn't one to talk through his problems anyway, so he tried to focus on the boxing match on the Telemundo channel. He had muted the sound. Maureen, who loved baseball, was not so enamored of boxing. Two Latinos fought, one smaller, older with tight muscu-lature and one a tall, younger man – almost boyish with an undeveloped chest. They weren't tentative. They were mixing it up. Shanahan was sure the older one would take it. He wasn't swinging as wildly. He was getting his jabs in. And he wasn't getting tagged. The younger one caught more head shots that he should have. He went down in the second, but was up quickly, flailing away.

It was over, Shanahan thought. The older boxer would out-point his younger opponent. Or he'd drop him. But it didn't happen that way. The young man caught his elder with an uppercut. The older man looked shocked, and while he was considering this surprise development, the younger boxer threw an overhand right and the older man not only went down on his back but also seemed to slide a few feet across the ring. Now it was over.

There was something unsatisfying about the bout. Perhaps it was that age and wisdom failed to trump youth and luck.

Maureen surfaced from wherever she was in Paris.

'What are you thinking?' she asked.

'Wondering how Howie is doing in New Orleans?'

'You ever have crawfish?'

'Nope. Don't want any,' he said. 'You know, we used to see them in the creek. We called them crawdads. They were ugly and never once did we think about eating them.'

Cross checked a couple of other bars nearby and then two bars on Rampart at the outer edge of the Quarter and close to the police station. One was a transgender bar. Festive. Loud. Well lit. The other was relatively quiet. None of those tending bar knew anything about Michael LaSalle. Neither did their patrons. If he had only three strikes, he'd be out twice. He'd saved the Corner Pocket for

103

last. It was on the way back to the hotel. There were other bars scattered around New Orleans and the surrounding area. He had hoped to limit his travels because of time and expense.

The Corner Pocket was dark and crowded. He looked for a seat at the bar, but decided against it when he saw a dozen young men dancing on it, encouraging customers to tip them by stuffing money in their shorts.

The clientele was diverse. Old men in comfortable clothes. Young men in jeans and T-shirts. Yuppies in blue button-down shirts. Guys with girls. Guys with guys.

The bar itself formed a square. Inside were two bartenders. An older man and a young black woman. They kibitzed with the dancers and the customers. The people standing around the outside of the bar were three and four deep, which made wading through the crowd difficult. The room behind the bar was the poolroom. Others gathered there, chatting, including others in their underwear or shorts, waiting for the shift change on the bar. Everyone seemed to know each other. Off the tourist track, perhaps, Cross thought. This is good.

A young, well-built youth with long blond hair and wearing only a pair of Calvin Kleins, smiled at Cross. Cross asked him about Michael LaSalle. He shook his head 'no', and slid through the crowd, maybe to smile at someone else who was more interested in him than in some guy named LaSalle.

Cross was about to edge between barstools to talk to the bartender when he saw three well-dressed black guys. Suits, ties. Looked as if they just got off work. They were more interested in talking and laughing with each other than the parade of male pulchritude prancing just above them on the bar.

'I wonder if I could trouble you?'

The largest of the three smiled. 'I hope we're not talking trouble. Nobody needs trouble on a Friday night.'

'No, no. I'm trying to find somebody.'

He gestured to the bar. 'Some of the finest in New Orleans.'

'Michael LaSalle.'

The man's head went back as if he'd been tapped on the chin. He nodded. 'What you want with Michael?'

'You know him?'

'As well as anybody can, I suspect.'

Cross pulled the photograph from his shirt pocket. It was too dark to see. One of the guys brought out a lighter.

'That's Michael. What's wrong with him?'

'He's dead,' Cross said.

The guy nodded. 'How did it happen?'

'Bullet. You don't seem surprised.'

'No. A man who lives like Michael LaSalle did courts death in any one of a number of ways. Then again, I guess maybe I didn't know him that well.'

'How did you know him?'

'Used to come in here occasionally, when he needed something to get him through the night. It was his last stop, that is, if something better, more profitable didn't come along.'

'He was a prostitute?' Cross asked.

'Not formally,' the man said. 'In his own way, yes. Somehow, whatever you did with Michael, you always managed to pay.'

'You?'

'No. Witness to the crimes,' the man said, leaning back, remembering.

'Who was closest to him?'

'His wife, maybe.'

'His wife?' Cross asked.

'His biggest catch,' the man continued, gossiping with gusto. 'She was from the Manchette family. Big, old money. Big, old power. Didn't last long. Shamed the family when they learned of the boy's proclivities. Maybe it wasn't so much his whoring, mostly it was just that he wasn't from the right family.'

'Got a class system down here?'

'Boy, do we?'

There was some jostling as one set of boys dismounted the bar and another climbed on.

'Does Miss Manchette have a first name?'

'Joan. Lives out in the Garden District. On

Audubon Boulevard.'

Cross thought he must have looked confused. What he was thinking was how this guy should know so much.

'Only the best live out there.'

'Really? You have the address too?'

'No, only way I'd make it past the guard would be to be on the service staff of one of the homeowners.'

'She lives there?'

'Family does. She probably lives with them.'

'You know a lot.'

'I read the papers. And I know Billy Dean.'

'Who is Billy Dean?'

He grinned big. 'I'm so easy, just blabbin' on like a songbird. Who are you?'

'That's fair,' Cross said. 'I'm investigating the murder.'

'Not a cop?'

'Nope,' Cross said.

'Why haven't I read about this murder?' the man asked. One of his friends had moved in close and was listening intently. The other had turned his attention to one of the dancers, who had knelt down and exposed himself.

'Officially, it is the murder of Morgan Lee. And it happened in Indianapolis.'

'Indianapolis?' the man asked, more surprised about where he was murdered than the fact he was murdered. He shook his head, turned back into the bar and sipped his drink.

'So, about Billy?'

'They had a business together. Didn't go well.'

'Billy who?'

The man was tired of talking, it seemed.

'Billy Dean, you'll find him in the book.'

The dancer who had entranced his friend was now in front of the man who'd talked to Cross. The dancer dropped to his haunches, pulled down the front of his shorts.

Cross, returning to his hotel, stopped for a margarita to go, went to his room and out on to the balcony. He sat and looked at the moon, heard the muted sound of music coming from somewhere, the sound of voices approaching and disappearing below.

He did have a plan now. Joan Manchette and Billy Dean. He'd gone all day, finding nothing. In the last hour, he got plenty. He stepped back inside, shut the doors, and took his thoughts to bed.

Cross woke up early. Not too early, but earlier than he needed to. He clicked on the television as he brewed coffee in the little gadget in the bathroom. The ABC Morning Show was on in all its insincere, fluffy splendour. People were dying and starving and being persecuted, but there was plenty of time for puppy psychics, Paris Hilton and anti-ageing creams.

He took coffee on the balcony despite the fact that the night had brought no relief to the heat. Across the street ferns were being watered automatically. It was quiet below. A few people came and went at the little grocery across the street.

Showered and dressed, he checked the phone book. No Manchette on Audubon Boulevard. But rich people don't list their numbers. There was no Billy Dean and no William Dean. He unfolded the larger city map and found several Audubons, but the Boulevard was off St Charles between Tulane and Loyola Universities. He knew about the St Charles streetcar and decided he'd save some bucks and get a tour.

He went to Bourbon and would head from Bourbon to Canal in order to get to the streetcar. Bourbon Street smelled of bleach, ammonia, garbage, and urine. There wasn't much going on, but it wasn't completely shut down. As he walked, he had to dodge guys hosing off the sidewalks, cleaning up before the afternoon. On the other hand, if he wanted he could still get a beer in a plastic cup or a T-shirt that said 'Jesus loves you, but everybody else thinks you are an asshole'.

The ride out was slow but pretty. The streetcars were a kind of military green, uncomfortable, and already crowded. The tracks were laid out on a center island of trees and grass that separated the lanes of traffic. The homes, especially after a distance, were graceful, beautiful and very Southern. The riders wore hats and T-shirts that suggested they were proud of their country or at least of their sports team.

Audubon was right where it was supposed to be. But coming up to the entrance, he noted how quickly his arriving by foot aroused suspicion on the uniformed man's face. He asked for Joan Manchette.

A call was made. There were questions from the person on the other end. Who was he? Who did he represent? There was a long silence after Cross mentioned Michael LaSalle. Cross figured he must have paced, under the careful watch of the guard, maybe ten minutes before the guard approached him. Beyond the gate were some of the finest homes one could find anywhere on earth. But he wasn't going to see them.

'They got in touch with Miss Manchette. She's at the shop.'

'The shop,' Cross said. 'What shop? Is she broken?'

'They said you could find her at Interiors Francais in the Quarter. Don't know more than that.' The accent was somewhere between Southern and New Jersey.

And back he went. Cheap transportation. The maids were in his hotel room, so he took the phone book out on to the balcony while they made the bed and cleaned the bathroom.

Yep, there was an Interiors Francais. He went in, closed the French doors and thanked them. They had been gossiping, but stopped to wish him a good day. People were polite. It seemed genuine enough. His feelings were confirmed at the hotel desk, where the lady cheerfully directed him to his destination.

The rain had stopped, Maureen was off to look at a house, Casey and Einstein were asleep, almost a full-time occupation for them as they got older, and Shanahan was antsy.

He drove the now familiar route to Bay Colony. He had an idea. When he got there, he pulled off and waited until he saw a car approach the gate. There was plenty of time to get in after the other car made its exit. Shanahan drove around and into the victim's driveway. The yellow tape was gone. He opened the rural-styled mailbox.

Bingo. The police had slipped up. The mail had not been stopped and there were likely a couple of days' worth judging by the stack. Shanahan wouldn't take it. That's a federal crime. But there was no crime in looking at the envelopes.

Indianapolis Power and Light. Some

charge card solicitations. Mostly junk. The curious piece was a newsletter from the Nash Family Values Institute. Shanahan knew of them. Anti-abortion, pro-prayer in the classrooms, opposed to stem-cell research, unfriendly to the theory of evolution and very, very anti-gay. Why was Morgan Lee on their mailing list?

Shanahan checked the address label. No mistake. It was sent to Morgan Lee – not to occupant – at this very address. Was he keeping track of the enemy? Or was he some sort of anomaly? A right-wing gay? Could be, he supposed.

He shuffled through a few more envelopes. Nothing strange. Coupons, magazine promotions. He put the mail back in the box and walked to the back of the house. He could hear cars whizzing by on 73rd just through the trees.

She was ravishing until Cross got a closer look. Joan Manchette was in her fifties, he thought. Not that older women were unattractive. He'd seen many gorgeous older women. And, in fact, she was good looking. It was just that Joan Manchette looked eighteen from twenty feet. Closer, she turned out to be tanned, in shape, and dressed to make the best of things, but still fifty.

Not that he was any great catch. At forty, he'd let a few extra pounds gather in unflattering places. He wasn't a smart dresser, was three weeks past a regular haircut, and most of his lines were more sarcastic than endearing.

'You're here about Michael,' she said, apparently surmising quickly he wasn't interested in the pricey French antiques that surrounded them.

'Yes,' Cross said.

'And you are...?'

'Cross. A private investigator from Indianapolis.'

She shook her head. Something wasn't registering.

'What's Michael up to?'

'Not much. I'm sorry to be the one to tell you,' he began, watching her eyes, 'but he's dead.'

Her face tilted upward, but her eyes were on him. Her chin jutted out. It was the prove-it-to-me look. Then she looked down, absorbing it, believing it. She lifted her head again, this time level with Cross. Blank.

'How'd you know I was here about Michael?'

'Word gets around.'

'Then you knew he was dead?'

'You hear a lot, but you don't believe all you hear,' she said.

Cross pulled out the photograph.

She looked. If she held four aces or two deuces, Cross wouldn't have been able to figure it out.

'Murder,' he added, ashamed at his hidden glee.

'In Indianapolis?'

'Yes.'

'Let's go into my office.' She turned and yelled mostly over her shoulder, 'Salvatore!'

A young man in a white shirt, tan slacks and sandals appeared.

'Take care of the front, would you?'

Cross followed her through the shop, into a sunny courtyard, where the faded paint on the walls, the sumptuous plants – some bearing fruit – the huge pots, and the rusted metal furniture seemed to sum up the decadent beauty that was Joan Manchette and New Orleans.

At the other end was an arched doorway that housed other antiques. In the back of that was a room that held a huge metal table. Behind it was a large ornate chair. In front of it were two, smaller matching ornate chairs. A ceiling fan stirred the air, moving the heat about. Classical music played not quite imperceptibly. Behind her was a six-foot-tall mirror in a gold frame that gave him full view of the room he'd just passed through.

She moved behind the table and sat in the Queen's chair. He sat in one of the smaller chairs.

'What on earth was he doing in Indianapolis?' she asked.

'Living as Morgan Lee.'

'How creative,' she said with an abundance of disdain. Her Southern drawl was softer, smoother than that of the guards. It was very lady-like.

On the desk was an Apple Computer, a stack of manila folders, and another stack of business cards in a clear plastic holder.

'May I?'

'Why not?' She looked at him curiously, picked up the top business card and handed it to him. 'You expect to be buying some French antiques?'

'You married now?'

'No, but thanks for asking,' she said. 'You know I am in the market. Perhaps you know of someone.' She gave him the look.

'Judging from your past, I'm guessing that I'm a little old for you.'

'Forty, right?'

'Thereabouts.'

'You're bad, you know. I like that in a man.'

Behind her on an ornate table that acted as a credenza was a photograph of two children. A boy and a girl aged eight or nine. The girl was older.

'Are these little LaSalles?'

'No they are little Manchettes. Mark and Sarah. First husband. Taken quite a long time ago. Now, they're out on their own. I prefer to look at them in their innocence, and I suppose to make me feel a little younger than I am. Incidentally, Michael and I were never married. People thought we were. He wanted them to think that. It was horrible enough for my family to see me with him.'

'He was living pretty high on the hog, as we say where I come from,' Cross said.

'We say that here too.' She allowed a grin, but retrieved it quickly. 'How was he able to do that?'

'Settlement from you?'

'No. Not really. Not enough to last very long. So how did he stay afloat?'

Cross couldn't imagine why she wasn't asking the obvious questions: who murdered him or why?

'I don't know,' Cross said. 'He seemed to be independently comfortable, but hiding from someone or something, don't you think?'

'You're not with the police, you said?'

'Not lately. Private investigator.'

'Yes, that's right. Working for whom?' she asked, the questions coming quickly and clinically.

'A client.'

'You won't disclose.'

'No.'

'Then maybe I won't either,' she said, suddenly pleased with herself.

Cross stood. 'No problem, I'll get your side of the story from someone else. Billy Dean, maybe.' Cross bluffed.

'Oh, sit down,' she said. 'I'm just teasing.'
She was also flirting.

'You don't seem to be too broken up or too curious about Michael LaSalle's death.'

'It's been three years, maybe four years since I've seen him. And if you knew to come talk to me, then you probably know that our splitting up wasn't amicable. He was a taker,' she said, raising her eyebrows, 'and I had plenty to take. I was a fool. My mid-life crisis.'

She said it with more humour than bitterness.

'You mentioned Billy Dean,' she continued. 'After Michael was booted from the house – and he was,' she added, smiling, 'he latched on to his old friend and gay playmate Billy Dean. They hatched a plan to go into the mirror business. Poor Michael had a head for using people, but somehow he couldn't translate that into business. He used Billy Dean's slight inheritance to start the business – none of his own money. Basically he wrung poor little Billy Dean dry. And Billy forgave him. That shop – they only sold mirrors, big, old mirrors, painted gold. Not gold leaf, mind you. Gold paint and trying to sell them for what you'd expect gold leaf to go for ... Am I boring you?'

'No,' Cross said, nodding his head back. 'There's a fellow who has been standing back there since we sat down.' Cross could see him in the mirror.

'That's Antonio. He's just being protective. Antonio,' she yelled, 'our friend here is harmless. You are harmless, aren't you?' She gave Cross a sexy smile. 'Or is this my lucky day?'

'Why do you think Mr LaSalle decided to go into hiding?'

'I have no idea,' she said. 'None. But I'm not saying that I'm surprised. He could make enemies easier than friends and turned most friends into enemies in the end. Only Michael LaSalle truly existed ... in his eyes, that is. He'd make you think he loved you, really. Then one day, he'd suddenly go cold. Either he became bored or he didn't need you anymore.'

'He didn't need you?' Cross asked.

'No. He did. He needed my money, my family's standing in the city. That gave him special entree to many places. His life was getting just too tawdry.' She looked at him squarely in the eyes. 'For me to say someone's too tawdry, now that's something.'

She smiled, gave him the look he interpreted as being game for an afternoon delight. Cross didn't consider himself much of a catch, but she was more than willing to have a little afternoon tumble anyway.

'I don't know much about Michael La-Salle, or Morgan Lee for that matter,' Cross said. 'What were his interests?'

'I told you. Himself.'

'Anything else?'

'He liked to sail. We belonged to the Yacht Club. Well,' she showed the face of equivocation, 'he liked to be seen on board and he liked to wear the clothes that people on yachts wear, but he didn't do anything. He didn't know fore from aft – at least on sailboats.'

'Anything else? Gambling, guns, stamp collecting?'

'He wasn't into games where people obeyed the rules. No. Even when they built the casino, Michael couldn't be bothered. Oddly, he'd rather go to church.'

'Church? After all you've said?'

'Devout Catholic. Cynical. Complained constantly about the hypocrisy. But he was there every Sunday.'

'The rules didn't bother him?'

'I don't know if he broke all the commandments, but he broke some of them many times.'

'When was the last time you saw Michael LaSalle?'

'Three years ago. The last time I remember seeing him he was making a fuss at the Yacht Club. I had him eighty-sixed and he had a problem with that.'

'Where were you last Saturday night?'

She smiled, gave Cross a naughty look.

'Sweetheart, if I wanted him dead I'd pick up the phone and place an order.'

'Tell me about Billy Dean. What happened to him?'

'Still around. Still has the shop, but he's not selling mirrors. Coffee cups and cute little pieces of art for the tourists. Not a bad location, near Austerlitz on Magazine, if you want to pay him a visit. He'll tell you some things, I'm sure. Is that it?'

'For now,' Cross said, standing. 'But what did you see in him?'

She stood as well, grinned. 'I saw the most stunning occasional beauty I've ever seen.'

'I don't quite understand,' Cross said.

'I don't quite either,' she said. 'But some days or maybe just some moments, his beauty would take your breath away. And at other times, he was just some guy on the street. I can't explain it.'

Cross left his card.

'Call me if you remember anything else.'

'I spend most of my time forgetting these days, intentionally and unintentionally.' She smiled. 'But not you. I'll remember you.'

# Nine

With a little help from one of the people at
the Central Library on St Clair, Shanahan
was able to locate media stories about the
Nash Family Values Institute. He had
remembered them correctly, but he had not
thought of them as being as powerful as they
claimed to be. From the stories he read, they
sure seemed to live up to their claims.

H. Ray Clarkson was the executive director
and spokesperson. And while he was just one
of the many gainfully employed, only Clarkson was quoted in the stories. It was his
picture all over the website and all over the
media. Shanahan remembered him as a
regular talking head on the Sunday morning
news shows, *Larry King*, *Nightline*, and
others. He was both a local resident and a
national figure.

His most recent clips showed him to be in
his fifties, glasses, his embarrassing comb-
over seemed to emphasize rather than hide
his bald head. He was one of those Reverend
Doctors that make it confusing when trying
to address him with respect.

Shanahan would have Maureen find out

more on Google in the evening. He already knew that the institute was anti-everything but Ozzie and Harriet. Why would a young, gay guy, even a closeted one, be on this organization's mailing list?

Interesting, Shanahan thought. Maybe it was a joke or a form of revenge, like scratching your ex-girlfriend's phone number on the face of a public telephone. He realized how antiquated that was. It would be some sort of revenge on the internet. He'd ask Maureen to look up Morgan Lee and Michael LaSalle as well as the institute and its leader.

The door of Billy Dean's shop, Demimondaine, was posted with a handwritten note: 'Back in twelve minutes'.

Twelve? Cross thought. Was his absence so perfectly timed? Not good for business to be closed like this. But if he had a one-person shop, things do come up. The shop wasn't what Joan Manchette had described. The store window showed two mannequins in wonderfully sleazy costumes. Inside, as Cross peered in, were feather boas, masks, fishnet stockings, mirrored jock-straps, capes.

Cross was about to leave when he saw movement inside. He pressed his face to the glass only to be face-to-face with Billy Dean. The young man opened the door.

'How long have you been waiting?' he asked.

'Eleven minutes, fifty-eight seconds,' Cross said.

'*Voilà*, we are open, come in.'

Howie Cross had seen many Billy Deans. Billy could have been in his mid-thirties trying to look like he was in his early twenties, trying the same trick as Joan Manchette, but without the talent or perhaps the dedication.

Billy Dean wore a baseball cap emblazoned with 'Yacht Club' on the front. He'd been away, because as he came back to his seat he took off his cap to settle back into business. His blond hair began after two inches of brown roots gave it away. He wore a tight black T-shirt that clung to his skinny chest. His black jeans did the same. His black Keds High Tops were starting to wear through.

'You here about Michael?' he asked.

'Word gets around,' Cross said, not surprised. But who told him? Joan Manchette or the guys at the Corner Pocket?

Billy Dean shrugged like maybe he'd better not say. 'Word's around. It's OK. I cried all night long. It's all out, I think.'

Last night. That meant the boys from the bar, probably. Maybe he'd stopped by later. The night was still young when Cross left.

The young man lit a cigarette, looked at Cross, upset.

'Is it all right if I smoke?'

'It's your shop,' Cross said. 'Your lungs.'

123

He stubbed it out. 'Sometimes I don't think.'

'Let me show you something,' Cross said, reaching in his shirt pocket and pulling out the now tattered photograph of Michael LaSalle, eyes closed, asleep one might guess except for the blood.

Billy Dean looked, turned away as if he'd been slapped.

'I'm sorry,' Cross said, thinking maybe he didn't have to do this; but he wanted to be sure.

'He never had his photograph taken. Never.'

'Why?'

'He wouldn't allow it. He knocked a camera out of my hands once, because he thought I was going to take his picture.'

'Why though?'

'Said photographs were lies. The moment it's taken, that image is already wrong. I think it was something else.'

'What?'

'I think he was afraid it would make him one thing,' he said, picking up the dead cigarette and lighting it again. He took a drag, making a face, no doubt from the first nasty rush of bitter ash. His mind went somewhere else for awhile. He came back. 'Can I see it again?'

'Sure.' Cross handed him the photo then went to the counter where the cash register and charge card machine were among the general clutter. Billy Dean stared at the photograph for a long time. He held it delicately at the edges. He didn't want to smudge it. He stared as if in another world, until Cross gently reached over and took it from him.

'What does Demimondaine mean?' Cross asked, to get things going again.

'Oh, it's like Demimonde. Demimondaine means lady of the evening. It's sort of what we sell here. Ways to be someone you aren't, but want to be – at least for a few hours.'

'So what happens around here on week-ends, Billy? You go out to the bars?'

'Sometimes,' he said.

'How about last Saturday. Were you hanging out somewhere? Corner Pocket, maybe.'

'No, I go sometimes during the week when it ain't busy,' Billy Dean said.

'So, Saturday night, where were you?'

'With somebody I know,' he said.

'Who'd that be?'

'My personal life, OK? Anyway you said Michael was killed in Indianapolis.'

'You ever been there?'

'Indianapolis. Went through it maybe. On the way to Chicago. Didn't stop. Don't know much about it except the race. I got work to do.'

'Yes. OK. Give me another minute?'

Billy Dean nodded.

'You were close to Michael LaSalle,' Cross said.

'We went to school together, came out together – literally.' He smiled. 'I mean I came out and he came out and went in and came out and went in ... We were best friends. I could tell him anything. And he could tell me too. You know? You're a private eye, right?'

'At least the gossip is accurate.'

'They say he was murdered.'

'Shot in the head. We're trying to find out who did it. I'm trying to get some background on Michael LaSalle. He was going by the name of Morgan Lee. Did you know that?'

'No. He left three years ago. I was afraid something happened to him. He didn't say goodbye. He would have said goodbye. I told the police. I mean, I reported him as a missing person.'

'You did? What happened?'

'Nothing happened. They don't care what some queer does or says.'

'Does the name Morgan Lee mean anything to you?'

'No.' Billy Dean seemed to drift off again. 'I guess he wanted a fresh start,' he finally said.

'Did he have a reason to hide?'

'I don't know. He got himself in a lot of trouble off and on.'

'You were partners in business, right?'

'Yeah, it didn't work out so well.'

'You lost money?'

'No. Michael did. He put up the money.'

'That's not what I heard,' Cross said.

Billy Dean shrugged. He seemed embarrassed.

'Somebody told me,' Cross continued, 'that he went to church.'

Billy Dean laughed. 'Yes. I understood everything about Michael except that. *Every* Sunday. Hung-over. Still drunk. He'd have to go.'

'Did he ever say why?'

Billy Dean was quiet, thinking. His eyes did a little dance.

'No. But the way he talked, it was like he went because he hated it. He went to hate it. I don't know.'

'You go with him?'

'Sometimes.'

'Did he have any other friends besides you?'

'No, not real ones. He had pretend friends for things.'

'What things?'

'I'd rather not say.'

'He's in no position to feel betrayed. In fact, it might help find out who did this.'

Billy Dean seemed to be considering it, although he might just stay silent, Cross realized.

'I'm not passing judgement,' Cross said.

'Sometimes it was money, sometimes it was sex, sometimes to get something else.' Billy Dean looked down as he spoke. 'Sometimes, I mean later, he'd make friends just to embarrass Joan.'

'Joan Manchette?'

'Yes. Her and her family.'

'Tell me about Michael LaSalle,' Cross said.

Billy Dean shrugged again. 'I don't know.'

'You liked him. Why did you like him?'

'He was smart. And funny. And like I said before, I could tell him anything and it would be OK.'

'You could be you?'

'Yes. He knew me. He knew who I was. Completely.'

'You were close?'

'Yes. Real close.'

Billy Dean might have been trying hard to look younger. On the other hand, emotionally, Billy Dean was thirty-five going on thirteen. His face showed both the sweetness of understanding and accepting pain, and the sadness of someone who had been deserted too many times. While lines around his eyes confessed his age, the brightness of the eyes themselves suggested hope. Promise. Or maybe just a willingness to be fooled again.

'But he could be mean,' Billy Dean said. 'You know, when he was hanging out with the Manchettes, he'd go on their yachts and the boats of some of their friends. Once in a while I'd be crewing the boat and I'd come up and see him with his glass of champagne and it was like he didn't know me.'

'That pissed you off?'

'No. Really it didn't. He was just scamming them and he'd come back to me and he'd tell me everything.'

'Who else did he take advantage of?' Cross asked.

'Sometimes he'd go down to the Corner Pocket and get one of the boys, get them to do it with him for free. Get them to really like him and when they did, he'd lose interest. It was like a challenge, getting people to do what they didn't want to do, even if personally he didn't care whether they did it or not.'

'He made a lot of enemies?'

'Maybe, but you didn't want to be his enemy. He knew people so well, he knew just how to hurt them.'

'Why were you his friend?'

'Because he was different with me. He knew he could trust me.'

'You think you can help me find his killer?'

'You tell me what to do to help.'

'You have a business card?'

'No. People know where I am.'

Cross left his card anyway, as he had with Joan Manchette.

Before Cross went, he got the name of the church. It was in a quiet, middle-class neighborhood not considered New Orleans proper. The cab driver, an elegant-looking elderly black man, drove slowly deliberately, commenting on the weather, saying that it was best not to stand still on a sunny day for fear of getting wet.

Cross figured that moving slow in this climate wasn't lazy, it was smart. He had already learned to slow down his not particularly fast pace. Cross had the driver wait, gave him two twenties. The driver pulled the taxi a couple of houses ahead under a tree as Cross went into the church.

He probably should have called. He was glad to see there was a house connected to the church. He should be able to find someone to talk to who knew Michael LaSalle and what his story was.

This was the second time in a week that he'd been in a church. Times before that could be measured in years. The interior was far more ornate than the Lutheran church in Indianapolis where he talked with Rafferty. The ceilings were higher, the windows bigger, the altar grander.

No one was there, but Cross was content because it was cool and restful. If you didn't mind looking at the images that characterized the stages of the cross, one might have thought that this was designed to achieve peace of mind.

Hearing his own footsteps, Cross investigated the opening to the right. It led to a series of confessionals. He crossed back through the church to the other side and found an open door. Inside was lighter than the rest of the church. Cross could see two upholstered chairs and the edge of a table. Cross moved forward slowly, nudged the door open farther and peered around the edge of the door. A sixtyish man with the white collar of a priest was working away at a computer.

'Father?' Cross said, feeling very self-conscious. He's not my father, he thought. He often thought about how people took on special ways to be addressed. Ads in the paper that said 'please send résumé to Mr James', or PhDs who required they be addressed as doctors. Or medical doctors for that matter. Maybe he should add 'sir' to his name. Who are you? Well, I'm Sir Howard Cross. Sounded better than Howie. 'Father?' he said, out loud this time, acquiescing to protocol.

The man looked up. He had a fine head of red hair, a pair of horn-rimmed glasses, and a pleasant enough look about him.

'Yes, can I help you?'

Cross stepped in, though not very far. He felt shy. He also thought feeling shy was stupid. What was he? Eleven?

'I came here to ask some questions about one of your ... uh ... flock.'

Flock? Cross hadn't the right words for any of this.

The priest stood, came around the edge of the desk, and extended his hand.

'I'm Father Berry. Have a seat.' He gestured to the chairs.

They shook hands.

'I'm Howard Cross, a private investigator.'

'Private investigator. Really? I don't believe I've ever met a private investigator before. Thought you only existed in the movies.'

'You'd be surprised how many of us there are out there. Wayward husbands, businesses doing due diligence.'

'How can I help?'

'I need to get some background on Michael LaSalle.'

The priest shook his head. 'I'm sorry. I don't know him.'

Cross must have looked puzzled because the priest continued, 'But even if I did, I don't think it would be appropriate for me to talk about my parishioners.'

'I was given to understand that Mr LaSalle was very, very regular here.'

'Could be. When was this? Currently?'

'No, it would be maybe three years ago and for a while before that,' Cross said.

'Oh, well, that's it, you see. I came here

about three years ago. We had a bit of a turnover about then. Father O'Connor was here before me. He may have known your Mr LaSalle very well for all I know.'

'Father Berry, Michael LaSalle is dead,' Cross said. He wasn't going to say it unless it made a difference. 'We need to know why. I would very much like to talk with this Father O'Connor.'

'Perhaps we could reach him by phone. He's in Indianapolis now.'

'Father O'Connor is?'

'Yes, about three years ago.'

It was a foolish idea. And Cross knew it when he decided to do it. He walked back to the hotel. He crossed over from Magazine to St Charles and followed the tracks back to Canal Street. Once you crossed Canal at that point you were into the French Quarter.

He stopped at the little hotel bar and, this time, ordered two margaritas in go cups. Up in his room he opened French doors to the balcony and sat his drinks on the small table. He took a couple of sips. He realized he was soaked through. It was as if he had swam home.

The red light on the phone was flashing. He had a message. It could wait. He took a hot shower. That would raise his body temperature and the air would feel cooler afterward. After the shower, he slipped on his jeans, retrieved one of his drinks, sat on the bed and keyed in the code for his message.

It was Rafferty. Cross played it again to catch the number and called.

'Cross,' he said when Rafferty answered.

'What do you have?'

'Nothing until an hour ago. Maybe a New Orleans–Indianapolis connection.'

'What?'

'Let me follow it up a little first,' Cross said. 'I'll fill you in completely when I get back tomorrow evening.'

'What if your plane crashes?' Rafferty said. 'Then where am I?'

'In a better place than I am. How are you holding up?'

'I feel it. Any minute. I look at these guys, especially homicide, and I'm thinking they know something. And they probably don't. I'm paranoid.'

'You have every right to be. What did you say LaSalle did for a living?'

'Lee, Morgan Lee,' Rafferty said.

'Michael LaSalle. Got it from a kid who went to school with him. Call him what you want, but LaSalle is on the birth certificate.'

'Crap.'

'What did he do for a living?' Cross pressed.

'I told you. I don't know. Had investments.'

'What I'm trying to figure out is why someone who could make his living anywhere in the world would choose Indianapolis. Make no mistake, I like my little hometown. Great place to raise kids. Maybe most people would be fine to move here for a job. Or you might move to the big city from Greenfield, but from New Orleans? I don't buy it.'

'I'm not into speculating,' Rafferty said. 'What do you know?'

'You met in Indianapolis, right. He didn't move there to be with you?'

'No.'

'Don't hold out. I can't do my work if you hold out, and it's your life on the line.'

'I'm aware of that, Cross.'

'Just checking. What are you hearing around the office, Rafferty?' Cross took another gulp of his margarita. Nice, he thought.

'Nothing. That's another reason why I'm worried. They're keeping this investigation real quiet.'

'Swann's the lead, right?'

'Yep.'

'He always keeps it quiet, doesn't he?'

'I guess so,' Rafferty said, unconvinced.

'Hang in there,' Cross said, starting to feel a little sympathy for a guy he didn't much like.

'Christ, Cross. Hang in there. What are you? A fucking high school coach?'

'Hey, all I ask is for you to write the check before you kill yourself.'

'Stay off Bourbon Street.'

'I do my best.'

Cross went out on the balcony, careful not to trip over the electrical cord that connected the lamp to the plug behind the television cabinet. He sat down and sipped his drink, looking at the people moving below. Tourists strolling through the Quarter, residents bringing home groceries, delivery trucks delivering.

He'd take a nap. After that he'd call Shanahan, then find dinner. He thought about going over to the casino, but decided that was a bad idea. He'd just meander about the French Quarter like the rest of the tourists, come back, watch a movie on TV, and retire early.

# Ten

Shanahan was doing the dishes when Cross called. Maureen cooked. That meant Shanahan cleaned up afterward. Not exactly fair because when Shanahan cooked it was a one-pan, one-plate meal with minimal preparation. Fifteen minutes from start to finish. Maureen used half a dozen big bowls, smaller bowls for the ingredients, and every pot and pan in the house. He didn't complain – out loud.

'How's New Orleans? Are you staying sober?' Shanahan asked him.

'New Orleans is great, though I think someone should come up with the idea of a portable air-conditioner. You know, a water-cooled suit as opposed to a water-heated atmosphere.'

There was a moment of quiet.

'It's your dime,' Shanahan said, 'though if you want I have some news for you.'

'Go.'

'Maybe it's just a fluke,' Shanahan said, pacing as far as the cord on the wall phone would let him. 'I checked Mr Lee's mail. Usual stuff. Except maybe for a newsletter from the Nash Family Values Institute.'

'And what's that?'

'I think they think they are the ones gonna get taken up when the big rapture comes. And they're not too thrilled with the rest of us. Morgan Lee is gay, right? That is established?'

'Hey, you working for me?' Cross said.

'I guess.'

'Am I paying you?'

'No.'

'Good work. Tell me more.'

'I don't have a whole lot more. What do you have?'

'Morgan Lee is definitely Michael LaSalle

and he is whatever he has to be to get what he wants. I'm not sure there's a category. But I definitely don't see him cozying up to a group like that unless he had a reason. And he might.'

'You know something?' Shanahan asked. 'What?'

'I mean, do you know something about why he might be cozying up, as you put it?'

Shanahan cupped the phone with his chin and pulled a bottle of beer from the refrigerator.

'I'm going to ask you a favor,' Cross said. 'Some New Orleans Catholic Priest and Michael LaSalle left for Indianapolis at about the same time.'

'Priest?'

'Yep. And I want you to go talk to him.'

'You want me to do what?' Shanahan asked.

'I don't like talking to these guys,' Cross said. 'Especially about sex. You see where I'm heading here?'

'So, you're suggesting that our victim wasn't day-trading in the stock market, that he had something else to sell.'

'I don't know. You need to talk with a Father O'Connor at St Ignatius. I don't know where that is, but it's probably in the phone book. I'll be up tomorrow night. We can compare notes.'

'What are we looking for?'

'Whatever the connection is,' Cross said. 'Pretty weird the two of them leaving at the same time.'

Shanahan wasn't too keen on conversations involving sex and religion with anyone, let alone some priest, but he agreed. It was a way to keep himself involved. Maybe he was making too much of the newsletter. Unlikely, but not impossible as LaSalle could have been picked up on some random mailing list. Maybe he was put on the list as a kind of joke, or possibly he was doing a little research. That's what Shanahan would do. He would do a little more research on the Nash Family Values Institute as well.

Cross watched part of a movie on TV as he waited for hunger to fetch him. He felt good. He had uncovered a big chunk of the mysterious victim's life. Verified a name. He may have also uncovered the reason for LaSalle's move to Indianapolis. It was too much of a coincidence that the priest of the church he was obsessed with left New Orleans at roughly the same time and settled in the same city.

Outside, the air was still dense. Cross walked slower consciously, discovered that his eyes found plenty to absorb. Tiny Edwardian cottages, walkways that appeared to lead to lush back gardens or courtyards. In this quieter part of the Quarter, he was away from the partying, but the air was still full of sounds, including the muffled sounds of the twenty-four-hour celebration on Bourbon Street blocks away, horses' hooves clopping in the narrow streets, echoing from the buildings, snatches of conversation in accents that were foreign to him.

Dinner was found in a small restaurant in what was otherwise a pretty residential block. More expensive than the surroundings suggested, he didn't want to spend hours wandering around. He'd done that before and found that food wasn't cheap in the Quarter. Tonight he made do with an appetizer and a salad and two glasses of wine, while he watched tourists stroll by, stop and examine the menu and move on. A heavily tattooed man was entertaining what had to be his daughter. Around six years old, maybe. The restaurant staff, including the cook, came by to help spoil her.

Cross was tempted to go somewhere and drink and listen to music. His testosterone level must drop when the geography is below sea level. Finding someone to sleep with would be his only motivation for a night of smoke, loud music, and generally rude behavior. Maybe it was age.

He walked off dinner and ended up stopping at a strange-looking A & P. He went in, bought a bottle of wine and a cheap corkscrew.

'How late are you open?' he asked the woman.

'We close at three a.m., reopen at four fifteen,' she replied.

Back at the hotel, he sat again out on the balcony, sipping his wine, thinking about Elena in Miami. She would have been trouble, like most of the rest of the women he somehow got involved with. What was it about him that put him off limits for sensible, traditional relationships? Why couldn't he find someone like Maureen, for example?

Cross wanted to leave the door open, but he wasn't sure whether the air-conditioning could offset the thick hot air from the outside. He closed the doors and undressed. He slipped between the sheets. His eyes felt tired, but his brain wasn't ready to give up the day.

He clicked on the television, rummaged through the channels, settled on re-runs of *Hawaii Five-O*. He was asleep in less than two minutes.

'I'm going to church tomorrow, you want to come?' Shanahan asked Maureen as he climbed into bed. She looked up from her book.

'If they served ice cream for communion, I might consider it.'

'I have to talk to a Father O'Connor about sex, inappropriate sex.'

'You're going to confession?'

'Have I been inappropriate?'

'Not inappropriate enough. Does that count?' she said, fluttering her eyelashes in exaggerated fashion.

'You could come, you know, so I don't have to be alone in the room talking to him about sex with minors.'

'Having a woman around will help? That's what you think?'

'I don't know.'

'Guys talk about sex all the time, don't they?'

'Not with priests and not implying that they did something immoral and quite illegal.'

'With your victim?'

'Could be. Have to find out. I could be jumping to conclusions.'

'No, you are on your own,' she said. She leaned over and kissed him, clicked off the light. No baseball on television tonight. They'd be left alone with their thoughts as they waited for sleep, and with their dreams once they arrived.

Cross woke from a thick sleep, his body perspiring, his mouth dry. Three forty-five a.m. The alcohol that lured him into un-consciousness was out of his system. He was completely sober, completely awake. By the light of the flickering TV set, Cross slipped

142

from the damp sheets, naked, went to the bathroom. A few moments later he emerged, drinking from a glass of tap water. He went to the other side of the bed so the sheets would be dry and climbed in again.

Grace Kelly was sprawled on a desk top. She reached back to grab scissors and plunged them into the back of the intruder, a man sent to kill her.

Cross foraged the blanket for the remote, finding it in the folds. He clicked off the set. Darkness. Except for a faded light coming through the translucent drapery on the French doors.

He worried about not getting to sleep. It didn't matter, he convinced himself. He had put the 'do not disturb' sign on the door. The plane wasn't until late tomorrow. He could sleep as long as he liked.

Cross hovered on the edge of consciousness. He heard a scratching sound. Metal on metal. Could be teeth. Perhaps a mouse was in his room, looking for scraps. The scratching became a click and Cross allowed himself to climb out of the half-conscious twilight sleep.

He turned slowly toward the sound and saw first the shadow against the drapery, then the door open and a figure sliding in. Who it was and what did he want slowly gave way to more serious questions. Was he armed? If so, with what? If it was a gun, he didn't know what to do. If the man had a knife, perhaps Cross could use the bedding, and somehow gain control. The figure was not huge, medium maybe. Hard to tell.

The figure moved slowly, carefully. No doubt his eyes had to adjust to the dark. At the moment, Cross had that advantage. He held his breath, didn't move. What could Cross use as a weapon? There was nothing big enough on the bedside table that wasn't bolted down. For a moment, he thought of turning on the light, blinding the man, realizing quickly that the soft golden-hued bulb would do no such thing, only provide the intruder with a clearer view of a target. Cross could think of nothing. Maybe he could talk the guy into having a pillow fight.

'Christ,' Cross said in his head.

The fellow was inside, approaching him, then froze, looked around, moved to the chair where Cross had strewn his clothes. A burglar? Not seeing a gun or a knife, Cross sprung from the bed. The intruder was quick and Cross was momentarily trapped by the bedclothes. The stranger moved to the side, then toward the open door. Cross pursued, almost catching him at the door, but Cross's foot caught the lamp cord. He heard the lamp crash to the floor right after he hit it. By the time Cross righted himself and hit the balcony, the intruder was hanging, his fingers wrapped around the lowest bar of the balcony rail, gauging the distance. He dropped, landed with the grace of a cat, and scurried toward the intersection.

He ran past some drunken, but shocked lovers. They looked at the runner, eyes slowly moving up to focus, as best they could on Cross, who stood naked on the balcony. He smiled at them, nodded, waved as he watched the intruder disappear around the corner.

Dawn was well on its way. Cross could hear the click of flying bats, no doubt in the last moments of their day. A taxi cruised the street slowly. Inside, Cross turned on the light by the bed. He picked up the lamp that had fallen to the carpet. It was in one piece. His heart was beating loudly and he was out of breath. It was after five. It was a strange time to be fully awake. Then he noticed the dagger. It was old, very old. He went to his bag, plucked out a sock. He picked up the dagger at the tip and dropped it carefully into the sock. He'd have to check his bag at the airport, instead of carrying it on. He wanted it though, as a souvenir if nothing else.

He thought about calling the police. But there was really nothing they could do. He never got a good look at the intruder. Worse, they would ask questions he didn't want to answer. Maybe he'd have to stay over. No, he wouldn't call them. The threat, if there ever was one, was gone. He wouldn't stay on, wouldn't come back.

Cross was hungry. If he wanted to sleep, he'd have to eat. The town was open all night. He'd find something. There was the A & P. Some salami and a beer. He'd come back, climb back into bed and sleep in the comfort and security of daylight.

Shanahan thought the best time to talk with Father O'Connor was before the Sunday masses began. It would be the priest's busy day. He'd called the information line Saturday evening to learn that first mass was at eight a.m. If Shanahan could be there a little before seven, he could catch him in the quiet before the storm, perhaps cause a storm of his own.

The limestone church, located in a pleasant, well-kept neighborhood, was solid and well anchored on the street. Two great blue spruce trees framed the large entry. Since it was early, Shanahan easily found a place to park. He took a deep breath, girded his resolve and entered through one of the fourteen-foot doors. Quiet and much cooler inside, Shanahan stepped from the entry into the main part of the church. There were two young men setting books down on the choir seats. They turned. Shanahan's footsteps echoed as he walked down the center aisle toward them. One of the youths stopped what he was doing and came to greet him.

'Mass doesn't begin until eight,' he said.

'I know. I need to see Father O'Connor.'

The boy seemed to be considering options.

'It's important,' Shanahan said.

'Please wait here,' the boy said. He went around and behind the altar. Shanahan seated himself a few pews down and waited.

The man Shanahan presumed was Father O'Connor trailed the returning youth. Shanahan stood and the priest extended his hand.

'What can we do for you?'

'Answer a few questions, if you don't mind.'

'About?'

'Morgan Lee. Or Michael LaSalle. I'm not sure which name he used with you.'

'Both,' the priest said, surprising Shanahan with his candor. 'I was very sorry to read about his death.'

'That's why I'm here,' Shanahan said.

'You are not with the police.'

'No. Private investigator.'

'I have Mass in an hour.'

'I hope to take only a few minutes.'

The priest looked at the two young men, still preparing for the upcoming service.

'Let's go into my office,' he said.

Father O'Connor was a thick-set man in his mid- to late forties. He had unruly dark curly hair that spilled over a pale, almost gray

147

face. His eyes resided deep in their sockets. He went behind the desk and sat in a large leather chair. His teeth were yellow and un-even. His face was unreadable.

Shanahan sat in a smaller chair beside the priest's desk. It made him feel as if he were interviewing for a job. It was a lesser seat. Then again, the priest held the position of judge – of morality.

The light that came through the windows was filtered by trees, dappling the interior walls. A fern, fronds dripping to the floor, sat in a corner, where it had no doubt lived for decades and seen many priests come and go. A grandfather clock stood in one corner. On the wall to the side of the priest's desk were crossed oars, too small for a rowboat, too big for a bare backside. Shanahan guessed canoe or kayak. The good Father seemed fit inside his gray flesh. Broad shoulders, a surprising lack of gut for a man of his age.

'It seems as if the young man followed you from New Orleans. Is that right?'

'Yes.'

Father O'Connor looked sad.

'You want to tell me about it?'

'No, I don't,' he said. 'Who do you work for?'

'At the moment, I have to keep that to myself.'

'What motivates me to tell you anything?'

'Probably because what it looks like ... I

mean what was going on between you and Michael LaSalle may be less than what meets the eye.'

The priest nodded. 'Less and more.' He laughed wearily.

'Go on.'

'Ahhhh ... I don't think so. He's dead and the story deserves to be buried with him.'

'Except that it won't,' Shanahan said.

'Are you blackmailing me?'

'It's not a threat. It's the way it is with these things.'

'Really,' the priest said smiling, doubting.

'You are the only strand that leads back to New Orleans and Mr LaSalle's real identity. He's dead. Murdered. Police have to start somewhere. And the media will be interested.'

'You Catholic?' the priest asked. 'A name like Shanahan...'

'My father was.'

'And you backslid?'

'I don't consider it going backward,' Shanahan said.

'I see,' he said, sitting back, relaxed. 'You have questions, then?'

'Your relationship with Michael LaSalle.'

'He came to my Sunday Masses.'

'He followed you here.'

The priest nodded.

'He missed your little sermons that much?' Shanahan asked.

149

'He was emotionally disturbed. I was trying to work with him, get him help.'

'In what way?'

'In a minor way. The boy was confused,' the priest said, a smile of condescending benevolence.

'That's all? A guy packs up his life, leaves the city of his birth and follows you all this way. For what? A little paternal advice?'

'I'm aware of the nature of your inference, Mr Shanahan. I have always been faithful to Christ. And I'm not going to dignify this line of questioning with any answers.' He stood up.

Shanahan realized that he'd made a leap in logic if not in faith. Certainly not all priests seduced altar boys. On the other hand, he was finding it hard to figure out what drew the victim to Indianapolis and at the same time that Father O'Connor was transferred there.

'If LaSalle was attending church here every Sunday, then maybe you noticed if he ever came with anyone.'

'No. Alone. He was always alone,' he said. 'Now I must go.'

'A young man is dead. He's been murdered. We have nothing to go on. So far, you are the only one who knew him.'

'Just a minute more, Mr Shanahan. I have Masses. I have classes. It's a full day.'

'Is it possible he made friends at church?

Someone he hung out with?'

'No. He sat by himself. He didn't attend extracurricular activities. Just Mass.'

'No one. He talked to no one?'

'He talked with Mrs Clarkson. He took her aside, I remember. She didn't look too happy. And once I saw them talking outside long after the crowd had dispersed.'

'You have anything more than a last name.'

'She's the wife of Ray Clarkson. H. Ray Clarkson of that values institute, I can't remember her first name. She wasn't a regular. In fact I've only seen her here a couple of times. She is very well known in the city. I recognized her. Actually I was surprised she was here. Catholic isn't what the Clarksons are all about.'

'Nash Family Values Institute,' Shanahan prompted.

'Yes. That's the one.'

'Do you know how they knew each other, LaSalle and Mrs Clarkson?' Shanahan asked.

'No. She had a slight Southern accent. Could be New Orleans.'

'You never saw her there?'

'No. Not that I remember.' Father O'Connor was getting antsy.

'When was the last time you saw her?'

'I'm afraid I can't remember. I'm not sure if she was here last Sunday.'

'When was the last time you saw Michael

LaSalle alive?'

'Two weeks ago. Here. On Sunday.'

'Not last Sunday?'

'No,' the priest said warily. 'According to the papers he was killed Saturday night or Sunday morning. Not too many have risen from the dead in the last 2,000 years.'

'You remembered when he was killed that clearly?'

'Of course. I knew him. I read the article thoroughly. Why wouldn't I remember?'

'And Saturday night, you were doing what?'

He smiled, but it wasn't a warm smile.

'Mr Shanahan. So far you have suggested that I might be a pedophile and now a murderer. I can't imagine what would come next. Maybe the Holocaust? I think we should cut this conversation short before the list of my sins gets too long to keep track of.'

'That's all right,' Shanahan said. 'I'll keep track. And you're right about the list. It will contain everyone who knew Michael LaSalle or Morgan Lee in New Orleans and here. That means you're on it twice – or maybe four times, depending on how you keep score.'

The priest stood.

'Good-bye, Mr Shanahan. Unless, of course, you'd like to stick around for Mass.'

'Thanks. I prefer an honest game of baseball.'

# Eleven

Cross was about to do something foolish. He was waiting outside NOLA, an expensive restaurant. It was his last meal in New Orleans. He wouldn't expense it, but he wanted one last sensuous experience in a city known for its sensuousness.

A spirited, nattily dressed gentleman explained that they were booked, unless a counter seat was an option.

'You'll be able to watch the kitchen,' he said. 'Quite a show.'

Cross agreed. He had no one to talk to, no book to read. The check, with tip, came to $75. He'd never spent anything like that for what amounted to lunch. The charming woman who waited on him convinced Cross that a half bottle of a certain Chardonnay would work well with the crab cake. Cross was easily charmed. There might be something to this business of matching wines so carefully, Cross thought. The crab cake, surrounded by wood-grilled prawns, and sips of the cool white wine was almost as good as sex. Better than sex, he thought, though he wouldn't have minded a fresh comparison.

He returned to his hotel, light-headed, but mellow, having a last pleasant impression of the city, erasing the frightening, but as it turned out, harmless incident the night before.

The flight back was also pleasant. He was seated in the exit row, which gave him considerably more leg room and no one sat in the middle, which meant he could spread out a little. The change of planes in Chicago went without a hitch. Life was good, until the taxi dropped him off at home and he found the big black car parked in front of his house.

Shanahan sat at the kitchen table. Maureen, who was now fixing a late dinner, had printed out some information on the Nash Family Values Institute and H. Ray Clarkson she found on the Internet. Their own website was informative.

Clarkson was the spokesperson for the institute, but he was neither the founder nor the funder. That was Anthony Bridges II, now in his late eighties. Clarkson, who had a degree in theology and engineering, was hired as the institute's executive director ten years ago, after Bridges read several collections of essays on the essential relationship of Christianity, capitalism, and family.

Christianity was of the fundamentalist variety. Capitalism was an unrepentant free market. And family was one man in charge, one obedient woman, and as many home-schooled children as they could support. Bridges, who was a politician in his earlier years, trained Clarkson in the ways of legislatures so that he could lobby on a local and national level to incorporate those sentiments into law.

Shanahan had pretty much a live-and-let-live philosophy. But just as he didn't like bullies, Shanahan wasn't happy when a group of folks got together and decided that everyone had to believe and behave the same way they did.

Clarkson was an Indianapolis native. Went to Warren Central High School, then Purdue University. He married late in life to a woman named Marissa. No other details about her were provided. Not unusual considering the institute's guiding philosophy about the role of women in marriage and society. H. Ray Clarkson and Marissa had adopted two children, a girl and a boy.

H. Ray Clarkson had made quite a deal of the adoption. It was a way to deal with unwanted babies, he said, rendering abortion unnecessary and therefore more clearly immoral. So it was Marissa Clarkson, the mother of those two adopted children, that Michael LaSalle met in church, Shanahan thought. It was odd any number of ways.

'Marissa Clarkson is married to the head of

a kind of right-wing, Christian fundamental-ist organization,' Shanahan said aloud to Maureen who was cutting the tips off the asparagus. 'She takes time out to go to a Catholic church.'

'Couples don't always agree. You watch boxing, right? Where two men beat the hell out of each other for fun, and I think it's barbaric.'

'Yes, but...' The sentence fizzled. Shanahan had nothing.

'But what?'

'And how would Michael LaSalle come to know Clarkson's wife? And why would he have subscribed to the newsletter of an organization that believes his mere existence is a sin?'

'You're unusually talkative tonight,' Maureen said, bringing him over a beer.

Shanahan got up, went to the phone, punched in Cross's phone number.

The phone stopped ringing as Cross entered the little entry/office area of his home. Rafferty followed.

'Shanahan. I'm about ready to sit down to dinner. Call me in an hour or so,' came the message.

Cross would call him after he got rid of Rafferty.

'You and Shanahan all that close?' Rafferty said, sitting himself down in the big, upholstered chair, covered with a sheet. He examined the sheet close and seemed to lower himself in the chair with caution.

'We talk.'

'About the case?'

'Hey, I just had a long flight, you know, and I don't get a minute to breathe?'

Cross sat at his desk, the only other available place in the small room. He didn't want to invite Rafferty into the living room. He didn't want the big cop to get too comfortable.

'What did you learn?'

'Talked to his lover,' Cross said.

'Lover?' Rafferty said.

'Couple of years. A woman.'

Rafferty wore his poker face.

'A rich woman. Also talked to his best friend. I don't mean to speak ill of the dead, but nobody had anything nice to say about your friend.'

'Ex-lovers rarely do.'

'Talked with some bar buddies ... or at least some people who knew him. He was kind of an opportunist.'

'Go on.'

'Maybe the most interesting thing is that ... did you know that LaSalle went to church every Sunday?'

'Yes, I guess I did. So what?'

'The priest in New Orleans, the one who gave the Mass in his regular church down there, moved to Indianapolis three years ago.'

'Which priest is that?' Rafferty asked, squirming in the chair.

'Not yet.'

'What do you mean "not yet"?'

'I don't want you messing around in the case until I know more.'

'It's my case. It's my ass hanging out.'

'We've already had this conversation. So, what do you know?'

Rafferty sighed. He was giving in.

'They know that someone in the department had a connection to Morgan ... Michael.' Rafferty shook his head.

'But they don't know who?'

'No, you see I used a cell phone that belonged to the department, but it hadn't been officially assigned. They don't know who used it.'

'The bills. Can't they trace the calls?'

'I only used it to call Morgan.'

'Why is that?'

'I'm a careful guy.'

'What about the video tapes of cars coming and going from Bay Colony?'

'Kept for forty-eight hours.'

'How do you know that?'

'Morgan told me.'

'All right, so your past visits aren't recorded, the last and most important one was.'

'I went in with the lights off. All they could see was a big black car, a shadow.'

'When you got out and dialed the number for him to let you in?'

'I dialed from my cell phone.'

'You sure they can't trace those calls to you?'

'It was a phone used for drug busts. Like I told you, I didn't check it out. All the phone records would prove is that he received calls from someone inside IPD or that the phone was lost and the killer used it.'

'Let's get this straight,' Cross said. 'You dumped his computer or did the police get it?'

'I looked through it. Nothing connects me. That's what I thought. But I wanted to be sure.'

'What are you worried about? If you did it, it's a perfect crime,' Cross said, letting the cop know that he hadn't ruled him out.

'No such thing,' Rafferty said. 'I don't know what I don't know. Could be something somewhere. I need to find the murderer.'

'You know, if they find all this out. Lights out. Illegal phone. Computer dump. You're going to look a whole lot guiltier than if you went to them right away.'

'We've had *that* conversation, Cross.'

'Seems to me you took a big risk talking to me. And to Shanahan.'

'I had to think about it. Look, I'll always be thinking they can come for me until the guy who did it is convicted.' Rafferty stood up. 'That all you got for me?'

'Quite a bit really in a day and a half in a strange city.'

'Motives? These folks you talked to?'

'Maybe. He was an embarrassment to his live-in lover and her snooty family. There's this thing with a priest I have to figure out. And he's here. Listen, your late friend wasn't a nice guy, Rafferty. Who knows.'

Rafferty got up angrily, shaking his head. He started toward the door, stopped, turned around.

'Here's the person I knew. Beautiful. Delicate like crystal. I wanted to protect him. Make sure he was safe.'

'Protect him from what?' Cross asked, glad he had not told him of LaSalle taking pleasure in being cruel.

'The world. He looked like he needed someone to ... the thing I wanted to do most for him was to make sure he was safe.' Rafferty paused to stifle the emotion, then when he had it under control, he smiled. 'Funny, isn't it?'

Rafferty left. Cross wondered which LaSalle Rafferty knew. He found a beer in the refrigerator. Put on some Muddy Waters. He checked his watch. He'd call Shanahan in a few minutes, then he'd climb into bed. It wasn't that it was late. It was that he couldn't think of anything else to do.

* * *

Shanahan let Cross fill him in on the events in New Orleans. He was intrigued by the marriage and the descriptions. The victim was a con artist. 'Who do you think broke into your room?' questioned Shanahan.

'Could've been anybody. Maybe Billy Dean. Maybe one of the wife's little helpers. Maybe his sugar momma. She wasn't young, but she was fit. She also had a couple of loyal minions who might relish the idea of offing me or stealing whatever they thought I had.' Cross thought a moment. 'Then again, might not have been connected. I'm sure New Orleans has its share of burglars. What did you find out about the priest?'

'He knew Michael LaSalle. He's hiding something. Maybe a lot of something.'

'So where do we go from here?'

'Another visit, maybe, now that we know a little more about LaSalle.'

'Wait a minute. Remind me again, are you working for me?' Cross asked.

'Maybe.'

'Am I paying you? I forget.'

'No.'

'Then I expect a little more dedication to the case,' Cross said. 'Now, more important than the priest, LaSalle knew someone else here.'

'Go on,' Shanahan said.

'A woman. Marissa Clarkson. She's mar-

161

ried to H. Ray Clarkson.'

'And?'

'And he's the guy I told you about. Runs a lobby for what they're calling family values these days.'

'The newsletter.'

'They talked in church. Maybe she didn't like the conversations. You should talk to her. Saw her photograph on the web. Pretty.'

'Maybe so, but she's not likely to take a liking to the likes of me,' Cross said.

'There's a lot of likes in that sentence.'

'I'm tired. I can't keep coming up with new words. Good night. I'm going to bed and dream of crab cakes.'

'You're getting old, Cross. Dreaming of food.'

'What do you dream about?'

'I'm so old, I don't dream.' There was silence on the other end. 'Or maybe I'm dreaming that I'm sleeping. Oh, one thing. Ask Rafferty about LaSalle's passion for Sunday mass.'

Once off the phone, he asked Maureen if she could search the web to find Marissa Clarkson's maiden name. He wanted to know how she knew Michael LaSalle.

'Well, Mr Private Detective, I certainly will; but in the event I fail – which I am likely to do, because I searched the hell out of the Internet without success – you might consider the courthouse. They were probably married here. Think marriage license.'

'I've tried my best not to,' he said.

She grinned. 'What, you're worried I'd divorce you and take all your worldly possessions.'

'We would have custody problems. Casey and Einstein.'

Einstein walked through the kitchen, slowly, eyeing them in an unkindly fashion, Shanahan thought.

'I'm downtown,' Shanahan said, 'standing in a public telephone in the courthouse.'

'That's very nice,' Cross said. 'I'm in bed. I like where I am better.'

'But we're both some place. That's good, right?'

'And you interrupted a dream. Let me just say, your call is a tremendous disappointment.'

'You weren't dreaming about food.'

'No. Why are you calling so early?'

'It's nearly eleven,' Shanahan said.

'My point exactly.'

'Thought you might be able to use a little more information about the woman who talked with LaSalle in church.'

'OK.'

'Does the name Manchette mean anything to you?'

'Jesus.'

Shanahan interrupted the long silence.

'Apparently, it does.'

'I can make some calls. But Manchette is the last name of the rich, older woman he gigolo'd for a few years.'

'Daughter?'

'Sure. She had one. A daughter and a son by Mr Manchette who was wealthy and powerful until he died. Who knows though, could be a cousin. Coincidence, running into her. Probably a cousin, come to think of it. Mrs Manchette said her daughter's name was Sarah.'

'You'll see her anyway,' Shanahan said.

'I forgot. Weren't you working for me?'

'I forgot that too.'

'So, I'll go see her, but I have a call to make first.'

Cross walked naked into the bathroom, ran cold water over his face, looked in the mirror. He needed a haircut. Hell, who was he kidding? He needed plastic surgery. His nose wasn't quite the same after a couple of fights and one pretty intensive beating. Haircut, he promised himself. At least he had his hair, and his body was holding up despite the punishment he gave it.

In the little kitchen, he put on some coffee, looked out the window. It was a gray sun, he thought. Hot, humid, and polluted. Not the makings of a great day. He went to his bedroom, found his wallet, pulled out the phone number he'd jotted down for

Demimondaine.

He slipped on a pair of sweat pants and went back into the kitchen, where he downed a glass of orange juice while the last of the coffee was dripping through the filter.

Coffee in cup, body in pants, Cross went to his desk, turned on the computer. He clicked on the solitaire game that the counter indicated he had played 10,324 times.

He punched in the New Orleans number and waited.

'Demimondaine,' came the soft, Southern voice of Billy Dean.

'Billy Dean, this is Howie Cross...'

'The private detective.'

'Yes. I need some help.'

'I told you everything I know.'

'There's a question I didn't ask. Who is Marissa Manchette?'

The other end of the phone went quiet. Even the distant music Cross had heard in the background was no longer.

'Billy?'

'I'm afraid I can't help you,' Billy Dean said. The music was back. Apparently the young man had muffled the receiver. No doubt he wanted to make sure he made no sounds of surprise or shock.

'Ah c'mon. I know you do. Remember you said you'd do anything?'

'Not anymore,' Billy said.

'Hey Billy, your friend, remember?' Billy

wasn't biting. 'By the way, Billy, did you lose a knife?'

'What?'

'Did you lose a knife?' Cross wished he had the knife now. It would make him feel better. 'I found one in my hotel room.'

'I don't know what you're talking about.'

'I'm sure it still has fingerprints on it.'

'I wasn't going to kill you.'

'What did you want?'

'Where are you?' Billy Dean asked.

'I'm right around the corner, Billy. I can be there in a minute and a half.'

'Area code 317. Indianapolis. I don't think so,' Billy Dean said, not buying it.

Cross heard the click.

Undeterred, Cross retrieved the antique shop's number, dialed Mrs Manchette. Closed on Mondays, said the answering machine.

Cross didn't feel defeated though. Billy Dean's reaction meant there was something going on that related in some way to Michael LaSalle and Marissa Manchette. Maybe Marissa would tell him. She'd be easy to find, but hard to get to.

# Twelve

It was nearly noon when Shanahan stopped by Harry's Bar. Harry's daytime regulars had already taken their assigned stools at the bar and sat, mostly quiet, nursing their beers.

'Bring me one, Harry,' Shanahan said.

'My, oh my,' Harry said, 'you come into my bar and damned if you don't order a beer instead of wantin' to make a call or hangin' out until somebody calls you. What are you doing here?'

'Waiting for Maureen. She's going to meet me here.'

'That right?' He brightened. 'Gonna have lunch here?'

'No...'

'Listen, I think I found out what Delaney left out of his stew recipe. It's good now, Deets.'

'No, Maureen and I are going to go look at a house.'

'What for?'

'Maybe to buy it.'

'Buy a house. You got a house. All paid for. You got walls, a floor and a roof. What else do you need?'

167

'Maureen is interested.'

'Well, she shouldn't have to live in Elaine's place, should she?' Harry could shift gears quickly if it involved women like Maureen. In Harry's mind, Maureen could do no wrong. Most women could do no wrong unless he married them. Harry went quiet for a while and wiped the bar, more out of something to do while he thought than because it needed wiping. 'New car. New house. What's going on?'

'Changing, I guess.'

Harry shook his head. 'You're staying on the Eastside, right?'

'I imagine. The house we're looking at is on the Eastside. Let me ask you something? You grew up Catholic, didn't you?'

'You gonna start going to church too? I don't know you anymore.'

'No. Just something going through my mind. All this stuff in the papers about priests and molestation.'

'So?' Harry said.

'So, were you ever molested?'

'Nah. Anyway, the town I grew up in was too small to have a Catholic school. We did go to Mass on Sundays for a while. You hear things. Seems to me, there was some funny business being whispered about.'

'But not you?'

'No.'

'Too ugly?'

'You might have something there. I wasn't a pretty kid,' Harry said. He grinned. But the smile faded. 'There was this kid, looked like a little Jesus, he did. All dark, curly-haired. You know, just a little too pretty for us heathens.' Harry shook his head. 'There was some trouble. You know I just don't remember anything but him being all upset and pretty soon he didn't come back. And after that we got a new priest. Damn,' Harry said, 'what got you going? What is all this?'

'Some funny business.'

'I enjoy laughing,' Harry snapped.

'Can't now.'

'And now, when it gets interesting, you're not talking.'

'Not much anyway, Harry.' Shanahan took a sip of his beer. 'Just some nonsense I can't seem to shake.'

Harry started to press him, but Maureen came in and Harry forgot all about it in his new happiness.


Cross went to the kitchen, grabbed the peanut butter and jelly. He was forced to use a heel as the second slice of bread for his sandwich. He wondered what he would drink. A white wine, perhaps? He settled for a Coke. Back in his little entryway office, Cross thumbed through the white pages of the phone book. He didn't find the number for H. Ray Clarkson. This didn't surprise him. While nibbling on his sandwich, he did a computer search, using the most effective privacy invasion program. He hated the Big Brother aspect to the Internet; but it was there and he'd use it. Clarkson's address was listed – which Cross wrote down – but not the phone number.

Cross called one of the few friends he had on the police force, promised tickets to the Pacers next season, and got two unpublished numbers. He played some computer games until he finished his sandwich, then called the first. An answering machine: 'This is the Clarkson home. Please leave a message.' Cross thought about it, but didn't have a good enough message to get the call back. He tried the second number and got Marissa.

'Mrs Clarkson, I'm an investigator working on the murder of Michael LaSalle.'

'Who?' she responded.

'Michael LaSalle or Morgan Lee.'

'I don't know why you are calling me,' she said.

'Because you know him.'

'I'm sorry, I have no idea what you're talking about...'

He was about to lose her.

'You used to be a Manchette, I believe.'

There was a long silence.

'Who are you?' she asked, her voice cold with anger.

'My name is Howard Cross. As I said, I'm an investigator working on the LaSalle case.'

'Police?'

'No. Private.'

'I don't have anything to say to you. I don't know who you are talking about or why you are talking to me.'

'Maybe we could meet some place and talk about this.'

'I'm going to hang up now. Please do not call me again.'

'You were seen arguing with LaSalle at a Mass conducted by Father O'Connor, who used to practise his profession in New Orleans.'

'He told you that I knew Michael?'

'Well, not exactly,' Cross said. She gave it away. If she had only known him in Indianapolis, she would have called him Morgan. 'So you do know him and you know him from New Orleans, where the Manchettes are an important family. Are you related?'

'You should be talking to the priest, Mr Cross. Howard Cross, right?'

'Yes. Why would I want to do that?'

'If I tell you, will you leave me alone? Completely?' she asked. The anger had been replaced by something else. Fear, Cross thought. There was something desperate in her voice.

'If what you say is true and you had nothing to do with LaSalle's death and we find

171

out who did it, then you don't figure in this at all.'

'Michael was shaking down the Catholic church, claiming molestation when he was a minor. So maybe you should be talking to the priest.'

'You know this?'

'I know this. Take my word for it, but that's it. You and I are done.'

Click.

Cross dialed Shanahan, got the answering machine.

'Call me,' Cross said in his message. 'I need to talk to you about Father O'Connor.'

Outside, the earlier rains had lightened the air. It was pleasant enough to walk the three blocks through the residential neighborhoods to the little shopping area at 56th and Illinois. The spot had everything anyone would need. A supermarket, a restaurant, dry-cleaners, and liquor store. The rest of the little shops – a tennis shop, women's apparel boutique and ice cream parlor – weren't essential.

The house was brown brick, and looked to be two stories, though it wasn't. It rested somewhat into the small crest of a hill as if a seed were planted and the house merely grew there. To Shanahan, it looked English, but not too English. The asphalt driveway curved up and around the back to a separate

172

garage hidden from the street. Between the house and garage was a small garden.

He and Maureen went in through the back door, which brought them to a landing. To the right were the stairs to the basement and cooler air. Straight ahead and up a step was the kitchen with knotty pine walls. It was larger than the one in the little bungalow they would be leaving. It was updated in the 70s perhaps, when one could buy brown refrigerators and stoves. The countertops were red Formica, trimmed in metal.

The kitchen opened to a smallish dining room from one door, and a hallway that led to a bathroom through the other. The bathroom was tiled in white and black and had a big, deep tub. He'd have to install a shower somehow. He wasn't much of a tub guy; but Maureen would like it.

The place was empty. He could hear their footsteps on the dark hardwood floor. The hall also led to two large bedrooms and to the living room with a fireplace. The dining room opened up to the living room, which had high-beamed ceilings and windows that looked out over the grassy, rolling front yard and the park across the street. All in all, not too fancy. Warm. Comfortable. Shanahan felt at home. When Maureen inquired with her glance, he nodded his approval.

'That quick?' she asked.

'If you like it, so do I.'

'You're just appeasing me?'

'No. I like it. Can we do it?'

'If we sell your place and split the monthly payment.'

'Which is?'

She told him the amount. With his Army retirement check, his social security check and the occasional job, he could do it.

'We would own the house outright?' he asked.

'In both our names.'

'With rights of survivorship,' Shanahan said.

She gave him a sad look. She knew what he was thinking.

'What if you live to be a hundred?' Shanahan said. 'By then, I'll be a hundred and twenty-five. Will I get enough work at that age to make the payments by myself?'

'Will you take a younger wife?'

'Will I have a choice?'

'So be serious.'

A clean break from the past. A fresh start. Seemed odd at this time in his life, but he couldn't think of a reason not to do it. He knew Maureen would get all the right inspections and make the best deal possible.

'I'm serious.'

'You want to do it.'

'I want to do it.'

He wondered if they should get married. They never talked about it. Never needed to.

But if it weren't clear before, it was clear now. She wasn't someone who just moved in with him for a while. And maybe marriage would provide some protection for her when he departed the earthly realm for whatever.

As Cross walked back, he saw the big black car parked in front of his house – Rafferty, overdressed as usual in his dark suit, a little too formal and a little too tasteful for most cops. It was summer weight, but a few seconds out of the air-conditioned interior of his car and sweat appeared over his brow.

'What'd you buy me?' nodding toward the bag.

'Shaving cream,' Cross answered. 'I thought maybe you'd want to change your looks, shave off the beard.'

'Funny, looks like a big bottle to me. You going to invite me in?'

'No.'

'Hey!'

'Listen, if you move in with me, I'm going to have to get a bigger bed.' Cross started to the stone steps leading up to his place.

'Your idea of a gay joke?' Rafferty asked.

'No. Just back off a bit, give me some room to get the job done.'

'They're not backing off. They're getting closer. They're sure it's somebody in government, maybe a cop. And with the cell phone missing?'

'How do they know?' Cross asked, stepping back down.

'People in the neighborhood saw a big black automobile coming and going late on a number of nights. They could say for sure the night of the murder.'

'Other people have big black cars,' Cross volunteered.

'Maybe big black Lincolns, or Mercedes. But not a big, black Ford Victoria. State, city officials drive those kinds of cars. They're pretty sure it's a police car and the only cops that drive them are plain clothes and under-cover. The fish they're after ain't swimming around in a very big pond.'

'No plates?' Cross asked.

'I pulled into the garage. Two-car garage. Morgan ... Michael had one car.'

'What else do you know?'

'Internal Affairs are into this big time. They know the time of death. Midnight. Twenty-two caliber. They know that Morgan Lee was not Morgan Lee, but they don't know he is ... was Michael LaSalle.'

'Midnight. You were right there at midnight.'

'Amazing, isn't it?'

'Scary.'

'I heard something in the back.'

'That's not original. You making this up as you go along?'

'I thought it was the dog.' Rafferty pulled a

crisp white handkerchief from his back pocket. Wiped his lips, then his forehead. 'What you got? And it better be more than milk.'

'I've got stuff.'

'Cross...' There was warning in his voice. Anger too.

'I don't want you charging in like some bull and messing this up. There is movement, I promise.'

'What if you die? You got all the information right in here,' Rafferty said, poking his head. 'Won't help me as they turn your flesh into ashes.'

'Somebody else knows.'

'Crap!' Rafferty screamed. 'Why don't you put out a news release?'

Back home, Shanahan returned Cross's call and learned more about Father O'Connor. Would he go talk to him again? Cross asked. Cross also told him everything else he found out, including what Rafferty told him.

Shanahan went to the back yard with Casey; but it was still too hot for Casey to catch the tennis ball. The dog walked out, and before he was fully outside, he turned around and walked back in.

'Wimp,' Shanahan said.

Casey gave him the 'don't-mess-with-me' look.

Maureen was in the shower, cooling off.

Einstein was in the bedroom, catching what was left of the cool from the air-conditioned night.

'Is the new house air-conditioned?' Shanahan asked a little louder than usual to be heard through the sound of the shower.

'Yes. It's not quite our house yet,' she said. 'I'll make a formal offer this afternoon. And you know, my dear friend, almost everyone in the city has an air-conditioned house.'

Conditioning the air. What condition was the air in? Not too good, he thought. Shanahan looked in the white pages to get Father O'Connor's phone number; but decided to visit in person. And now was as good a time as any.

'I'm going to confession,' Shanahan said.

'Whose confession?' She turned the shower off, stepped out, looking like a fantasy he didn't deserve to have.

'A priest, if I'm lucky. Good thing I'm not Catholic or I'd have to confess to a few things myself.'

She smiled.

'I'll be back in a couple of hours,' Shanahan said. 'Your turn to cook.'

'You just want an excuse to drive your new car,' she said, drying herself off.

She wasn't all wrong. But he felt foolish and ashamed for wanting to. He wasn't a teenager.

'You jealous?' he asked her.

'Yes, I am,' she said, turning her back to him to wipe the mirror of its condensation. 'The car has air-conditioning. Nice seats.'

'You have a nice seat,' he said.

She came to him, kissed him lightly on the lips. 'Don't be too long. It's really your turn to cook.'

He hoped he was enough for her. It's hell getting old. It made him think again about marriage. Maybe it wasn't the right thing to do.

Cross punched in the area code for New Orleans and followed it with the number for the shop on Magazine Street.

Billy Dean answered. 'I don't want to talk to you. Stop calling me.'

'If you're smart, you'll listen,' Cross said.

There was quiet. Cross took it as a temporary agreement.

'I know a lot of cops up here. I can get the fingerprints on the dagger read and identified. You've been arrested before, right? Probably something minor, but your prints are on file. And if not, I'll have them take them. My cop friends here will call their cop friends there. I can get you arrested for attempted murder.'

'No way,' Billy Dean said. 'Nothing happened. Not a jury in the world would convict me.'

'Billy,' Cross said, 'who said anything

about conviction? I don't care. I don't want you spending time in jail. So, you beat the case. What kind of chunk does that take out of your life and your pocketbook?'

'You'd do all that?'

'Yep. I'm very frustrated. I need some answers.'

'I don't know anything about the murder. I told you that.'

'I want to know about Marissa Manchette Clarkson.'

Another long silence.

'I don't know about the Clarkson part of it, but you're talking about one of Mother Joan's kids,' Billy Dean said.

'Joan Manchette said her daughter's name was Sarah.'

'Not daughter. Son. Mark.'

# Thirteen

The church was locked. Shanahan followed the brick walkway from the church to a wrought-iron gate that wasn't. Beyond it was a building made of the same materials as the church – limestone – and of, roughly, the same style of architecture. Built in the forties or fifties.

Thick drapery covered the window. The maroon velvet pressed against the window as if it wanted out. A straggly flower garden occupied the small space on either side of the walkway that ended at a door that seemed grander than the rest of the building.

Shanahan lifted the brass knocker and tapped gently twice. He waited.

When the door opened, Father O'Connor was there in the welcomed rush of cool air, wearing gray sweats. There were perspiration pools at his armpits and his face was damp.

'Oh, I thought you were the pizza.'

'A new prescription for your contacts would help.'

The priest nodded, but didn't smile.

He pulled the towel from his shoulder. 'I was working out,' he said, putting the towel back, then sternly: 'Unless you have news for me, I don't know why you are here.' He frowned.

'I have news.'

'Come in, I can't cool off the entire city.'

Shanahan followed him in. It wasn't a large living room, more of a parlor. The worn upholstery on the sofa and stuffed chairs and faded wallpaper took the edge off the cold formality of the room. A slim but harsh light slid through the gap in the drapery on one of the windows as if it were slicing up the threadbare oriental rug.

Father O'Connor sat in the larger chair,

and nodded to Shanahan to find a seat on the sofa.

'Let's get whatever it is over with,' the priest said.

'You or the church paid for the victim's silence?' Shanahan said.

O'Connor's face was stone. 'Mr Shanahan, young Mr LaSalle was a stalker.'

'That's a little more straightforward. Why?'

'It changed over the years,' Father O'Connor said.

Shanahan could tell the man was debating whether to continue or not, or perhaps measuring just how much he was willing to tell. He got up, went to the door to another room, shut it, returned to his seat.

'Once, many years ago ... Michael was fifteen or sixteen ... the last service of the day was over. Michael came into the little changing room and asked if he could help. I was removing my vestments and preparing to get into my civilian clothes. I had no idea. When I turned around he was naked. I was speechless. Shock. The surprise, the suddenness of it all. And yes, it was all quite beautiful ... but oh no, Mr Shanahan, not sexual. A strange embodiment of ... what ... I don't know. But it's what he said that stunned me more. He said his soul and his body were mine.'

The priest was silent for a moment, then continued, 'Don't believe all that you hear about priests. I'm aware of what's been going

182

on and how the church has played three-card monte with priests who take advantage of altar boys, switching them from church to church. And it is true that I moved here to get away from him, but I had no idea he would follow. Mr Shanahan, I want to make this clear: we never had a homosexual relationship.'

'What did you have?'

'I had my duty to attend to him spiritually. I tried to get him to counselling.'

'That's on record somewhere?'

'No. I should have. I had no idea where that moment would lead to. After I asked him to get dressed that day, he became even more obsessed. He wrote me letters, some of them quite lurid. He tried to find ways of getting me alone. This went on and on for years. Then one day it changed.'

He leaned forward, looked Shanahan in the eyes.

'I'm telling you all of this because it's important you understand his nature. He went from love to lust to hate to cold, calm hustle. He started blackmailing me.'

'You gave him hush money?'

It was a guess on Shanahan's part. But it would help explain how Michael LaSalle could subsist without a job.

'Yes.'

'May I ask how much?'

'A substantial amount.' Father O'Connor

was in pain. 'It wasn't my money. It was considered an out-of-court settlement by the parish in New Orleans.'

'How was the payment made?'

'Cash. The full amount, the amount everyone agreed to, was paid off three months ago.'

'Went on that long?'

'Yes.'

'But he wanted it to continue, didn't he?'

'Yes, he did. He also wanted to up the payment.'

'How did you resolve it?'

'It wasn't resolved.'

'It's resolved now, though, isn't it?'

'Yes. But let me make things clear, Mr Shanahan. I never wanted to have the church pay him. I told them I would face him. I would face him in court if I had to. Apparently, he told the parish there were others. He told them that he could corroborate his complaints by convincing others to come forward. The church was getting overwhelmed by these charges. They wanted them to go away.'

'Were there others?' Shanahan asked.

'There was no one. None. I told you. Michael made it up, all of it, first as revenge for being continually rejected. Then, as I said, he turned it into a money-making scam once stories started leaking to the press about the priests in Boston and he saw the opportunity to exploit it for his own purpose.'

'On the other hand, Father O'Connor, your career would be over once this got out. You had the most to lose. If I talked to the parish...'

'They would say nothing.'

'Not even to defend you against those charges?'

'No. They would say something vague and mystical, perhaps,' he smiled, 'something completely incoherent. On the other hand, as you say, they could never be sure.' The priest paused. 'They knew how easy it was to be seduced by a beautiful young boy or girl.'

'Are you gay?'

'I have no orientation sexually. I love Christ.'

'But Michael stunned you, you said, with his nakedness.'

'He would have stunned you too. Anyone. Beauty is beauty. Look at Michelangelo. I thought I had explained it. Because I deal in sin, I can only find solace in innocence. That both good and evil resided in the beautiful and so innocent young body, caused me deep confusion, caused me to question beliefs I thought I had made solid.' Father O'Connor looked tired. 'I'm not sure what was going on in that boy's head at that moment. I'm sure he was undergoing some personal difficulties and perhaps my handling of the affair caused him greater anguish than he should have been asked to bear. Perhaps I handled it badly. But it seemed that innocence was tempting me to sin.'

'Michael wasn't innocent,' Shanahan said. 'Not even then, I suspect.'

'No, maybe not, but he could play the role convincingly. There's grave danger in that seduction.'

'As he found out. Now, once again. Where were you Saturday night between eleven and midnight?'

'With Mr Shumley. At St Vincent's hospital. His wife was dying. I was there from eight in the evening until five the following morning.'

It was a call Cross dreaded to make. He'd almost rather tell little Timmy that Lassie had died. He dialed the number that got him Marissa the first time. She answered.

'This is Cross again.'

'Wrong number,' she said.

'Wait. I promise you'll want to talk to me.'

'I've asked your company to put me on the don't call list, and it agreed. Please check your records.' She was masking the conversation, keeping the substance from whoever else was in the room with her.

'You'll be sorry if you hang up.' He understood that she couldn't talk, thus the code,

186

but he had to keep her on-line.

He waited. She finally said, 'Make it quick.'

'Meet me in Broad Ripple on the little bridge by the Firehouse. You know it?'

'Why?' she asked.

'We've got to talk about Mark Manchette.'

Another moment of quiet.

'Certainly, I'll reconsider. Thank you for your call. I have a meeting in an hour in Broad Ripple. I'll get back in touch after that.'

Cool, Cross thought. Cool as a cucumber. He was glad he remembered to make it a public, very public meeting place. If she was the killer and killed Michael LaSalle to protect her new identity, there's no reason she would spare his life.

Shanahan sat at the bar with a beer and a jigger of J.W. Dant bourbon. As a former regular, he knew the others who passed their afternoons here rain or shine. Harry talked to someone who wasn't a regular, had perhaps been in the area and wandered in to cool off and grab a beer.

'So there was this big crash,' Harry said. 'Huge. Right out front here. I called 911 right away and then went out to see what I could do. Well, the Lord must have been watchin' out for these two. They both stepped out of their mangled vehicles unscathed. Not a scratch. A miracle.'

Harry hunched over the bar in a posture suggesting this was a story intended only for the customer directly in front of him; though the volume of Harry's voice was carefully calibrated so that he could be heard throughout the bar.

'I started to go over to them,' Harry continued, 'but they started talking to each other. The rabbi recognized the priest by his collar and told him that he was a rabbi. And the priest said that God must've wanted them to meet or he wouldn't have saved their lives like that. So, the priest went back to his car, reached through the broken window and pulled out a bottle of wine, opened it. He put his arm around the rabbi's shoulders and handed him the bottle. The rabbi took a deep swig of the wine and tried to hand it back to the priest. "Ah, take another," the priest said, making a gesture of generosity. Soon after, the priest suggested another. Finally, the rabbi handed the bottle back and insisted the priest take a drink. The priest put his hands up. "No thanks," he said, "I'll just wait for the police."'

Harry didn't get the expected applause and he was pissed.

'He gave the rabbi the wine,' Harry said.

The ringing of the bar phone saved the awkward silence that followed the repeat of the punch line.

'Hello to you. Thank you. Yes, he's here.

But you know, he don't deserve you,' Harry told the caller, then motioned for Shanahan to come to the phone.

'I step out of the shower,' Maureen said. 'I step out completely naked and glistening. I was glistening, wasn't I?'

'You were. Maybe even twinkling.'

'Let's leave it at glistening,' she said, 'I don't do twinkling.'

'Glistening, it is.'

'And you go for a drive in your very new, very sexy automobile.'

'You are much sexier,' Shanahan said. 'But sometimes I need something more.'

Harry gave Shanahan a sharp and intense look.

'Howie called, said he has some important news. He wants you to call him. Dinner at seven?'

'With Howie?'

'No, dummy. Two separate thoughts. Call him. Dinner is at seven. Swordfish.'

'Got it.' He put the phone back in the cradle. He looked at Harry. 'The car, Harry. We were talking about the car.'

Harry ignored him, grabbing the remote and clicking on the television.

The Braves against the Cubs, the team who finds great athletes and then trades them away, Shanahan thought, to guarantee the Cubs never play in the World Series.

'Why do I care, Harry?' Shanahan asks.

'Because she is a wonderful woman.'

'The Cubs. Why do I care?' He picked up the phone, punched in the number for Howie Cross. Got the answering machine.

'You don't make any sense,' Harry said. 'You haven't been making any sense for a long time now.'

Cross wanted to be there first. He wanted to see if she brought friends. He wanted to be more familiar than she was with the terrain.

The bridge was concrete. It crossed a narrow canal that ran from downtown out to Broad Ripple Village, once another town, now a desirable and entertaining neighborhood. Broad Ripple Avenue, the main drag, plays host to a number of bars that at night make the place a little too boisterous and a little too drunk. A decade ago, he hung out here when he was off duty – at a little bar called the Alley Cat.

South of the main street is residential – small, solidly-built expensive bungalows. North of Broad Ripple Avenue is an inter-mingling of homes, shops and restaurants of a random and eccentric nature. The bridge is on this side, near a fire station that is large enough to house one small fire truck.

Cross went to the bridge, settled in, leaning against the concrete wall, sometimes watching the ducks below in the murky, otherwise quiet water and sometimes scanning the area for signs of an approaching Manchette.

Mid-afternoon in August. This was the hottest time of the day during the hottest time of the year. Today there was a faint breeze though there was nothing cool about it. It was just good that the air moved. The tables and chairs outside the Corner Wine Bar were empty. People moved slowly. Even the ducks were quiet. The only energy Cross could see was the occasional bicyclist heading up to the Monon trail, a refurbished railroad bed that went on for miles and provided a ride or a run without the interruption of auto traffic.

She approached wearing a gauzy pantsuit. Her long palomino hair added to a kind of relaxed look, an elegant hippie. They were obvious to each other though they hadn't met. Who else would be standing out there in that heat but some sleazy private detective?

She didn't smile. Her green eyes were without emotion. Blank. Much like her mother's. A guy? Cross asked himself. Hard to believe. He gave a polite smile to show he wasn't a mean man, that he wasn't out to harm her. He wanted to be trusted.

A shirtless, perspiration-coated skateboarder roared between them.

She smiled.

'Here we are, living dangerously,' she said.

Cross tried to keep in mind that this was

once Mark as he was nearly taken in by the charm. A lot like his ... her mother's.

'You Cross?' she asked.

'Most of the time,' he said.

'Thought we had a deal,' she said.

'We did. I think I said something about being able to rule you out. What I learned pretty much rules you in. Best motive yet.'

'Let's go have a drink,' she said.

He followed her to the Corner Wine Bar. It was quiet. They found a seat in the corner by the windows – panes of translucent glass with stained glass crests. Dark wood panelling alternated with deep red walls. Black leather chairs. Whatever look they were going for seemed to work. Pan-European maybe. They had wine. That's what counted at the moment.

'I never order white, but it's too damned hot to drink red,' she said, as she found a table.

They waited until the waiter took their order before talking.

'So you knew Michael. Almost his ... daughter,' Cross said after the waiter noted their order and disappeared. 'You meet here in Indianapolis?'

'New Orleans. We were friends from the eighth grade. Later, we had a short, boring affair. We both wanted to be the center of attention. And when it was just the two of us ... well, you can imagine.'

'You stayed friends?'

'We were connected somehow. I don't know if I'd call it friendship. We understood each other. That's something, maybe enough.'

'Was he blackmailing you?'

'No.'

'You're gay and married to a right-wing what? Social conservative, right?'

'Half right,' she said. 'I am not and never was gay. I was female who just happened to get some wrong parts, that's all. Nature does that all the time. You know, six toes on a foot. When that happens, you fix it.'

'Four leaf clover,' Cross said, trying to suggest he got the concept.

'And that's good luck, right?' She smiled. 'You know we're born into this world without a whole list of rights and wrongs and people write the list for you. They say what's normal and what isn't and we are conditioned to buy into the program or suffer the consequences. There isn't a norm. Dig deep and we'll find something very different than the way you are expected to be.'

'You could find that out with a toy shovel.'

'Normal is just what a group of people decide it is.'

'I consider myself educated,' Cross said, 'we can move on.'

'I hope so,' she said, smiling at the waiter as he arrived with two chilled glasses of Pinot

Grigio. 'He probably would've extorted me if he could, but he didn't want to be exposed either.'

Cross couldn't help but try to figure out if he would have known about her if he hadn't been told. Could she have fooled him?

'The surgery in Thailand is really quite remarkable,' she said, as if she'd plucked his thoughts out of the air. 'I was small-boned. That helped. They worked on the Adam's Apple,' she said, looking right in his eyes, seeing right through him.

'Does your husband know?' he asked.

'No. It would kill him. Destroy all of his trust, all of his work.' She kept her eyes on Cross as she sipped more wine. 'Does that provide you with an opportunity?' She raised her eyebrows, playing tough. Or perhaps she was.

'Sort of.'

'How much do you want?'

'Not money. Just truth. A lot of it.'

'How noble.'

'No. I've been hired to find it.'

'And who decides what truth is?'

'At the moment, I do.'

'Go for it.'

'How did you and Michael LaSalle end up attending the same Mass in Indianapolis?'

'I know what brought him here. And so do you. I came by accident by way of Chicago. I relocated as far away from my family in New

194

Orleans as I could. I wanted to be in a big city after the surgery. I chose Chicago. I had a friend there who would help me integrate into mainstream society. That's where I met Ray.'

'H. Ray to be exact.'

'Yes. I worked for him. He was a corporate attorney who I found out later spent every Wednesday night at a soup kitchen.'

'Really?'

'The man has a soft side. He's a good man.'

'I'll take your word for it,' Cross said.

'When I met him, all he could talk about was that he was in the wrong field. He wanted to help people.'

'We're still talking about H. Ray Clarkson.' She gave him a look. 'Seriously,' Cross said, 'what happened? I've seen him on television. He has about as much compassion as a meat grinder.'

'He looks at the world differently now. Something happened.'

'What?'

'God spoke to him.'

'What did God say?'

'That Ray must do everything he could to purify the world, get it ready for the rapture.'

'Do you believe him?'

'I believe he believes it.'

'That's enough?'

'Enough for now,' she said. 'It is hypocritical, ironic even, I'm sure. But I've never been happier. Mind and body are one. I'm a married woman living the life I knew I had to live. I have children. Adopted, but mine and I love them. Politically, I disagree with Ray, but how many other husbands and wives have these kinds of disagreements?'

'You've been very, very open. I know more about you than I know about me.' Cross looked at her.

'I want you to understand. I want to answer all your questions and then I want you to leave me alone. Nothing personal. But I don't want to visit that time in my life again. I'm not that confused little boy anymore. So if you have questions, get them all in now.'

'I'm just trying to find out if you killed Michael LaSalle. You had an argument in church.'

She laughed. 'Father O'Connor told you that?'

'Mmmmm.'

'Good old Father O'Connor didn't even recognize me, I bet.' She smiled.

'What?'

'From New Orleans. I used to go to his church there. Like Michael. I often went with Michael, many, many places. All right, shift to the present: Michael and I had two arguments at church. Then I stopped going. One was when he asked me to have sex with him. He said he wanted to be the only one

196

who fucked me while I was a male and then again as a female.'

Cross said nothing. He couldn't for the moment. He had trouble getting his mind around the idea.

'I said "no".'

'And the other argument?'

'Michael wanted me to corroborate his story that Father O'Connor molested him, by saying that I witnessed it.'

'True?'

'Yes. Michael said we could make some money. He wanted me to tell the Cardinal that I had been molested as well. That we were molested together, forced to do things.'

'True?'

'Forced, I don't know. Convinced maybe. Coerced possibly. We were excited too.'

'How many boys did he seduce?'

'I don't know. Father O'Connor had a thing for the sensitive boys. And he could be very persuasive. And, of course, these were the boys most likely to volunteer to help with the services or join the choir. Some were devoted to him, felt privileged that he chose them.'

'How old were you?'

'Early teens, mid teens, I think.'

'Why didn't you want to bring him down? Father O'Connor?'

'Then, I was afraid. Now, it would ruin my life as well as his. You'd be surprised how often that happens.'

'You didn't tell your parents?'

'It would have killed them. They were already horrified that I was wearing Mother's lingerie.'

'You're taking all this well,' Cross said.

'I'm sorry Michael's dead. In a way, I can't imagine any other end for him. He was very self-destructive.' She sipped her wine. 'You know,' she continued, 'looking back on it, I should have helped Michael. He didn't know how to deal with his feelings for Father O'Connor.'

'You were the same age. What makes you think you could have done something?'

'I was tougher than he was. I was already dealing with my differences, my place in the world. I should have protected him. Maybe gone to the authorities. Who knows what would have become of him had he not been seduced by a priest?' She smiled, shook her head at the world, it seemed. Then she looked up, nodded.

'What?' Cross asked.

'Oh, nothing,' she said, smiling.

'No, what? You're saying maybe he might not have been gay? Or you might not have...'

'No, no. You're way off. Father O'Connor may be a horrid man and maybe he screwed up a number of lives, but he didn't make anyone gay and he certainly didn't make me want to be a woman. I was. So we were whatever we were. But without that experience, it's quite obvious Michael wouldn't have been in Indianapolis, perhaps not even dead.'

'I'm just surprised you're not bitter,' Cross said.

'I can't afford the emotion.'

'Amazing,' Cross said.

'The world isn't fair,' she said. 'So you deal with it. That's what you learn if you pay attention. Do what you can, but don't let the fuckers screw you over.'

'Going back earlier in our conversation, you never answered one of my questions.'

'I'm sorry.'

'Why didn't Michael just blackmail you? You have access to some big money.'

'Same reason we didn't attack Russia or the Russians didn't attack us. What did they used to call it during the Cold War?'

'Mutually assured destruction. MAD. You really couldn't be sure though, could you?'

'I knew Michael very well. He wouldn't take on the devil unless he was absolutely sure he could win. This was lose–lose for him.'

'And he lost anyway, didn't he?'

'Everybody's got a day when they come for you. You ready?'

'Is that a threat?'

'I'm not a murderer, Mr Cross. I was just speaking about the inevitability of it.'

'You still in touch with the old crowd?'

'Old crowd?' She smiled. 'How old do you think I am?'

'The guys at the Corner Pocket?'

She grinned. 'What a time? It was tough, but I'm glad I went through it, but in the end, Mr Cross, that was the old life.'

'So, you have no contact down there?'

'Not really.'

'What about your family?'

'My kids or my folks back in New Orleans?'

'The New Orleans branch.'

'They're not part of my life.'

'Who decided that.'

'They wanted to hold on to Mark and I wanted to forget him. So, in their minds, I'm dead. Now they can have him, and I can have a new life. I doubt if they know where I am.'

'Could your mother have had Michael killed?'

'My God, is there no end to your questions?'

'Soon.'

'Does she have the capacity to kill him personally? No. Is she cold enough to have him eliminated? Yes. If he was a recurrent problem, she'd have him swatted like a mosquito.'

'You have a sense that this is all incestuous ... you sleeping with Michael, Michael sleeping with your mom?'

'That's New Orleans.'

'There's a lot of coincidence here. You both end up in Indianapolis. You run into him in the same church. How did that happen?'

'He came for Father O'Connor, like I said before. I came down with Ray when they offered him the job to run the institute. It fit in with his plan.'

'God's plan.'

'Yes. You have a better explanation?' She smiled.

'But the same church, come on?'

'He saw me in the newspapers. Some charity events. He looked me up. Just like you did.'

'So you weren't going to church for spiritual guidance and happened upon Michael?'

'No. I gave up the church a long time ago. He got a hold of me and we agreed to meet there.'

'And here you are with H. Ray. Life is cruel.'

'It is. A little bit of black humour. But I love Ray. I'm in it for life. Unless...'

'Unless what?' Cross asked.

'You. What are you going to do about all of this?'

'I don't know yet.'

'You going to destroy my life?'

'I hope not.'

'I hope not too,' she said getting up. 'Thank you for the wine.'

'You're welcome. One more thing. Did you know Michael subscribed to the Nash Family Values Institute newsletter? You have to be a member, right? I mean to get it.'

She looked at him blankly, but for too long. She didn't know what it meant, he was sure. He was also sure she knew that this wasn't a good thing.

She left without responding, without saying 'goodbye'. Cross thought he could still see the boy in the woman. It was a curious thing for him. When he was in vice, he had to deal with transvestite prostitutes. He had never given any thought to the young males who may have quietly and successfully 'passed' into straight society as women. In his own wild and sometimes debauched life, had he slept with someone who was once a man?

Some questions are better left unanswered, he thought. He liked Marissa, as he had her mother, but he wasn't attracted to her. Too much bosom for him. Hmmmh, he thought, as he paid the tab and headed for the door.

He stopped, came back to the table and retrieved her glass. He asked the waitress if he could buy the glass.

'I'll check,' she said. She left him standing there, but was back in a moment, carrying a clean wine glass.

'Fifteen dollars, if you want?' she told Cross.

Cross reached in his pocket, found a five and a ten. She took the money and wanted to exchange glasses.

'No, I want this one,' Cross said.

She looked puzzled.

'Sentimental,' he said.

She smiled, nodded.

# Fourteen

Too early to start dinner. It would be quick when he got around to it. Some variant of pasta and fish or chicken, a salad.

So long gone, dead to his memory, and now his brother kept popping to the surface, as were many images from quite another century. Random and out of order, an uncle stirring his coffee at his mother's table, the smell of apples being cooked for apple sauce, the golden brown cow in the barn.

Calming sometimes, unsettling other times, these images wafted in and out of his consciousness at their own will. There were moments when he felt more than just tugged back in daydreams, but moments when he seemed to occupy the space and time. They say, when you die, he remembered, your whole life flashes before you. Perhaps when you die slowly, your life flashes in front of you in slow, spasmodic episodes. Putting it all behind you. Finishing business.

Thing was, he'd finished most of it. He'd made peace with his mother and father. Good thing, at seventy, to get by that. The relationship with his son Ty in California was good and getting better. He understood why Elaine left him those many years ago. He would have done the same in her shoes. There was one thing left – and he'd forgotten until the dream. He was reminded again by the photographs in the basement. Young Fritz Shanahan was beginning to nag at him.

When Maureen came home, Shanahan asked her to look up Fritz Shanahan on the Internet.

'Fritz? Who's that?' she asked, a mysterious Mona Lisa smile on her face.

'They have this people search thing, don't they?'

'They do,' she said, her mind racing. 'You have another son?'

'No.'

She put down her bag on the sofa. It was stuffed with papers and it tipped, spilling out forms and photographs and real estate books. As she gathered them back up, calmly, she asked again, 'Who?'

He walked into the kitchen, tossing 'a brother' out as he passed from her view.

She followed. 'You never told me...'

'I ... forgot.'

'A brother? You forgot you had a brother?'

'It's easier than you think.'

Cross opened his eyes in the darkness, turned his head toward the bedside table. The glowing numerals said 12:44 a.m.

The pounding came again. More forceful. It was the front door. Cross couldn't imagine who or why. He was between girlfriends, a thought that he immediately understood was overly optimistic. He had no other friends. And he had only one client. Rafferty.

Cross rolled up so that he was seated on the edge of the bed. He leaned down, felt around, and found the baseball bat. One night not all that long ago, he answered the door late and ended up with a broken nose and some dangling teeth, not to mention days of pain and ugliness.

It was Rafferty.

'Somebody call you in to pinch hit?' Rafferty said. He was moderately dishevelled, which meant he was a lot dishevelled by his usual sartorial standards. He fit every stereotype of the drunk – eyes finding it difficult to focus, a body listing from side to side, mouth agape. He was so drunk he didn't know he was drunk.

Rafferty nudged himself inside, not waiting for an invitation that wasn't likely to come.

'You got reservations, buddy?' Cross asked

205

half in jest, half in anger.

'About you? Plenty. Who was that woman?'

'What are you talking about?'

'At the restaurant. In Broad Ripple.'

'You tailing me?'

'You won't tell me anything,' Rafferty slurred, his head dipping a bit and coming back like a prize fighter dodging a punch – all in slow motion.

'Some woman I know,' Cross said. The last thing he'd do was to tell Rafferty these kinds of details. Certainly not now, when the cop had time to screw it up.

'You playing around on my dime?' Rafferty tried to stand in the middle of the room, but the room wasn't having any of it. 'You got anything to drink?' He stumbled toward the short set of stairs that led to the living room. And apparently with enough moonlight filtering through the pines and the big glass doors to the patio, he did a running stumble to the sofa.

He crashed and fell silent.

There was no way Cross was going to get a 300-pound man anywhere else. He should just be thankful Rafferty didn't find the bed. He pushed Rafferty's stone-weight body further into the sofa so that he wouldn't fall out of it. It was warm enough without a blanket, but Cross found a clean sheet and used it to hide the evidence from himself.

★   ★   ★

Shanahan was up with the sun. Earlier than usual. The night was haunted. A mix of gray, cloudy dreams in which shadows moved. Vague identification. Brother Fritz on the other side of the door where there were shouts and cries. A silver-haired man with a black leather bag. When he was awake, he seemed still half in that world. He was glad to see the sun and he didn't trust sleep.

Coffee. Two puzzled animals, both normally very schedule-driven. The dog was happy to go out, sensing this might be the coolest part of the day. The cat decided that since Shanahan was up, food could be served earlier. The half-awake human satisfied both Casey and Einstein and checked to see if the paper had arrived.

Grapefruit juice, Raisin Bran, whole-wheat toast. The *Indianapolis Star.*

It was a hopeless cause, Shanahan realized in the faint pink light of early day. He was a hopeless cause. His brother was an old man too. Probably dead. Drooling in some nursing home or, if his life had somehow turned lucky, playing golf and bridge in Boca Raton.

After he finished his breakfast, he went out the kitchen door to the back yard. The rains made it unnecessary to water the grass and garden. It was warm and he could feel the humidity inching back in. He sat in the white wood lawn chair. He unfolded the newspaper. Working his way from front page to international and finally to local news.

Casey pulled up beside him, letting his body drop on the grass.

Shanahan read Dan Carpenter's column. The guy wasn't taking the views most popular in a conservative midwestern city. Shanahan liked that. Too many people were sheep, unable to think for themselves. They needed somebody to piss them off from time to time.

Done with the editorial section and the sports, Shanahan went back through the paper. With his earlier than usual start, he had finished the paper before he normally would. He thumbed back through it, seeing if there was something he'd missed. And there it was. The police spokesman said that the victim's name, Morgan Lee, may be an alias. According to their investigation, there is some connection between Lee and Michael LaSalle, originally from New Orleans. Scant details about the crime are available. However, an unnamed source indicated there is serious speculation that the perpetrator works for a government agency.

Shanahan figured that the police were now on the trail. These were important discoveries. And it's likely, he thought, that they knew more. Usually, Rafferty was the official spokesperson for the Indianapolis Police Department. And when he was, they would use his name. Rafferty wasn't mentioned in the story. Did they already suspect him? He looked at his watch. Still too early to call Cross. He'd wait until eight, which of course, was still too early. But it was hard to tell when Cross slept.

The ringing of the phone awoke both beasts currently inhabiting the former chauffeur's quarters-turned-PI office and home.

'What the hell am I doing here?' came the voice of papa bear. Rafferty continued to growl something as Cross headed toward the phone.

'Everyone has to be somewhere,' Cross said, as he picked up the phone.

'Cross.'

'This morning's paper suggests the police are narrowing their investigation. They know Lee is LaSalle. And they think the murderer is in government someplace.'

'It may be worse than that. They also know the phone came from the IPD.'

'Who are you talking to?' Rafferty asked, stumbling into the small middle room where Cross had his computer.

'Who's there?' Shanahan asked.

'So many questions, so little time,' Cross said. To the phone, Cross said, 'Rafferty, because everyone has to be somewhere.' He looked to Rafferty: 'Shanahan, because ... because ... I don't know why. I'll call you back, Shanahan. I have to tell Rafferty why he's here.'

He hung up.

'Coffee?'

Rafferty looked around as if he could find some alternative to the offer. 'Yeah, I guess.'

Cross went to the kitchen, dumped some coffee into a filter, filled the tank and pushed the button.

'Drunk, huh?' Rafferty asked, hovering behind Cross.

'Rip-roaring, or should I say, falling-down drunk. I was glad you made it to the sofa. I don't think I could have gotten you there.'

'Why did I come here?' Rafferty said, then looking at Cross's puzzled face, 'Yes, of course, I don't expect you to know. That was rhetorical.'

'Your friend's death just now sinking in?'

'No,' Rafferty said softly. 'Just one more thing.'

'What's that?'

'Nothing. When will coffee be ready?'

'Couple of minutes. Come on.' Cross guided him back to the little living room where there was room to sit comfortably. He opened the sliding doors to let in the early morning breeze, and the sounds of the morning. Rafferty sat on the sofa.

'I'll be off. Sorry to have bothered you.'

'Well, something happened. I think you need to keep me informed.'

'Why? You don't keep me informed,'

Rafferty said.

'What you fail to remember is that I'm the one trying to keep you out of the newspapers and out of the electric chair.'

'Lethal injection.'

'What triggered this drunken rampage? Or is this normal?'

'No. I can usually control my drinking. In public anyway.'

'Get your head together,' Cross said. 'I'll get our coffee. I want you to talk, Rafferty. Shanahan says the police know Lee is La-Salle and they have connected it to someone in public service.'

'I told you that.'

'If they are putting those facts out there, what are they holding? Why aren't you making the public statements? Isn't that your job?' Cross left Rafferty to think. When he came back with the coffee, Rafferty was hunched over, head in hands.

'You have to work this morning?' Cross asked.

'Yeah. I do. But it's getting tougher to go into the office. I don't know what they know except that they know enough to keep me from knowing.'

'What did you find out that made you want to drown your sorrows?'

'More anger than sorrow,' Rafferty said. He went silent, apparently still trying to figure out if he should talk about it.

'Max. It's not helping you or your case to keep stuff inside.'

'Morgan stiffed me.'

Cross bit his tongue.

Rafferty continued. 'He milked my accounts. Charged on my card.'

'What did he get?'

'Cash. Airline ticket.'

'To where?'

'You were fucking right. He was using me.'

'Where was he going?'

'Paris. He was leaving the morning after he died. He knew he'd be gone before I got the bank statements.'

'Shit.'

'Yeah. More ways than one.'

'Traceable. Connection to you, not to mention motive.'

Rafferty stood.

'I must have killed him,' he said. 'If I were investigating this case, my ass would be in jail and the district attorney would be blowing me goodbye kisses. Closet case cop, afraid of being outed, victim of fraud. Hell, if I had known, I might have killed him.'

All the case was missing was an eyewitness, Cross believed. Who wouldn't believe that a cop was capable of shooting someone? 'Slam dunk', as some are inclined to say about 'sure things'.

'I can't believe I bought it,' Rafferty said.

'Love is blind,' Cross said.

'Stupid. Love is stupid. Only weak people fall in love.'

'No, the song is "only fools fall in love".'

'Thanks,' he said, shaking his head at what appeared to be his fate.

'Don't start feeling sorry for yourself. We've got work to do.'

'Shanahan helping?'

'Yeah.'

'What is it with you guys? You working on sainthood?'

'Me, I'm in it for the money. As for Shanahan, he wants to get to the truth.'

'Even if incriminates me?'

'Yep. That's why he didn't take the case when you offered it to him.'

'So you think him helping is good?'

'Only because I believe you didn't do it. You didn't do it, did you?'

'No. I would have strangled him, not shot him.' Rafferty was trying to pull himself together.

'It looks like you slept in your suit,' Cross said.

'Don't you ever give it up? Being around you is like being in a Bugs Bunny cartoon.' Rafferty headed toward the door. 'Oh,' he said, 'I forgot to give you this. I found it in Morgan's ... dammit ... LaSalle's wallet.'

It was a crumpled piece of paper with a phone number.

'Whose number? Nash something institute. I don't remember. Don't know if it will help.'

Everything that Rafferty did bring was tainted. Was this in LaSalle's wallet? Or did Rafferty plant it?

'Anything else in the wallet?'

'Nothing but the usual.'

'You wiped off any prints?'

'Yes. I told you I cleaned the place. Every place I'd been. Wiped the prints, made sure there were no strands of hair.'

'I know. Killer's prints too, right?'

'Maybe. Maybe not.'

'What?' Cross asked.

'If I heard what I thought I heard, the killer ran out the back door. Likely as not the killer came in that way. I didn't wipe those prints. Or the front door either. Never used them. Came in through the garage.'

'I see.' Maybe there was something there.

Shanahan picked up the phone on the first ring. He was at the door, letting Casey out to the back yard.

'I'm hoping I can talk you into interviewing H. Ray Clarkson,' Cross said.

'Why is it that you give me all of the religious guys?'

'They give me hives.'

'Why is that, you think?' Shanahan asked, amused.

'The Book says it, so it's true.'

'And you write your own book?'

'More than that. Smirking condescension.'

'Yours or theirs?'

'Both,' Cross said.

'Supposing I could survive the smirk, why would somebody like Clarkson be willing to talk to me?'

'Oh, c'mon. You find ways. Tell him you are prepared to make a huge donation to his cause. Tell him a murder victim named him in his will. It doesn't matter,' Cross said. 'I just need to find out if there is any connection.'

'Is there?' Shanahan asked. 'You're holding out on me,' Shanahan said to the long silence.

'I ... uh ... there's a piece of this that ... I uh ... need to keep to myself. I don't know how else to say it.'

'All right.'

'Rafferty came over last night roaring drunk, passed out on my sofa.'

'You two are getting close.'

'No, it's getting bad, really bad. Young La-Salle was emptying Rafferty's bank account and was about to pack his bags when he was killed.'

'Maybe no eyewitnesses,' Shanahan said, 'but a bushel of motives.'

'Yep. And it's all going to be traced back to Rafferty. There's too much. Somebody's going to find something and the rest of the cards will come tumbling down.'

'If I were on the jury, I'd vote for the prosecution. I've been thinking. He wiped the place down, didn't he?'

'I know. He wiped off the killer's prints either way you cut it. But please talk to Clarkson. Find out what some gay guy is doing on his member's list.'

There was another quiet stretch.

'Did I forget to say please?'

'And thank you,' Shanahan said.

'One other thing. I found another source that said Father O'Connor did molest young Michael and maybe a few others.'

'Who?'

'I'll let you know later. But the person was convincing, had no real axe to grind.'

'So you want me to talk to the good Father again?'

'Would you? Please and thank you.'

When Shanahan placed the little wall-mounted princess phone back in its receiver, he let his eyes focus on the screen door, but his mind was on the case. Rafferty had a slew of motives to kill LaSalle and he had crippled any real investigation by tampering with evidence. Rafferty was smart enough to want to throw suspicion somewhere else. What smarter move could he make than to hire a private eye to explore the possibilities.

It was entirely possible that Rafferty killed

in a moment of rage or, because of the execution nature of the killing, in cold, white anger, Shanahan speculated. After the killing the veteran policeman went into cop mode and began sanitizing not just the scene but also any known connection. He may have come over when LaSalle wasn't expecting a visit and when Rafferty knew the young man would be asleep.

What Cross was doing was uncovering others with a motive. All that Shanahan could do, try to do that is, is be sure that they were legitimate suspects, and not a scapegoat to ensure Rafferty's freedom.

Then again, this revelation about Father O'Connor ... He had a few more questions to answer.

Through the screen door, Shanahan could see Casey sniffing around the garden. Einstein came in from his spot of sun in the living room – so old, so slow, so deliberate in his steps – to get his morning vittles. The sixteen-year-old, bony feline could still leap on to the countertop to watch Shanahan open the can, staring as if he could provide instructions should his old keeper forget.

Not long after Einstein got his breakfast, Maureen came in, half awake, going to the refrigerator for the orange juice, while Shanahan poured her a cup of coffee and, while she remained half in the unconscious world and unaware of his eyes on her, he drank in her beauty.

The little bungalow on the East Side of Indianapolis was coming alive – as much as it could.

# Fifteen

Cross wasn't sure how smart he was to send Shanahan to see H. Ray Clarkson without knowing some of the particulars. Clarkson's wife having once been a man – at least in the eyes of the law – might have been one of them. But he wanted to honor a largely unspoken agreement with Marissa. He didn't want to wreck a marriage, though he wouldn't have felt half so bad about wrecking the man's career.

Shanahan was good at reading character, the best as far as Cross was concerned. He'd find out something. Cross went to the table in the middle room, picked up the scrap of paper with the phone number Rafferty had given him. Rafferty had told him that the paper found in LaSalle's wallet was the foundation's number; Cross hadn't tried it.

He dialed. The answer couldn't be clearer and couldn't be more interesting. The female voice said, 'Nash Family Values Institute, Mr

Clarkson's office.'

'Sorry, I have the wrong number,' Cross said, realizing he didn't have the wrong number at all, but a far more meaningful number than he thought. LaSalle didn't have the main line into the institute. He had the office number, the main line into Mr H. Ray Clarkson himself.

This would give Shanahan more ammunition. It also made Cross wonder if LaSalle went behind Marissa's back or worse, Marissa lied to him about mutual assured destruction. Maybe it was just who could destroy whom first. And she did it. There were a lot of maybes. Maybe LaSalle got a hold of H. Ray Clarkson and H. Ray killed off the little blackmailer to save his career.

Didn't really matter who it was at the moment, Cross was unable to conceive of what the business world calls 'next steps'. Unless Shanahan came up with something solid, Cross would be stuck with his speculations. Could be her. Could be him. Could be Rafferty. Could be someone completely unknown.

Cross was stymied, yet the net was closing in on Rafferty. Cross let his mind wander through the list of those he knew on the force – those that were still there, those who would talk to him. But once he did that, they would be on to him as well.

Again, he called Shanahan, who was about

to leave. 'What about Swann? Can you find out where the police are with your friend?'

Shanahan said he'd figure something out. Cross hung up the phone. Then it hit him. He truly didn't know what to do next. Not just on the case, but in the next moment, the next few hours – about anything. The case was stymied. He was stymied.

So this was mid-life crisis? Well, he didn't want a red sports car. He didn't want some young blond bimbo. He didn't want to find some nice girl and settle down. He didn't want to be a private detective living hand to mouth from case to case. He didn't want to be anything else. He didn't want to have lunch. He didn't want a drink. There was nothing he wanted or felt he needed. What was the point of it all anyhow?

Shanahan sat at the kitchen table, a cup of coffee in front of him, the telephone cord stretched to the maximum. It took three calls and the correct combination of words to get to talk to H. Ray Clarkson. Eventually, it was murder, homosexuality, Nash Family Values Institute member, Clarkson's office number on the body, and the names Morgan Lee and Michael LaSalle. Shanahan didn't know which ones carried the most weight; but maybe he'd find out.

Clarkson was adamant about not meeting at the institute, which was a sprawling modern building on the northeast side. Shanahan suggested Clarkson meet him at a quiet, little neighborhood bar where nobody would know his name.

'I don't drink, Mr Shanahan,' he said.

'I know the bartender. He won't make you. If you're nice he'll even make you a Shirley Temple.'

Fact was, Shanahan generally didn't like people who didn't drink at all unless they were recovering alcoholics.

'I don't like your attitude,' Clarkson said.

'I don't like my attitude either,' Shanahan said. 'I have a feeling that's the only thing we have in common. When can you get away?'

'Let's make it four.'

Shanahan told him how to find Harry's little place on 10th Street. He got up from the table, went back to the wall mount, dialed the police department. Swann was out. Shanahan left word.

He called back within ten minutes.

'You have something for me?' Swann asked.

'Listen, I'm curious about what's going on. Not a lot in the papers.'

'You know it's a felony to obstruct justice. You know anything about the case?'

'I know what people tell me.'

'What people?' Swann pressed.

'People who have opinions. I don't have any facts for you. Just opinions and you

221

probably have enough of those already.'

'You working for Rafferty?'

They knew something.

'On what?'

'On the case.'

'What does Rafferty have to do with this?' It wasn't dishonest to ask a misleading question, was it?

'Just thought I'd throw that out,' Swann said, realizing what he'd done. 'Means nothing.'

'Why would Rafferty hire me? For anything?'

'You're not working for Rafferty?' Swann asked.

'I told you, I'm not getting paid a dime. I'm not working for Rafferty or anybody.'

'I don't get it,' Swann said.

'So, you were leading me on thinking I knew something and then you were going to pull my chain,' Shanahan said.

'Yeah. About right.'

'Well see, you pulled and what did you get? Why are you asking about Rafferty?'

Quiet.

'Nothing,' he finally said. 'You better not be lying to me. We've always played it straight, you and I. So let's not mess up a good thing.'

'I'm not. I've got no facts.' Shanahan hadn't told a single untruth.

'Why are you in this?' Swann asked.

It was Shanahan's turn to be quiet.

'I let you in on this,' Swann said, 'because you did me a favor, a big favor. But this is getting hot.'

'Close to home?' Shanahan asked and instantly regretted it.

'It's not a time for games. I can't return a favor by not doing my job. I have to do my job.'

'I understand.'

'But nothing?'

'For now,' Shanahan said. 'I promise you I'm on the right side.'

'And what side is that?'

'Whatever it turns out to be.'

Now Shanahan faced another dilemma. Should he tell Cross that the police knew at least something about Rafferty? He felt like he was playing both sides against each other – and he guessed he was. It was as if the truth could be squeezed out by putting pressure on both ends.

He called Cross.

'I've got an appointment with Clarkson,' Shanahan told him.

'When?'

'Four p.m. at Harry's.'

'I wish I could be a fly on the wall.'

'You could be a barfly. He's never seen you.'

'All right,' Cross said.

'You might suggest that Rafferty get a

lawyer.'

'You're telling me this because...'

'Because Swann was worried, thought I was in the employ of their not quite beloved fellow officer.'

'Damn.'

'Don't tell him how you know this. And you, have you found out anything from your sources?'

'No. Either nobody knows or nobody's talking.'

Next on the list was Father O'Connor.

He picked up on the second ring.

'This is Shanahan.'

'You're not done with me yet?'

'Information keeps popping up. Where were you the night Michael died?'

'I told you.'

'Yes, a Mr Shumley.'

'I'll need his full name.'

'And you are going to interview a man who just lost his wife about who was with him when she died?'

'There are others who said you did molest Michael LaSalle.'

'There are people convinced they've been beamed aboard alien spaceships. And there are others who say they saw it happen.'

'I can find Mr Shumley.'

'Be my guest. Please don't call again.'

Shanahan was glad to be off the phone. It was rare that he'd talk to so many people in such a short time. It was tiring. In general, he thought people talked too much.

When the two guys came in the bar, it was as if they interrupted a Hopper painting. Seated, facing the door, at a booth far inside, Cross saw the two regulars who sat down in the shadows near the front door, heads bowed as if in prayer over their Budweisers. Harry, a white towel over his shoulder, leaned on the bar, eyes up on the Cubs game. Shanahan sat at the bar, farthest from the door and within a peanut shell's throw of Cross, who returned his eyes to the open copy of *NUVO*, Indianapolis' alternative newspaper.

When he looked up again, he saw that Harry's eyes had momentarily picked up on the newcomers as the swatch of white light and a blast of heat swept in with them. One guy was the burly type, dressed in a cheap suit. The other was skinny, sharp featured, and cloaked in a better suit. Harry eyed them again when they approached Cross. Cross looked up, then back down at his newspaper.

'Shanahan?' the skinny guy said to Cross.

Cross looked up, 'Nice to meet you, Shanahan, Jones here.'

'No, I'm not Shanahan, I'm...'

'Then you shouldn't introduce yourself that way. It's confusing,' Cross said.

'I'm Shanahan,' Shanahan said, not looking at them, but having caught them in the corner of his eyes earlier and knowing instinctively that neither of them was Clarkson.

'You?' the heavy-set guy said.

It wasn't new to Shanahan for people to be surprised at his age. It was the rule rather than the exception at times like these.

'Mr Clarkson wants to meet you outside,' the skinny one said.

'That wasn't the deal,' Shanahan said.

'It's the new deal,' the skinny one said.

'Tell Clarkson that he can meet me here or I'll take my questions elsewhere.'

'You talk tough,' the skinny guy said, smiling.

Shanahan turned back to the bar, took a sip from the shot glass now half full of J.W. Dant bourbon.

'I don't have to talk at all.'

The two newcomers stared at each other a moment.

'We don't have a lot of time to play games,' the heavy-set guy said.

'Your mother calling you?'

'You're an ass,' the heavy guy said.

'You buying a drink?' Harry said, coming into the conversation. 'If not, I'm going to have to ask you to leave.'

The two guys looked at each other again.

'Don't get your pants in a twist, Grandpa,'

the heavy-set guy said. 'We're conducting a little business of our own at the moment.'

'It's called the strong arm of the Lord,' Shanahan said, as he watched Harry duck under the bar top, then return with a baseball bat, heading toward the newcomers.

'Get out,' Harry said.

'The *friendly* neighborhood bar is down the street,' Shanahan said.

The two men looked puzzled. The skinny guy shook his head, turned, headed toward the door. The heavy-set guy followed. Harry went back to the game. Cross resumed reading. Shanahan waited for Clarkson.

After a few moments of quiet, the door opened again. The skinny guy stepped in, but remained by the door. Another man, tall, fit, in his late forties or early fifties came in, stopped, looked around, then continued toward Shanahan.

'Mr Shanahan,' he said.

'Yep.'

'Let me apologize for sending in security first,' he said.

Shanahan turned to look at Clarkson. He wore a light tan suit, with a blue button-down shirt, open at the neck. His thinning hair was spread over the skull feebly trying to hide his baldness. He looked clean. Really clean. His skin was wax-like. He had piercing blue eyes and thin lips.

Shanahan waited for Clarkson to continue.

Clarkson sat on a stool. Harry came over. 'A cola of some sort,' he told Harry. 'I've achieved, if you call it that, a little bit of celebrity. Just enough to put me in danger. It won't surprise you to know that a lot of people dislike me a great deal. So, since I'm meeting you in a place of your choosing, I needed to check it and you out first. I really thought this was some sort of shakedown.'

'Why didn't you call the police?' Shanahan asked, letting his eyes meet Clarkson's.

Clarkson looked away.

'You have something to hide?' Shanahan asked.

Clarkson was quiet for a moment, searching for something.

'Sometimes people make up things. You know how it is.'

'How is it for you?'

'You don't like me, do you, Mr Shanahan?'

'No, I don't. But that really isn't important.'

'What is it you want?'

Harry brought the glass of iced cola.

'I'm trying to figure out why a young gay man would become a member of your organization.'

'I don't have an answer for you. Could be he believes homosexuals are committing serious sins and destroying the fabric of American life. Many homosexuals know what they are doing and are trying very hard to mend their ways. We often help them find an organization that can change their orientation.'

'You know Michael LaSalle?' Shanahan continued.

Clarkson thought a moment, then said, 'No.'

'How about Morgan Lee?'

'No. Am I supposed to know them?'

'Morgan and Michael are the same person and he had this on his body when they found him dead, a bullet in his head.'

Shanahan handed him the crumpled phone number.

'Yes, anybody can call the institute.'

'Odd that he'd have the number of your office, not the general number.'

'Not impossible to get. Did he have my private line or my cell phone?'

'No, but he had this number tucked in his wallet like it was something special.' Clarkson, poker-faced, didn't bother to respond. 'You do any travelling to New Orleans?' Shanahan asked.

'I do a lot of travelling for the institute. New Orleans pops up now and again.' Clarkson smiled. 'So, now I have answered a few of your questions. I have one of my own. Why are you asking them?'

'We want to find out who killed him.'

'Who is "we"?'

Shanahan was caught. 'We, meaning the

public. General we. Now, I have another one for you.'

'Go ahead.'

'Why did you agree to meet me?'

'From what you said on the phone, it sounded serious. I wanted to clear up any misunderstanding,' Clarkson said. He took a deep sip of his drink, stood up. 'I have to catch a plane. Anything else?'

'Is it possible that your wife knew Mr LaSalle AKA Mr Lee?'

Clarkson's look of quiet arrogance switched to bitter anger.

'What makes you ask that?' He didn't raise his voice, but clipped the words with his teeth. More snarl than growl.

'She's from New Orleans, isn't she?'

'Hundreds of thousands of people are from New Orleans,' Clarkson said. He looked back at the door. The skinny guy was still there. He looked back at Shanahan, his face moving closer to Shanahan's. 'I'm sorry for the death of your friend. The world's a dangerous place.'

'I know. And all we need is a few more religious radicals.'

Clarkson smiled an unfriendly smile, pursed his lips as if he were about to kiss someone. 'There is good and evil, Mr Shanahan. And you are on one side or the other.'

'What just went on here?' Harry asked, after Clarkson left, followed by the skinny guy.

'Cross's case,' Shanahan said, nodding over to the smiling Cross.

'Who told you about Mrs Clarkson being from New Orleans?' Cross asked.

'Research,' Shanahan said.

'I asked what was going on?' Harry insisted. 'You asked me about Catholic school earlier. Now you have this Clarkson character in here with his ... his...'

'Christian soldiers,' Cross said.

Shanahan would trust Harry with his life, but sometimes not with sensitive information. The elder detective saw no reason to talk about Rafferty's problems.

'I'm helping Cross with a case, Harry. That guy who got shot at Bay Colony.'

Harry turned to Cross. 'Who are you working for?'

'Hey, I'm supposed to keep that quiet,' Cross said.

Their plates were empty, yet Shanahan and Maureen sat at the kitchen table. She sipped her second glass of wine. He was finishing his second beer.

'They accepted the offer,' Maureen said.

'We have the house?' Though there was no reason for him to be surprised, he was. Somehow this made it suddenly real. He was also surprised she waited for so long and said it so nonchalantly.

231

'You okay?'

'Sure.'

'You know you didn't put up an argument?'

'I know,' he said, puzzled.

'We never argue.'

'Yep.'

'You think that's healthy?' she asked.

'Isn't it?'

'I guess I'm wondering if we're really being honest, exposing ourselves.'

'Why would I want to expose myself?' he asked.

'C'mon, what do you think?'

'About?'

'About us not arguing.'

Shanahan shrugged.

'Well, I think we should argue sometimes,' she said.

'We could set aside a time. Tuesdays at seven.'

'Now you're being silly,' she said.

'Me?'

'So, you're saying I'm silly?'

'OK. You're silly,' Shanahan said.

'Now we're getting somewhere,' she said. 'Why do you think I'm silly.'

He stood, walked over to her and kissed her on the cheek.

She grinned.

'Are you all right with the house?' she asked again.

He nodded. 'It's Saturday night,' he said. 'What do you want to do?'

'Let's see,' she grinned. 'We could find a disco palace somewhere, smoke some marijuana, and listen to the Bee Gees and dance.'

'No, let's do something different for a change. How about we watch a video and go to bed?'

'Where do you come up with these crazy ideas?'

# Sixteen

Howie was crossing a river of naked people, guiding his small wooden boat through the tangle of bodies when the phone rang. He looked around the boat for his cell phone when he was pulled groggily from sleep. He pulled the metal chain of the lamp by the bed, was blinded by the sudden light. He picked up the receiver, but the ringing didn't stop.

Cell phone, Howie. Cell phone, he told himself firmly. He got up, tripped over the sheets twisted on the floor, then wandered into the small room, clicking on the light next to the computer and finding his cell phone, he flipped it open. Two things registered immediately. It was four eleven in the morning and he didn't know the caller.

'Hello.'

'Mr Cross?'

That threw him for a moment. So did the voice that hovered between male and female. Oh.

'Marissa.'

'Yes. I need to talk,' she said, reluctance of some sort in her speech.

He almost said that it was four o'clock in the morning, but he guessed she knew that.

'Can you give me five minutes to wake up?' he asked. 'I'll call you back, then we can talk as long as you like.'

'Please meet me at the bridge in Broad Ripple. You know, where we met before.'

'When?'

'Now,' she said.

'Listen, why...?' He struggled to get the words out, but she'd already disconnected. He punched automatic redial. It rang until he got an answering system.

Cross stood naked in the room, staring blankly at the phone, his mind paralyzed by indecision. There was something wrong here. He thought about calling Shanahan, but it would be cruel. Maybe she had some information.

As he slipped on his jeans, a T-shirt and his tennis shoes, he couldn't help but think that everything about this was wrong. Late-night, urgent meeting in a place sure to be absent of people. In the movies, this was the moment when the idiot went down the dark stairs to the cellar after twelve other people in the house have been bludgeoned to death there.

The situation called for rational thinking, but there was no time for it. He grabbed his wallet and his car keys, but stopped at the door. He went back for his gun, a new SIG Sauer P220. He checked the safety, tucked the .45 in the waistband just above his butt. That meant he needed a jacket. Back in the bedroom, he grabbed a light jacket and headed out.

He rarely opted to carry a piece. Only when he thought there really might be danger. Tonight qualified.

Cross put the window down rather than turn on the air-conditioning as he drove along Westfield Boulevard, paralleling the shallow, narrow canal occasionally lit by the street lamps. Cross lived only a few minutes from Broad Ripple and the bridge where Marissa was waiting, or so she said. Not another car on the road. Even the drunks were home.

He followed Westfield as it angled left at College Avenue, slowing as he entered the little village. He turned on Carollton, expecting to see Marissa standing somewhere on the bridge or perhaps seeing a car parked near there. Nothing. He parked up on Carollton and strolled back on to the bridge. The place was empty. No skateboarders, no ducks.

It was a strange place for a bridge really. The canal stopped twenty or thirty feet to the east of it – ending its run from downtown at a concrete wall. There was no sound of running water. No sound of anything really, except Cross's own breathing. The humidity was low, the night was clear, the moon full and sharp.

Was it just a prank call, he wondered? Could be that because he lived so close, she misjudged how long it would take him to get there. He realized he was standing in a puddle of light from a street lamp, giving a gunman a clear view. Cross moved into the shadows. There were moments when he wished he hadn't quit smoking. This was one of them. That's what people are supposed to do when they stand waiting for someone in the middle of the night. Except that he should be wearing a trench coat, and it would be cold and damp and he'd pull the collar up to protect his neck. Nope, he was there in a T-shirt and jeans, feeling an odd mix of anxiety and boredom.

He scanned the area around him. He could take in quite a bit of real estate. He turned to look over the west side of the bridge, let his eyes find patterns in the black water. Slowly, as his eyes scanned from the faraway to the near, he saw her. Face up. Hair and forehead in the water, she was sprawled on the small rocks that lined the canal at unnatural angles. It wasn't likely, but it was possible she was alive. He moved around the wall and down on the embankment on the north side of the canal.

The descent was more vertical than he thought. The angle and the darkness conspired to trip him more than once. He tried to catch himself with his hands only to feel the sharp rock cut into them. The warm wetness he felt had to be blood. The closer he got to the body the less likely it was that she was alive; but that was his first goal.

Finally he was down. Feet now in the water, he dropped down on his haunches. He knew better than to touch her or the handle protruding from her chest. The murderer, judging from the angle of the victim's head, might have snapped her neck first.

'Fuck,' Cross said. She had made it this far, trying to be who she was and now she was no longer.

He'd call 911 once he got his way to the top. He began his climb. As he found the top and level ground, he heard them. The whoops were stereophonic. Lights flashed from every direction, down Carollton from both directions and the same for Westfield Boulevard. No need to call 911, he reached in his coat pocket for his cell phone. He could barely concentrate. He punched the number for Shanahan and hoped the old guy would answer before the cops could get him sprawled on his belly on the street.

A groggy and tentative hello. It was Maureen.

'It's Cross. I think I'm being arrested. If I don't call...'

Tires screeched to a stop, car doors opened. Police emerged, flashlights, guns. They were taking no chances.

'Get down on the ground now,' the voice came from an electronic megaphone. The command could be heard in the next county.

Cross raised his hands. 'It's a phone, don't shoot.'

'Get down on the ground now.' A voice from an angry God.

He got down on his knees then stretched out as he knew he was supposed to. He left the phone on.

Two cops approached, one with a German Shepherd struggling against its leash.

'I have a gun tucked in the back of my pants,' Cross said.

'Don't move an inch,' one of them said, kneeling down beside him. 'He's got blood on his hands.'

Cross was all out of smart-ass responses. He knew how it looked. And any words that may have formed on his tongue dispersed silently in the atmosphere like dandelion fluff in a strong wind.

One of the cops pulled up the back of his coat jacket and pulled out the gun.

'Nice. Anything else?'

'Nothing that would hurt anyone.'

The cop noticed the cell phone, nudged it away from Cross's grip, left it open on the concrete.

Another cop came over, pulled Cross's arms behind him. He felt the handcuffs lock over his wrists. The cop then felt around Cross's shirt, legs, crotch, feet, removing car keys, money, and wallet.

'PI,' said one of the cops to the crowd.

Cross couldn't see what was going on, but imagined there were cops finding their ways down the embankment. More sirens in the distance. Someone had called in homicide. No doubt the medical examiner was on his way.

He was pulled to his feet. He could barely see anything, caught in the crossfire of headlights. But he could see uniforms moving down the embankment. Then, through the light, he saw a big black sedan. Standing just outside the door of the car, staring into the scene from just outside the periphery, was Rafferty.

When Rafferty saw Cross looking his way, the cop looked away, then got in his car and backed it up a few feet before making a U-turn and heading away.

What was he doing there? Cross wondered. How did Rafferty know to come to the bridge?

Secrets. Odd now. Cross was holding two secrets – both now threatened by his arrest.

For now, no one was asking him any questions. They were waiting for someone higher up. The questions would come though. If he kept the secrets entrusted to him by Rafferty and Marissa, he was in deep trouble.

Maureen had awakened Shanahan, handed him the phone. 'It's Howie. He's in some sort of trouble.'

Shanahan heard voices, obviously not directed at him. 'It's a cell phone, not a gun.' There were shouts. Shanahan heard a voice say, 'Don't move an inch. He's got blood on his hands.'

'Howie!' Shanahan shouted into the phone as he sat up, swinging his legs over to sit on the edge of the bed, but all he heard was scratching sounds, indistinct shouts, and distant sirens.

Shanahan hung up the phone, looked at the clock – still early – then back at Maureen, who was sitting up in bed, wide awake.

'Nothing we can do until later,' he said. 'He won't be processed until eight or nine. That'll take a while. I guess I should get him a lawyer. Kowalski, maybe.' Shanahan said all of this to himself, as much as to Maureen.

He got up, went to the bathroom. When he came back, she was sitting there, waiting for him.

'What's this all about?' she asked.

'I don't know.'

'Does it have to do with Lieutenant Rafferty?'

'Probably. He's got the anti-Midas touch. The minute he touches a piece of gold it turns to manure.'

'You going to try to sleep?' she asked.

'I don't know. But you go ahead. You need your ten hours.'

'I need a little melatonin to calm me down.'

'You want the one prescribed by Dr Haagan Dazs?'

'Yes,' she said. 'Yes, I do. You're getting it for me?'

'I am.'

Maureen seemed pleased that the forceful pounding on the door came after the treasure was delivered and she had sampled two spoonfuls of Swiss Almond Vanilla. Shanahan crept to the table he used as a desk, removed a .45 from the drawer and brought it back to Maureen. She slipped it under her pillow.

'If I sleep on it, will I have money in the morning?'

The knocks came again and Shanahan

241

slipped on his robe and went into the living room, stood to one side, flicked on the light and again caught the countenance of one Max Rafferty, Lieutenant.

'I saw lights on,' Rafferty said.

'What are you? A moth?' Shanahan asked as he stepped aside so Rafferty could enter.

'We need to talk.' Rafferty went to the center of the room and turned. 'Cross has been arrested.'

Shanahan said nothing.

'You don't seem surprised?' Rafferty waited for some sort of response and getting none, continued, 'Looks like it could be a murder charge. Thought you might want to get your Harley-riding lawyer pal downtown.'

'You know all of this, how?' Shanahan asked.

'I'm a cop?' Rafferty said. 'You suppose?'

'It's five in the morning. This isn't your shift. I mean you really don't have a shift, do you?'

Casey walked into the room, gave Rafferty a sullen stare and walked out.

'I saw him getting arrested.'

'You're not making me feel any better,' Shanahan said. How would Rafferty know Cross's whereabouts at this hour? 'You set him up?'

'Why would I do that? I need the bastard. I was following him.'

'You sitting in front of his house all night long in case he sleepwalks?'

'I put a locator on his car. I pick it up electronically. The car moves, I hear a beep. I follow him on this little screen.' Rafferty showed him a little hand-held device with a screen.

'You hire a PI, then tail him?'

'Looks like I should have done more, don't you think?' Rafferty said, beginning to pace. 'Cross was close-mouthed. Thought I'd fuck it up if he told me too much. Now he's in jail and I'm expecting a call from Internal Affairs. Unfortunately, Mister Shanahan, I don't know anymore about the case than the day I hired him.'

'Why are you here?'

'You have to help. I'm sure Cross didn't kill anybody, but he was found in the middle of the night climbing out of the canal. There was a body down there. Cross had blood on his hands.'

'Who's dead?'

'I don't know. But, Shanahan, he's sitting in a cell and I'm his get-out-of-jail-free card.'

'I doubt he'll use it, the fool,' Shanahan said.

'You going to help?'

'I'll help him. If that helps you, I can live with it. But if it comes down to you or him?'

'I know. Do what you can.' He started toward the door. As he opened it, he turned back. 'I don't know if I can convince you, but I didn't kill Morgan or whatever the hell his name really was. And I don't know whose body ended up in the canal. Somebody is pretty clever though. Two bodies and some innocent schmuck on the line for each of them.'

In the bedroom, Maureen pulled the .45 from under her pillow, handed it handle first to Shanahan.

'I hope you didn't want me to shoot him. I was busy,' she said, nodding toward the empty ice-cream container.

'Good thing he didn't come in here and want a bite of that.'

He switched off the lamp. He'd call Kowalski at first light.

Cross walked ahead of the guard who escorted him up the walkway between cells. Unlike in the movies, nobody paid any attention to him. He was just another number in prison whites.

A huge iron gate with bars that seemed thicker than his bones made a sound locking in place that had to have echoed throughout the floor. This was the second such gate he had passed through. This one led to an open space with a couple of concrete tables. There was just one person in the open space. An attorney named Kowalski.

'Nice of you to visit,' Cross said, sitting

down. He looked up to see the face of a guard looking out of a high window, close enough to see everything, far enough away to afford some verbal privacy.

'You look splendid in white,' Kowalski said.

'Well, it's a lie. It might surprise you, but I'm not a virgin. You my lawyer?'

'If you want. Shanahan sent me.'

'James Fennimore Kowalski, I want you more than you know.'

Kowalski was a big man, barrel-chested, dressed in a white shirt, open at the neck and a black suit. He had a full head of wild hair with silvery-white streaks at the side adding a dramatic touch. He had a thick beard, also streaked. He looked like a Roman general or god of war. He knew Kowalksi and he knew of Kowalski. When Cross was on the force and testifying – sometimes reluctantly – against prostitutes and drug peddlers, his testimony was being attacked by the man who now sat across from him.

'What's up?' Kowalksi asked.

'Marissa Clarkson, who I questioned the other day on another case...' Cross looked up at the guard, smiled, then looked back to Kowalksi. 'She called me in the middle of the night...'

'What time exactly?'

'Four eleven a.m., and wanted me to meet her at the bridge. When I queried her, she said "Right now", and hung up before I could argue or think. I was stupid. So stupid.'

'You found her already dead,' Kowalksi said matter-of-factly.

'I did.'

'How did you end up over here so quick?' Kowalski asked. 'Usually you're in a holding cell at the police station for a while.'

'I'm special. You know, this place is so crowded they're letting people out just to make room for the new ones. And they have me in a cell with just one inmate.'

'You are special,' Kowalski said. 'They want you to get chatty.'

'There are other reasons I'm special. I'm an ex-cop. And the victim is the wife of H. Ray Clarkson.'

'They got the wrong spouse,' Kowalski said. 'Why were you talking to her? What case?'

'Shanahan can fill you in and if this goes any farther, you and I can talk. There's a lot of strange things about the situation.'

He'd told no one about the sex change. He shook his head. Poor Marissa, he thought. She had excised all her ghosts – except one apparently.

'I'll try to get you out by this afternoon,' Kowalski said, mistaking Cross's mood as being depressed about his incarceration.

It would be, of course, Cross thought, if it

lasted more than a few hours.

'You know there's a billboard outside my window that says "Escape to Hawaii?"' Cross said.

'These ad guys, they have a great sense of humour,' Kowalski said.

# Seventeen

It was early yet. Too early to try to call anyone. Sunday morning's TV talking heads. What made it so interesting to Shanahan, who sat at his little table-like desk in the living room, was that one of the heads was H. Ray Clarkson. He was debating Constance Westerhaven on the rights and wrongs of same-sex marriage.

The wizened moderator and his two guests spoke in front of a sky-blue scrim with vague suggestions of Washington DC behind them.

*Clarkson: Same-sex marriage not only jeopardizes marriage, the concept of family, and the health and welfare of our children, it threatens to tear down all that Western civilization holds dear.*

*Westerhaven: This is profoundly silly. We're*

247

*asking to change nothing about heterosexual marriage. Is the institution so weak that it cannot abide the idea that two people committed to one another and choosing to make it legal has anything at all to do with marriage as it stands today? It's ridiculous. Western civilization, goodness, Mr Clarkson. One by one the nations of the West are choosing to finally provide equal rights to gays and lesbians.*

***Clarkson****: It's not only against Biblical teaching. And that should be enough. It is against everything our founding fathers stood for. They were Christians. The country was founded by Christians. This process will destroy religious faith as a value for future generations and it is completely against the Constitution.*

***Westerhaven****: Reverend Clarkson...*

***Clarkson****: I'm not a reverend...*

***Westerhaven****: Whatever you are, first, the founding fathers were not uniformly Christian. Jefferson actually wrote his own bible with all references to the supernatural removed. Benjamin was no fan either. If you'll recall your history, people fled to this country because of religious persecution by people like you...*

***Clarkson****: Come now...*

***Westerhaven:*** *This hysteria. It is difficult to understand where it came from. There's absolutely no mention of homosexuality in the Ten Commandments. You'd think if it were so important...*

***Clarkson:*** *It's mentioned throughout the Bible.*

***Westerhaven:*** *The Old Testament. Why do you hang on to the Old Testament? Where is there mention in the New Testament where your beliefs are supposed to be founded?*

Shanahan was only half engaged in the argument, though he was surprised at some of Westerhaven's statements. He rarely thought about gays and lesbians. They weren't very much part of this life. His attention drifted. But he was interested in their faces as they debated. Westerhaven's face revealed anger, sometimes impatience. Clarkson, despite the smug smile, had to restrain his passion, as if at any moment, it would all just blow up. A man perhaps capable of murder?

***Clarkson:*** *Listen, Ms Westerhaven. I don't hate gays and lesbians, but we must face facts. Several leading research institutions suggest that this is an illness. We know that orientation can be reversed. We are not angry with people, we are angry with behavior. Homosexual behavior is just not acceptable in a civil society.*

*Westerhaven: The so-called research people you quote are charlatans. The books are cooked. I'd rather listen to respectable institutions like the American Medical Association and the American Psychiatrists Association. Listen, Mr Clarkson. I pay my taxes in full. I want my rights in full. So does every other gay and lesbian who do their part to build schools and highways, pay for our police, and our armies. Do your children go to public school?*

*Clarkson: That's not the point...*

*Westerhaven: If they do, we contribute our fair share, but you would deny us children of our own...*

*Clarkson: You can't have children.*

*Westerhaven: We can and do. We also adopt. Your children are adopted, aren't they?*

Shanahan shut the set off.

Maureen sat at the kitchen table. She sneezed three times. After each, Shanahan blessed her from his seat at the little desk table in the living room. After the fourth sneeze, he came in.

'I think,' Maureen said, putting down a piece of toast, 'I'm allergic to wheat.'

'Really?'

'At the moment,' she said, 'it is an unsub-

250

stantiated rumor.'

'I see.'

The phone rang. Shanahan answered it. 'Shanahan.'

'Kowalski. Cross is in deep.'

'How deep?'

'He isn't getting out anytime soon,' Kowalski said.

'What's going on?'

Shanahan looked at Maureen who was staring at him anxiously.

'The weapon that killed Mrs Clarkson was a screwdriver. That screwdriver matches the set Cross has at his home.'

'And there's a screwdriver missing in the set, right?'

'That particular screwdriver,' Kowalski said. 'A Philips head.'

'Jesus,' Shanahan said.

'I didn't know you were a religious man, Shanahan.'

'Buried real deep, I guess.'

'Truth is he's gonna need Jesus or someone to perform a goddamn miracle. Scene of the crime. Weapon traced to him. You know him better than I do. Could he have flipped out?'

'No.'

'That's unequivocal?'

'Yes, he is not a violent man. If he was, he'd probably still be on the police force.'

'OK.'

'Meet me at Harry's, would you?' Shana-

251

han looked at his watch – eleven forty-five. 'At noon. You have time?'

'I can rearrange some things, but it'll take me longer to get to Harry's. Before twelve thirty. I've arranged a meeting with Cross later.'

Shanahan put the phone back on the hook, feeling powerless. He knew very little about the dead woman.

'I'm going,' Maureen said. 'It's about Howie, isn't it?'

'Yep. Not good.'

Harry's place was bustling. Eight guys sat at the bar staring at their drinks instead of the usual four. The booths were full and Harry was carrying bowls of something – chili or stew – to the rear booth. The juke box, more often than not sitting quietly in the corner, spouted Johnny Cash going down in a burning ring of fire.

'What happened?' Shanahan said, as Maureen found a stool near the cash register.

'Get Robinson a Budweiser, will you?' Harry asked Shanahan. 'He's crying in the Doritos.'

Shanahan was rarely allowed in that sacred space on the other side of the bar. 'He drinks Budweiser. No wonder he's crying.'

'Shut up and mind the bar a moment.'

Harry rushed to the back bar where he ladled more stuff into bowls and balanced three on his way to another booth.

'They actually eat that stuff?' Shanahan asked.

Harry looked up, grinned. 'I got the message. Nobody likes homemade stew. They want it out of the can. This here is canned. I just heat it up.'

'You found your calling. Heating things up.'

'Shush,' Maureen said.

'Coming from you,' Harry said, 'the man that ate spaghetti every day for ten years until Maureen came along.'

Shanahan looked at his watch. Not quite twelve thirty.

'Get me another Miller's,' one of the non-regulars said to Shanahan.

'That's better,' Shanahan said, clipping the cap off the bottle, using the opener mounted on the back bar. 'What brought you here?'

'Thirst,' the guy said.

'I haven't seen you before,' Shanahan said.

'You don't know what you missed.'

'You walk into the wrong bar, maybe?'

'Starting to look that way,' the guy said.

'Hey, hey, hey, don't be running off the customers, Deets.'

'Just trying to figure out what a nice old guy is doing in a dirty little place like this.'

'Kramer croaked,' the man said, chugging half of the bottle. 'Nobody to run the bar.'

Kramer's bar was two blocks to the west on

10th. 'They closed it down, the relatives, I guess.'

'That's the way to get new business, Harry. Kill the competition.'

'Maureen, my sweet,' Harry said turning to her, 'when are you going to leave him for me?'

'If what you say is true about eliminating the competition, Shanahan,' she said, 'you better watch your back.'

'We all do,' said James Fennimore Kowalski, coming up to them. 'We got a place to talk?' He looked around.

A booth was clearing near the back. Shanahan and Maureen cleared the table, then sat. Kowalski asked Harry for a coffee, waited for it, and brought it back to the booth.

'Mrs Clarkson complained to her husband that Cross was harassing her.'

'Why? Did she say?' Shanahan asked.

'No.'

'That's odd,' Shanahan said. 'He wouldn't ask why.'

'Or she wouldn't tell him,' Maureen said.

'Cross was investigating a murder,' Shanahan said, and explained what he knew about LaSalle, how he died, and the priest and how he likely molested young boys. 'There were ties to New Orleans. The victim, a gay guy, was interested in the organization that Clarkson ran. He was a member.'

Kowalski sipped his coffee.

'I remember the story now. Out by the reservoir?'

'Right,' Shanahan said.

'Why was Cross investigating?' Kowalski asked.

'Somebody asked him to.'

'Who?' Kowalski asked. 'You know.'

'I know.'

'I can keep a secret.'

'Even if you don't want to?' Shanahan asked.

'Even if I don't want to. I have to know these things.'

'Let Cross tell you.'

'I'm never convinced that discussions between attorneys and prisoners are confidential in a jail environment.'

'Max Rafferty,' Shanahan said.

There was a long silence.

'Go on.'

'Rafferty was having an affair with the guy,' Shanahan said. 'Found the body.'

'Doesn't want to come out to the force?' Kowalski was unfazed by the news.

'Doesn't want a needle in his arm,' Shanahan said. 'Rafferty has more motive than anyone, it seems. It was a race. Cross was trying to find the murderer before the police made the link to Rafferty.'

Kowalski stared at his coffee cup.

'That ass Rafferty gives gays a bad name.'

'Michael LaSalle wouldn't have made a

255

very good spokesman either. Nasty little guy. He was about to run out on Rafferty with a chunk of the lieutenant's money, and he was blackmailing the Catholic priest who molested him.'

Kowalski smiled. 'So what did the guy do wrong?' He looked at Maureen. 'You mind if I smoke? Not going to be able to do that in a bar all that much longer.'

'Go ahead,' she said. 'Blow a little this way. I quit eight years ago, but I still miss it.'

'How do you know all this?' Kowalski asked Shanahan.

'I helped Cross out. Interviewed the good Father and H. Ray.'

'Come with me, Shanahan,' Kowalski said, lighting a brown cigarette. 'This is almost the same as quitting. Thanks.' He smiled at Maureen and turned to Shanahan. 'You need to be with me when I interview Cross. Fill in the holes.'

'You have to get him out,' Maureen said.

'Nobody's got that kind of money ... or influence,' Shanahan said to Maureen. 'Why don't you take the car? I'll ride with counsel.'

Kowalski smiled broadly.

'Why don't you get a car?' Shanahan asked, realizing he'd just agreed to ride behind the big lawyer on the big, loud Harley.

Cross again walked a couple of steps behind the guard – this time a man as wide and tall as a security door – through the drab, color-less world of the Marion County Jail. He hoped he was walking toward his freedom but doubted it would work out that way. Otherwise he wouldn't be meeting Kowalski. He hoped the lawyer had, at least, news of his release. Though his internment wasn't a nightmare, more like limbo, he had yet to take a shower, yet to mix with the general population.

Life could get worse. Fast.

He found Shanahan and Kowalski waiting. They looked grim. Not a good sign, Cross thought.

Shanahan stood as Cross approached. Kowalski shrugged a hello. Neither smiled.

'I take it I shouldn't be packing my bags?' Cross said, sitting down with them.

'The woman was killed with a screwdriver,' Kowalski said.

'It was dark,' Cross said. 'If I told the police it was a knife, I was mistaken.'

'Your screwdriver.'

Cross couldn't speak. Couldn't move. But somewhere inside him, his stomach rose to his chest then dipped like the big drop in a monster roller-coaster. Now, the nightmare begins, he thought.

'They searched my place?' he finally said.

'Seems so,' Kowalski said. 'What else might they find?'

'Toenail clipper, an old *Playboy* or two, a

257

half-empty bottle of tequila, some moldy cheese, lots of dirty clothes.'

'Howie, c'mon,' Shanahan said.

'I didn't kill her.'

'You know the drill here,' Shanahan said. 'Think like a cop.'

'I've tried very hard not to do that.'

'You're up for murder,' Kowalski said.

'They're not going to take your word for it,' Shanahan said. 'This killing has to be connected to the LaSalle murder.'

'It does,' Cross said, nodding. His consciousness was only barely connected to the moment.

'Who knew where you lived?' Shanahan asked.

'I'm in the phone book. White pages, yellow pages. I gave everybody I talked to on this case my business card in case they remembered something. One of them apparently figured out where to find me. All they have to do is Yahoo my name.'

'Who are the players?' Kowalski asked.

'Father O'Connor, H. Ray Clarkson,' Cross said. 'I would have put Marissa on the list, but that doesn't seem likely now.'

'That's it? Short list,' Kowalski said.

'Then there's Rafferty,' Shanahan said.

Kowalski looked at Cross.

Cross shrugged. He felt like he was underwater.

'Just throwing out names,' Shanahan said.

'What about the folks in New Orleans?'

'Not sure they knew where he was,' Cross said. 'I suppose it's possible. Ex-girlfriend who was also Marissa's mother. An old friend who seemed to love him.'

'The good Father has an alibi,' Shanahan said. 'I checked it. He was bedside at the hospital with a dying parishioner.'

Cross took a deep breath.

'Since I'm no longer the keeper of big secrets,' Cross said, 'Marissa Clarkson was once Mark Clarkson.'

'She had a penis?' Kowalski asked, amused.

'At one time,' Cross said.

'Curiouser and curiouser,' Kowalski said. 'What we have here is a priest who molests little boys...'

'Allegedly,' Shanahan said half-heartedly.

'And a young gay guy who...'

'Bisexual,' Cross interjected.

'That makes it better. And a woman who used to be a man.'

'She would take issue with that,' Cross said.

'I'm speaking in legal terms or biological terms or just some terms to make it interesting,' Kowalski said.

'All right,' Cross said. 'It's actually more convoluted than that. Marissa's mother had a live-in relationship with the first victim. The second victim, Marissa, when she was still Mark, also had an affair with the victim.'

'Before he was the victim, I take it,' Kowalski said. 'Though that would add something to the mix as well.'

'So far, necrophilia doesn't play a role here,' Cross said.

'And in the middle of this mess we have a world-famous homophobe,' Kowalksi said.

'Who was married to...' Cross was trying to say it right, 'the son who became a daughter of the woman with whom our first victim had an affair.'

Kowalski grinned and shook his head.

'Who on your list – and maybe not on your list – do both victims know?' Shanahan asked.

Cross thought a moment.

'Everybody I mentioned. I don't know if Michael LaSalle ever met or talked to H. Ray Clarkson, or if he did, what was said. But everybody else knew each other. They both knew the priest. They both knew Joan Manchette in New Orleans. They knew Billy Dean in New Orleans. And how many others, I don't know.'

'And Rafferty?' Shanahan asked. 'Are you including Rafferty in this?'

'Rafferty knew LaSalle. We know that for sure. Did he know Marissa? He knew of her. He followed me twice. Once when I met her at a little bar in Broad Ripple and again when I found her dead body.'

Kowalski looked at Shanahan.

'I'll pick up where you left off,' Kowalski said. 'Of those people on the list, who has a motive to kill both of them? Or keeping it short, which ones didn't?'

'Rafferty didn't,' Cross said. 'We know why he might have killed LaSalle. But why Marissa? I don't know why, at this late date, Marissa's mother would want her dead. Plus, she's 800 miles away. Billy Dean didn't seem to have an axe to grind at all.'

'That would leave Clarkson and Father O'Connor,' Shanahan said. 'These were the two I interviewed. They didn't know about you. How could they set you up?'

'Shall we order a few beers and figure this out?' Cross said. 'What do you have on draft?' he yelled up at the guard.

'What have you said to the police?' Kowalski asked.

'Nothing. I was waiting for my attorney, or Rafferty, or something. Anyway, I knew I shouldn't talk. I know about that sort of thing.'

'The two of us need to talk with them, the prosecutor anyway,' Kowalski said to Cross. 'They're going to want to take a statement. I'll be with you, but we've got to figure out what we're going to say.'

'The truth?'

'That would be novel in these kinds of meetings. But the prosecutor will want to know how you knew Marissa.' Kowalski said. 'You wouldn't only out the lieutenant, you might make sure he joins you here. You for Marissa, him for LaSalle. You could be cellmates. Now that would be fun, wouldn't it? You ready for the truth?'

'No.'

'Why?' Kowalksi asked.

'I don't know,' Cross said. 'I made a promise.'

'What do you think he'd do for you if the tables were turned?'

'I'm not him,' Cross said. 'Put it off. Slow things down.' He looked at Shanahan. 'You going to track a few things down?'

Shanahan nodded.

'Slowing it down means you'll stay in here longer.'

'I've got nothing else to do.'

'Anything you want?' Shanahan asked.

'Yeah. Bring me something to read. There's a book I was reading on the plane. It's by the bed. I don't remember the name but it's by that guy ... uh ... Lewin. He writes about an Indianapolis private detective. That should be fun.'

# Eighteen

Another ride on the back of Kowalski's cycle back to the Shanahan house on the East Side left Shanahan's legs a little shaky. The deep bass sound of the engine rattled every bone in his body. But he'd survive.

He kissed Maureen on the cheek, promised to cook later, and drove up to the North Side. He didn't have a key to Cross's place, but he knew the lock was old and worn. It gave in to a lock pick easier than most. Inside, it was clear the police had searched the place. As sloppy as Cross was, his was organized chaos. This place was tossed with attitude. Drawers and cabinet doors were left open. Shelves were emptied on to the floor below. Books had been opened and tossed aside. Kitchen products had been inspected and left on the countertop. In the bedroom, piles of clothing had been tossed on the bed in search of something.

Shanahan had picked up the mail before he came in, sorted through it. Nothing important to the case, nothing urgent, mostly junk mail. In the bedroom, he noticed the answering machine blinking. Only one message. The fact that it blinked indicated it had come after the police visited.

Shanahan pushed the play button. It was the airline. They had found Cross's luggage and would he come pick it up at the airport. Shanahan made a mental note. Beside the answering machine were two books. He took them both. There was little reason to stay. If there was something to find, Cross would have told him what to look for, and if he hadn't the police would already have it.

Outside he found Lieutenant Swann coming up to the path.

He nodded to Shanahan. 'And you're here why?'

'Cross is a friend of mine. Watering the plants, picking up some reading material.'

'I keep running into you.'

'Life is funny.'

'Really? I don't think I've ever seen you laugh.'

'Not funny ha ha,' Shanahan said drily.

'Makes me uncomfortable running into you so often. Murder here. Murder there. Pretty soon, I'm going to think you are connected more than you admit.'

Shanahan said nothing.

'Or the cases are connected?' he asked, then suddenly understood. A thin grin crossed his face. 'They are, aren't they?' He shook his head.

'I didn't have a client when I talked to you at Bay Colony. I do now. Cross didn't do this.'

'I'm sure that's true. But that's not what it looks like. We're going to do a whole lot better if we work together to get to the truth,' Swann said.

'I'd like to. I'll help you when I can.'

'You don't have a choice.'

'I do,' Shanahan said.

'When is my debt to you paid off?' Swann looked squarely into Shanahan's eyes.

'Maybe you have. Maybe it's my turn to ask for a little credit.' Shanahan returned the look.

'Listen,' Swann said. 'Every murder is the same to me. Somebody steals a life that doesn't belong to him, they should forfeit theirs. But you know as well as I do that the world doesn't work that way. Nobody cares if some gay guy is murdered, especially if there's no family. Nobody pushing for the case to be solved. But folks care a whole lot if a high-profile guy's wife and mother of two is slain in the middle of the night in a part of town where that's not supposed to happen. All sorts of concerns, pressures, come into play. Your pal's ass is grass and if the two crimes are connected and he's innocent, you'd be smart to let me in on it.'

'I don't question your honesty. Never did.'

'He could go down on both.'

'You know better,' Shanahan said.

'It's not about me,' Swann said.

After an unpleasant dinner – and Cross was not a gourmet – he was given orange scrubs to wear and again pulled from his cell. He was handcuffed and transported in the back of a van the few blocks to the City County building where he sat in a holding cell for another thirty minutes.

He was brought into a room where Kowalski was waiting.

'What's going on?' Cross asked.

'They want your statement. At eight thirty in the evening, they want to talk.'

'And you agreed?' The guard led Cross to the seat beside his lawyer.

The room was small, had a mirrored wall, a table that could seat six comfortably if, that is, the government had spent more than twelve dollars for the chairs.

'I thought we ought to know what they want to talk about. I left a T-bone and a baked potato on the stove to be here for you. That's love.'

'Well, this is a night out for me, I guess. They even gave me special clothes.' Cross looked toward the door.

'You look good in orange,' Kowalski said. 'It brings out the red in your eyes.'

After a few moments of defense attorney and defendant staring at each other and the walls, lit by harsh, ugly fluorescent lights, two men in suits walked in. Cross recognized Brigham Lassiter, assistant district attorney. He had the look of a city politician. Conservative cheap suit, white shirt, unimaginative tie. At forty, he worked a lot of overtime and was unappreciated and bitter. He carried a Starbucks coffee cup with a plastic cone as a lid.

With him was a well-scrubbed, rested-looking sixty-year-old in a blue blazer, gray pants and a red, white, and blue striped tie that barely kept from looking like an American flag.

'Brigham Lassiter,' the assistant DA said introducing himself. He nodded toward his colleague. 'Thomas Easterly. You are?'

'James Kowalski and you know Howard Cross.'

Cross felt like Kowalski was introducing someone else. No one said 'Howard Cross'.

The two suits on the other side of the table sat down, Lassiter pulling a manila folder from his briefcase.

'Don't you have a briefcase?' Cross asked Kowalksi.

'No,' he smiled. 'You worried?'

'He's got a briefcase and a pal.'

'Good point,' Kowalski said. Then looking at Lassiter: 'What purpose is Mr Easterly serving today?'

'Friend of the court,' Lassiter said in a

dismissive tone.

'What kind of friend would that be?' Kowalski looked at the man directly.

Cross thought the man looked smug, as if he'd been asked to come to the monkey house and noted how much they were like humans.

'I'm Mr H. Ray Clarkson's attorney.'

'I don't think so,' Kowalksi said. 'It was kind of you to drop by, but you aren't invited to this little party.'

Easterly was unmoved, face frozen in kindly condescension.

'I do think so,' Lassiter said. 'He's a guest. Victims have rights. That's the way I see it.'

'Can ... may I have a word with you, Mr Easterly?'

'Certainly,' Easterly said.

'Outside,' Kowalski said.

Easterly looked at Lassiter and Lassiter looked back at him. Lassiter shrugged.

'We'll only be a moment,' Kowalksi said as he ushered the larger, better-dressed man out the door. The door shut.

'What's your handicap?' Cross asked Lassiter, who acted as if he were looking for something in his folder.

'Handicap?'

'Golf. You play golf right?'

Lassiter ignored him.

'More of a bowler, I bet,' Cross said. 'You look like a bowler.'

268

Nothing.

After a few more moments, Kowalski came in, shut the door behind him.

Lassiter looked around.

'Where's Mr Easterly?'

'He had second thoughts about the relationship,' Kowalski said.

'What relationship?' Lassiter said.

'Friendship. Wasn't sure he wanted to be a friend of the court,' Kowalski said. 'He wanted you to know that it was him. Not you. He hoped you'd understand.'

Cross looked at Kowalski. Knew what he had done.

'Hey,' Kowalski said. 'She wouldn't care. And...'

Kowalski stopped and whispered in Cross's ear, 'As far as I'm concerned H. Ray Clarkson is a suspect.'

Lassiter stood up, looked at Kowalski with unmistakable disdain and walked out.

Kowalski reached over, picked up Lassiter's cup.

'It won't be long,' Kowalski said, 'before people will entertain each other with their travel exploits. "I was in the Beijing Starbucks. Amazing," or "When you were in Barcelona did you get a chance to take in the Wal-Mart?"'

Cross smiled. Another political riff.

Lassiter came in, sat down, talked into the microphone. He gave the date, time, and the names of the people at the table.

'Let's get on with it,' Lassiter said.

'Coffee this late, you'll be up all night,' Kowalski said.

'Let's get down to business.' He looked at Cross. 'What was your relationship with Marissa Clarkson?'

'I didn't have a relationship. I interviewed her the previous afternoon with regard to a case I'm working on.'

'And what case would that be?'

'The Bay Colony murder.'

'Morgan Lee?' Lassiter asked.

Cross nodded. He found it interesting the prosecutor didn't have the victim's real name yet.

'And who is your client?' Lassiter asked.

'I'm his client,' Kowalksi said.

Cross was careful not to look surprised. Lassiter looked down at his notes, stunned.

'And who is your client?' Lassiter asked.

'I'm not at liberty to reveal that.'

'I don't think that will fly. You will regret it.'

'I have many regrets. It is hard to get through life without them,' Kowalski said.

'Even Frank Sinatra had a few,' Cross said.

'You met Mrs Clarkson where? When?' Lassiter wasn't slowing down for snide remarks.

'Broad Ripple. Like I said, that would be yesterday afternoon. Corner Wine Bar. We had drinks. I asked a few questions. Received some answers.'

'How is she related to the Lee case?'

Cross looked at Kowalski, who nodded and smiled.

'She knew the victim. She knew him from a previous life.'

'And why would you ask her about the murder?'

'I haven't been able to locate very many people in Indianapolis who knew the victim. I needed to get as much background information as possible.'

'So she was helpful?' Lassiter asked. He took a sip of his coffee as he waited for the reply.

'I guess.'

'Why would a woman of her stature agree to meet some, pardon me, two-bit gumshoe.'

'Why would anyone meet with a tired old shyster?' Cross looked at Lassiter, nodded. 'But I did, didn't I?'

'Actually he met with two tired old shysters,' Kowalski said. 'Listen, what we want here is justice, that's all.'

Lassiter winced at the word justice. Anybody in the legal system – judge, attorney, cop, whatever – talked about law but never about justice. That word was reserved for politicians who knew the power of grand-sounding words and used them shamelessly.

'It will be in your best interest to co-operate, Mr Cross,' Lassiter said, looking as if he had swallowed vinegar. 'Why would she meet with you?'

'I asked her nice.'

'Where were you on the night of Mr Lee's death?' Lassiter looked at his file.

'You want a double?' Kowalksi interrupted. 'You don't even have one and you're trying to pin both on him?'

'I'm trying to get to the facts of the case.'

'He was in Miami,' Kowalksi said. 'And he was in bed, asleep when Mrs Clarkson called him, begged him to meet her. He found the dead body, Mr Lassiter. He didn't make it dead.'

'Why were you in Miami, Mr Cross?'

'Vacation.'

'And you went to New Orleans shortly thereafter,' Lassiter said. 'Why were you in New Orleans?'

Cross was perplexed, then remembered the cops searched his house. No doubt they found the airline ticket stub. He looked again at his attorney.

Kowalksi leaned over and whispered, 'Give them something to keep them busy. New Orleans won't lead them where you don't want them to go.'

'The case,' Cross said to Lassiter.

'What case?'

'The same case.'

'Tell me more,' Lassiter said.

'Some leads in the case suggested there

was a New Orleans connection. Since the victim was gay...'

'How do you know that?' Lassiter asked.

'I checked some of the gay haunts in New Orleans.'

'I'm asking you, how did you know the victim was gay?'

Cross started to answer. Kowalski put his hand on Cross's forearm, then spoke directly and intensely to Lassiter.

'What you have here is a chance to solve both murders. But if you keep Cross in jail any forward momentum in his investigation will end. Stop. Kaput.'

'If you think for one moment he's going to get out, you need to give up criminal law. The weapon that killed Mrs Clarkson belonged to your Mr Cross, who was not so incidentally found by himself at the scene of the crime. If we have to dig a little to find a motive, fine; but I'm not sure we need one.'

Shanahan decided to swing out by the airport and pick up the bag before going home. He loved driving at night, when it was quiet, when it was cooler. He would drop off the books at the jail in the morning. And he'd check the bag. Perhaps there was something of value in there and no one knew at this point when or if Cross would be let out. He was also a little antsy. He wanted to do something about the situation, but was unsure what he could do. What would be the point of traipsing over to Father O'Connor's cozy little rectory and quizzing him again? Or H. Ray Clarkson, for that matter. He had no idea what to ask them other than check for alibis. Both had possible motives.

O'Connor would perhaps have gotten rid of two victims of his molestation before they could testify – that is if Marissa wanted all the truth to come out. Clarkson might very well have felt that Marissa was better a dead wife than a live transsexual. That would destroy his career.

The drive to the airport would help him sort things out, he thought. It didn't. He stopped by Harry's. The Cubs were playing in California and the game was still on. He had his bottle of Miller's and a shot of J.W. Dant. He let his mind drift into the game, where it hovered tenuously, occasionally re-turning unproductively to Cross's situation.

At home, he found Maureen already asleep. He let Casey out in the back yard to guarantee he could make it through the night. He had another shot of whiskey in the kitchen while he waited for the dog to sniff out the appropriate spot and do what he needed to do. He'd have to press O'Connor and Clarkson. If they weren't it, then Shana-han wasn't going to come close to helping Cross. The idea that Cross would spend the rest of his life in some dark, dank penitentiary was more than depressing.

Though he wasn't there, and despite the fact he didn't want to, he pictured the scene. The dimly lit bridge in Broad Ripple. Poor Cross crouching over the sad dead body of Marissa. What horror she must have felt when she was stabbed. But how surprised was she? Did she know her killer? We'll all be surprised at our deaths, Shanahan thought, even when we know it's coming.

Casey pressed his nose against the screen door and Shanahan let him in.

'Get some sleep, old man,' he told Casey. He turned off the lights.

Shanahan worked his way through the darkness to his bedroom. He undressed, climbed into bed, the warmth of the night enhanced in temperature and pleasure as he moved toward Maureen's sleeping body. The smell of her hair was intoxicating. He put his arms around her as if he were protecting her from demons.

Tomorrow, he thought. Tomorrow he must do something.

# Nineteen

Sleep ended too early and unhappily for Cross. In the thickness of his emerging consciousness, he had forgotten he was in jail. The discovery was rude and disheartening. He had to get used to it, though, didn't he? He had to prepare himself for the possibility that this was what he faced for the rest of his life, however long or short that might be.

He closed his eyes again. What did he know that he might not know he knew? He let his mind go back to the night of the murder, retrace each and every movement from the phone call to his arrest. Could there have been anyone else around? Was there a movement or sound that he could retrieve from his memory that would help? The only odd note was Rafferty's presence. It bugged him, but he didn't know what to make of it.

Back he went to the phone conversation. Was there a hint that she was forced to call? Was there background noise? Nothing new anywhere here. He replayed his interview with Marissa word for word as best he could. Nothing came out of it that would focus on anyone who might want to kill her – and Michael LaSalle. Cross was convinced the murders were connected.

In the darkness, Cross went back to New Orleans. Let his mind drift over the faces he saw, the conversations he had. Marissa's mother and her young protectors. What was it that Marissa said about Joan Manchette? She couldn't kill someone herself, but she wasn't above having it done. Then, there was Billy Dean. Poor, foolish, used Billy Dean. The inept burglary, the clumsy escape.

Just as Cross's eyes were about to close and he could feel himself losing his grip on thought, gray light came in the slit of a window. He would have only minutes now, perhaps only seconds of sleep. That saddened him. Sleep was his only recreation, his only escape. It was, during the day, the only thing he looked forward to.

Maureen came into the kitchen at eight thirty, after Casey and Einstein had been fed, after the coffee was made, the newspaper was collected from the front porch, and the morning operations were settled.

Shanahan, freshly showered and shaved, kissed her on the cheek, poured her a glass of orange juice and a cup of coffee.

'If you ever left me, I'd have to get a butler,' she said.

He didn't mind doing these things. He'd

done them for himself for years after Elaine left with her hairdresser boyfriend – decades now – and before he met Maureen. He liked getting up before she did. An hour or two of quiet anticipation. He wondered if it would be the same at the new house. It was hard to imagine.

'You ate light this morning,' she said, looking in the sink, then at the cabinets.

'I have a favor to ask,' he said, choosing not to explain how he felt – about Cross in jail with the possibility he'd never get out and the thoughts of his brother with the possibility he would never know anything other than he was last seen escaping a photograph.

She nodded. His behavior wasn't out of the ordinary, so she didn't feel she had been merely buttered up for the request.

'I need to get to Clarkson. But he's not going to let me in the office or his home behind the gates. But if I can get to him with one short sentence, he'll talk to me, I'm sure.'

She nodded again. She sipped her coffee.

'What sentence is that?'

'Mr Clarkson, did you know the woman you married was once a man?'

If Maureen hadn't already swallowed the coffee, Shanahan thought that he would be wearing it.

'What?'

'Simplest way to say it,' he said.

'The world's moral compass? The second or third most self-righteous human on the planet...'

'You are not including me?'

'That's why I said second or third.' She shook her head. 'How do you know?'

'Cross found out. He was gallantly trying to keep it a secret, as he is with Rafferty's little thunderbolt. But now that she's gone, he feels less guilty about revealing it.'

'It's a motive,' Maureen said. She took a quick sip of the orange juice, went to the wall phone. 'What's Clarkson's number?'

Shanahan fished the little slip of paper from his wallet and recited it.

'Hello, this is Maureen. I'm trying to set up a time to visit Mr Clarkson today.' She waited. 'I really prefer to discuss it with him. It's personal.' A brief pause. 'I know. Our thoughts and prayers are with him.' Another pause. 'Well, if I had his cell phone number with me I would have used it. This is the number Johann asked me to use.' She turned to Shanahan, shrugged. 'Johann,' she repeated into the phone. 'Well it doesn't matter. Either he's in or he's not.' She waited, a mock-patient smile on her lips. 'I see.' Pause. 'No, I'll ask Johann for his cell phone.' She placed the phone back on the receiver.

Shanahan looked at her expectantly.

'He's apparently not keeping regular hours today or perhaps the rest of the week...'

Maureen said.

'Understandable.'

'...other than maybe ten minutes at his office around noon to sign some checks.'

'You're wonderful.'

'And clever.'

'Very clever.'

'And beautiful.' She grinned, gave him a sideways glance. 'Well.'

'I thought that was a statement, not a question.'

'And if it had been a question?'

'I would have answered it.'

The day was set. He'd wait at the institute for Clarkson to arrive. And at some point after that, he'd make his move. Then he would find Father O'Connor and have another chat. First he'd stop by James Fennimore Kowalski, drop off the books for Cross.

Kowalski was in his office, drinking coffee from a cup that looked as if it hadn't seen suds in a month or two. A cigar was perched on an ashtray. Thin spirals of smoke climbed into the stale air.

'He's being arraigned this afternoon,' Kowalski said. 'A press conference has been set up afterward. Your pal Swann, the police chief, and the prosecutor. This is tough. The problem is that it's so fucking simple.'

He took a gulp of coffee, picked up his cigar, kept it in his mouth.

'If it wasn't his screwdriver, we'd have a real chance,' Kowalski continued.

'You get a coroner's report?'

'Not yet. They're still processing the body.'

'What if they find someone else's finger-prints on the screwdriver?'

'That would be great, but I'm betting they don't find any, or worse, partials of Cross. I assume he screwed light switch plates or something once or twice in his life.'

'I brought some books,' Shanahan said. 'Also, picked up his lost bags at the airport.' He put the bag on the desk, pulled out two books.

'What else is in there?'

'Dirty clothes, as far as I can tell.'

Kowalski grabbed the canvas bag and pulled it to him. He set the cigar back down and rummaged through the contents. A little black fake leather bag contained toothpaste, shaving cream and the like. Kowalski swirled his hand around for more. He brought out a sock with something hard and long inside. Delicately, Kowalski pulled out the dagger.

'Hmmmph,' Kowalski said. 'What's this?'

'I think we should ask him.'

Kowalski put it back in the sock, holding it by the tip only. He shook his head. 'Strange. Very strange. What in the hell would he carry this around for? It's a little too theatrical to be a real weapon.'

Shanahan shrugged.

'You suppose your good pal is a little twisted?' Kowalski asked.

'Who isn't?'

'True. Rafferty's a prime example ... not that I think being gay is twisted, but somehow it seems twisted with Rafferty.'

Shanahan had time to kill. He'd be at the institute at eleven thirty and hopefully sit unnoticed in his look-like-all-the-others automobile and wait for Clarkson to leave. He had some time to engage in his little infidelity. He felt guilt, but also excitement.

His secret stops at Burger King were justified. For it was true that Maureen ate considerably more Haagan Dazs Vanilla Swiss Almond ice cream than she admitted. Now, away from her, he could engage in a bit of sin of his own. Afterward, he drove to Clarkson's institute, hoping no one would notice him in his silver sedan.

The fries were good, the sandwich so-so. Maybe Maureen's attempt to convert him to healthier, better food was working.

Men in conservative suits and women in conservative suits came and went, the pace of their gaits purposeful and business-like.

At twelve ten a navy blue Lincoln Towne car pulled up to the main entrance. Clarkson got out, went in. The car didn't move. That was a good sign. Clarkson wouldn't be long. Shanahan took the last bite of his sandwich and the last fry, washing it down with the last of the coffee. He was careful not to spill anything on the leather seats, a luxury that still made him feel not only pretentious but also fussy – and fussy did not sit well with him.

Shanahan was able to tail the Lincoln easily as it cruised ahead, never over the speed limit, never making sudden lane changes in its steady, patient pace west on 38th Street. Clarkson probably used the time productively and his driver was keeping things steady so he could work in the back seat.

The car pulled into Crown Hill Cemetery, an old and respected burial ground where many of the city's most illustrious dead spent eternity. The tombstones and monuments tended to be a bit grander than other cemeteries.

Shanahan wasn't happy. It was one thing to accost the grieving husband at all. It was quite another to do so when he is obviously working on his wife's burial plan. But the car didn't stop at the office. Instead it wound around the curving drives that snaked through the grounds. Deep inside now, the car stopped.

Clarkson got out, walked up a slight grade to an area that had few grave markers. He stood, stared down, looked around, then down again as if to determine what the view would be.

Shanahan, who had pulled up just before the last turn, got out and walked up toward Clarkson. He felt a hand on his shoulder.

'Now's not the time,' the man said solemnly. It was one of the guys from the bar – the one in the better suit.

'I have no choice,' Shanahan said.

'You're right. You have no choice,' the man said, attempting to turn Shanahan in the opposite direction.

Shanahan turned back. 'Don't do that.'

'I think you have a little repressed rage problem, old man.'

'I think you have a repressed stupidity problem, but you can tell your therapist it's bubbling to the surface.'

'Here, here,' Clarkson said, coming over. 'Pretty low, coming here like this. Even for a private investigator.' He was wearing sunglasses.

'It's going to get lower,' Shanahan said, respectfully. 'I'm sorry. You might want to suggest your friend here take a walk.'

The man looked at Clarkson, whose look was questioning but also showed warning.

'It's all right, Bill. I don't think it will get physical.' A thin, bitter grin crossed his lips. Clarkson took off his glasses. There were deep, dark bags under his eyes that weren't there the last time Shanahan saw him.

Shanahan waited for Bill to walk out of hearing distance.

'I have a tough question, Mr Clarkson. I'm sorry I have to ask it.' Shanahan was rarely sorry, even more rarely said it. But he meant it.

'I know,' Clarkson said.

'You know your wife was once...'

'I know,' he said.

'When did you find out?'

'Right before I married her.'

'She told someone else you didn't know.'

'That's right,' Clarkson said. He seemed relaxed, surprisingly so. Perhaps just defeated. He leaned back against the car. 'I didn't tell her I knew. I had her investigated before the marriage. I was going to break it off, but I couldn't. I loved her. And I could never tell her that I knew. I didn't want anything to change.'

'Isn't that kind of counter to everything you profess to believe in?'

'One doesn't always get a choice when it comes to love.'

'Imagine that,' Shanahan said drily.

Clarkson didn't respond.

'That gives you motive, though,' Shanahan continued.

Clarkson looked around slowly as if he could find the answer somewhere other than inside himself. Then he nodded. 'I don't know what to say, except that I wouldn't, couldn't. You have no idea what this has done to me.'

'If the truth had come out, you would have been destroyed.'

'Even the threat of scandal seems trivial at the moment.' He laughed. 'I am destroyed, Mr Shanahan. I am already destroyed.'

'Howard Cross didn't kill her.'

'And why would I believe you?' He looked directly into Shanahan's eyes. 'I don't mean it personally. But some stranger's word that says the obvious isn't true – I'm sorry. And does it matter what either of us think?'

'Maybe you sent your boys out.'

'I have two children, Mr Shanahan. I loved my wife. I believe in God and I live by the rules He set down.'

Shanahan wanted to ask which ones, but it would be of little use. There was nothing else to ask except to try to get alibis for him and his two cohorts. At three or four in the morning, most people don't have alibis.

Clarkson was believable. A guilty man of Clarkson's temperament, when faced with these kinds of accusations, would puff up in pompous outrage. But Clarkson seemed truly deflated, too hurt to care that someone doubted his purity.

In the end, it wasn't about who he was but what had been lost. Then again, maybe he was just terribly sorry he did it, Shanahan thought. No. Bringing her to the canal after having carefully retrieved a weapon for the person he was setting up – that was premeditation of the first order.

The other thing was: it was Cross who was set up. Did Clarkson even know Howie Cross existed? Shanahan had handled the H. Ray Clarkson interviews. Would Marissa have told her husband about Cross? Possible. Anything's possible; but not likely.

The same could be said of Father O'Connor. Unless someone told him, he wouldn't know to set up Cross. And he had an iron-clad alibi for the time LaSalle was killed.

Cross, wearing his orange public scrubs and seated beside James Fennimore Kowalski in the courtroom, was arraigned. He was charged with murder in the first degree – having lured her to the bridge to die being a sign of premeditation. What was missing, as Kowalski pointed out to the judge, was motive.

'He was called by the victim to meet her there,' Kowalski said. 'We have the telephone records to prove it.'

'Do you have a record of the conversation?' Lassiter asked rhetorically.

The room was surprisingly empty. Just the judge, the bailiff, another police officer and a recorder. For Cross, it seemed as if this was something being done secretly.

'Your honor, Mr Cross came to Broad Ripple at the request of Mrs Clarkson. He was not told why, but he could tell from the tone of her voice that she was in trouble.'

'Normally, people would call 911 in those circumstances,' Lassiter interrupted.

'When you are awakened in the middle of the night by a hysterical woman, your first instinct is to do as you were asked. Maybe she didn't want to involve the police. It's obvious Mr Cross was set up to take the fall. What motive could Cross have had to kill her? The case is extremely weak...'

'Scene of the crime, ownership of the weapon. What more do you need? He was leaving the scene of the crime when he was found. There was still no call to 911. In the age of cell phones, this is inexcusable,' Lassiter said.

'He was going to call. He was making the goddamn call when he was arrested,' Kowalski said.

'He wasn't calling 911, Mr Kowalski, he was calling another private detective. What was that about?'

The judge, a pleasant-faced, balding man with black-rimmed glasses, gave the bearded defense attorney an almost humorous admonishing look. He had said nothing so far, continued to let the attorneys chat.

Cross looked at Kowalski. Kowalski's look said it all. Motive or no motive, the screwdriver, if not his presence on the bridge, guaranteed it would go to trial and pretty much eliminated any chance of bail.

'Sorry, Mr Cross,' the judge said. 'You'll

remain in custody until the trial.'

'Judge,' Kowalski managed to say before being stopped.

'As I understand it,' the judge said, 'Cross has no family, no steady job, no ties to the community. And this is first degree murder. Bail is out of the question.'

Cross knew that even if he were granted bail, it would be so high as not to count. So this wasn't devastating. But it did seem pretty sad the way the judge defined his life on the planet. Disposable.

He whispered to Kowalski, 'I didn't even know where the screwdrivers were. I forgot I had them.'

'Someone found one,' Kowalski said.

As Cross was escorted out, he shouted over his shoulder, 'Ask Shanahan to see who was poking around my house or if the neighbors saw any strangers in the neighborhood.'

# Twenty

Shanahan stopped by Harry's place, had a long-neck Miller's High Life, 'The Champagne of Bottled Beers', as it was once advertised, and a shot of J.W. Dant whiskey. He had come to think of his little ritual as medicinal. If it was the old Shanahan, the pre-Maureen Shanahan, he might well have drunk the afternoon away. These days he paced himself. A little in the afternoon. A little more in the evening.

The old regulars were there as were the new regulars, quietly watching television. The Cubs afternoon game was in the early innings. As much as he loved the Cubs, Shanahan was beginning to lose track of all the new players. In the old days, a player stayed with a team all his life. In the old days ... he let his mind drift until Harry popped back to ask about Cross.

'They're previewing the press conference,' Harry said, using his head to point to the television. 'Serious.'

Shanahan nodded.

'You have anything?'

'No.' Shanahan took a sip of cold beer.

Always tasted better in the summer.

Halfway through his beer, Shanahan called Maureen. No answer at home, he dialed her cell. He hated the cell, hated how it could interrupt any time any place. But it was handy.

'What are we doing about dinner?' Shanahan asked when she answered.

'I think we should eat it.'

'But who will fix it?'

'Let's let some stranger fix it, in some strange place.'

'Not too strange, I hope,' he said. 'I'll pick you up at home at half past six and you can tell me where we're going.'

He settled on the stool, getting a comfortable angle on the TV screen. He'd catch the good Father tomorrow morning. He'd ask Harry to switch over when the local news came on.

There were several microphones on three stands – all the local channels, the networks. This was the taped, edited version; but it was story number one on this newscast. An attractive woman introduced the segment, switched it over to a pleasant-looking man who stood against the wall of the little bridge over the canal in Broad Ripple.

'Media interest was high,' he said, 'but were they disappointed? This is Craig Nelson here in Broad Ripple where an hour ago, the mayor, police chief, and other government officials told us they had someone in custody for the brutal murder of Marissa Clarkson. The victim, wife of the well-known leader of the Nash Family Values Institute, H. Ray Clarkson, was stabbed and killed last night very near where I am standing now. The name of the suspected assailant was not disclosed, pending additional information from the medical examiner's office.'

There was a cut to tape of the conference. The mayor, another in a long line of young business types to hold the job, spoke seriously. 'We are here in Broad Ripple,' he said, 'to grieve with the family, to let the people of the city know we are on the job, to emphasize that our city streets are safe. The suspect has been arrested. Our police department is doing its job.'

The mayor spoke in simple word groups, to clearly communicate each point. What he was saying was, 'We are sorry, but the city is safe because we did our job.'

'Craig?' The woman's face now appeared on the set.

'Yes, Natalie?' Switch back to the reporter in the field.

'Is there any information at all about the alleged murderer?'

'Nothing but speculation, Natalie. We have heard that he was a drifter and we have heard that he was a stalker. We're not sure.

But one thing is sure. People in Broad Ripple will sleep more soundly with the suspect in jail.'

'Thank you, Craig. We have some news about NASCAR.'

Harry flipped the channel, finding a national newscast. And a few minutes after the first commercial, there were side-by-side photographs of Marissa Clarkson and H. Ray Clarkson. As the anchor spoke, file footage of H. Ray Clarkson with the President, then with various senators, ran. The anchor spoke of the shocking murder of Marissa Clarkson in a quiet Indianapolis community.

'The murder has stunned the citizens of Indiana's capital city and while they have the suspected murderer behind bars, authorities are revealing very little in these early stages of the investigation.'

They did a bio on Clarkson, his influence as a social conservative, also his books on family values and his crusades against abortion, homosexuality, and anyone who criticizes his views on Christianity.

Shanahan lifted his bottle of beer for a sip and was disappointed that the bottle was dry. Time to go.

'They have Cross down as a stalker and a drifter,' Harry said, shaking his head.

Shanahan thought that Cross would be amused. He might agree with the characterizations. Though the younger detective had lived in the same place for at least a decade, he embodied the mind of a drifter.

The afternoon – all of it – had put him in a bad mood. He was sorry he had agreed to a dinner out.

'You are out of sorts,' Maureen said, before putting a bite of halibut between her lips.

'Not much gets by you.' He meant it sincerely, but she smiled at what she thought was witty sarcasm.

There was a light buzz of talk and silverware on china plates around them. Behind the buzz was a hint of calming classical music. All of it made for a bland background for their own conversation.

'What's wrong? Cross?' she asked after a moment and after a sip of chilled white wine.

The room was warm and smelled of garlic and basil. The lights were dim and golden. Maureen was at her sensuous best.

'Cross, yes. The victim. It's all screwed up.'

'And you talked with Clarkson?' she asked.

'Nothing's right. I even felt bad for that son of a bitch.'

'You don't think he had anything to do with her death?'

'He's sorry now, I think, whether he did it or not.'

The waiter came by, noticed the empty bottle of beer and the empty glass. Shanahan nodded.

'Could you get me a shot of J.W. Dant?'

'I'm sorry, sir, we don't carry it.'

'Whiskey. You pick.'

'Now what?' Maureen asked, poking at an asparagus spear.

'Father O'Connor,' he said. 'I feel like I'm going in circles.'

'What color should we paint the living room?'

'You pick.'

The whiskey arrived. It was fine. Maybe better than his own special brand, but he wouldn't ask what it was. Then he might be tempted to change. And some things had to remain the same.

'Maybe you're going in circles because the answer is inside it.'

Night came early to Cross. His cellmate was morosely quiet now, a reversal from earlier when he was trying to engage Cross in exchanging personal information. He'd either given up or found out enough to lose interest. The guy's position on the bed was slightly fetal, face to the wall.

By nine the sounds from the other cells had diminished, as if someone turned down the volume. He had books to read, but no light to read them by. If living was going to be like this for the rest of his life, he knew he was getting a first-hand peek at limbo.

★  ★  ★

295

Shanahan's answering machine had one message. It was from Kowalski.

'Cross wants you to canvass his neighborhood. Did anyone see anything, anyone out of the ordinary in the few days leading up to the night of Marissa's death?'

There was a pause. For a moment Shanahan thought that was it.

'It doesn't look good. I got nothing.'

Shanahan was sure that wouldn't help him sleep.

He went to the kitchen, let Casey out for his very short but important last constitutional of the day, and waited for him to come back. Afterward he locked up, took a beer from the refrigerator, went into the dimly lit living room, sat in a chair. Casey clunked his body down beside him.

He didn't tell Maureen that his brother Fritz was invading his thoughts more frequently and that he wasn't sure, but he thought he might have lost a few moments of time today.

'You coming to bed?' she asked from the bedroom.

'Soon.'

Maureen was a woman of rich passions. Shanahan regretted not being up to them all. But she was quite capable of engaging in some of them all by herself – food, gardening and sleep. She went to bed at night before Shanahan and remained in bed hours after he got up. Her sleep was passionate – deep and long.

Today, he left her in bed shortly after dawn, going through his morning routine machine-like until the coffee was brewed. He sat at the table. The paper was full of the murder, the quiet and secret arraignment of the alleged perpetrator, the lives of the victim and of her husband and the tortuous logic that hobbled fact and rumor together with leaps of faith. Without the facts, he thought, one was free to speculate.

After coffee and tending to the needs of his aging two-animal herd, he wrote Maureen a short note. Shanahan showered, shaved, and hopped into his shiny semi-new automobile and headed for Father O'Connor's. The earlier he arrived, the more likely he'd catch him at home, he thought. He was at the rectory by eight.

'You're like a dog tugging at a trouser leg,' Father O'Connor said at the door. His hair was wilder than usual. Gray stubble indicated his beard line. His eyes were red. It was difficult to tell whether his expression was pain or exhaustion or both. 'One of those stubborn breeds that won't let go.'

'I just keep learning more about you. And it's not very nice.'

'Lord knows I didn't kill your boy,' he said. 'Check the alibi.'

'I did.'

'So you're here for what, confession?'

'Yours if you're willing. Marissa Clarkson.'

Shanahan tried looking beyond O'Connor, but the strong light outside and lack of it inside rendered the interior a blank. He made a move as if to invite himself inside.

O'Connor's expression didn't change, nor did he move. 'I don't have the time or the inclination for this. So, *adios.*'

He started to shut the door. Shanahan put his foot in the jamb.

'Look, I'm going to call the police,' O'Connor said.

'I'll give you the number. You have an alibi for her murder?'

'Let get this straight. You plan on stopping in to check my alibi every time there is a murder in Indianapolis?'

'No, just when the victim is someone you molested.'

'Well, that's interesting. You have two people you claim I molested and they are bound to be silent on the issue.'

'Yep.'

'I didn't know the lady in question.'

'I'll make it easy for you to understand. Born Mark Manchette, died Marissa Clarkson.'

Another poker face. This time it didn't hide the truth. It condemned him. If he hadn't known about Mark/Marissa, he would have at least been puzzled, most likely surprised.

'Coincidence? Now about that alibi?'

'You know full well, and if you don't I'll remind you, that a celibate, unmarried priest is not likely to have an alibi for the middle of the night. I live alone. I sleep alone. If you were to tie one murder to the other, you have a problem. I have an alibi at the time young Mr LaSalle was killed. If you've been doing your job, you know that. Seems to me they would have shared the same killer.'

He had a point, though Shanahan thought the conclusion was arrived at all too quickly.

'You and I are through,' the priest said. 'You come back this way and I promise you will regret it.'

Shanahan could have taken a solemn promise easily. A threat to call the police would have worked. But he didn't much like the bullying tone as if the priest would do it personally.

'If I come back by here, your life – as you know it – is over.' It felt good to say that.

Shanahan smiled at the man. He rarely smiled.

Canvassing Cross's neighborhood involved a little déjà vu. It wasn't that long ago that Cross suffered a beating in his home by unknown thugs. Asking a few questions of neighbors revealed a car with Illinois license plates. It helped.

People in the neighborhood tend to recognize cars – and people – that aren't regulars. The problem was that Cross's screwdriver could have been pilfered anytime, not necessarily near the time Marissa was killed. The folks across the street saw nothing that registered as odd or different. Then again, once someone walked up those craggy steps, he, or she, couldn't be seen.

Shanahan walked up the steps, back to a rusty gate, and inside a kind of second yard. There was a nice house next door. Someone wandering around on the south side of that house could see anyone hanging around Cross's porch or trying to get in the front door. The only other view would be from the second floor of the house behind him, which faced the next street over.

The woman next door was helpful. She was an older woman, but cheery. She had a slow-walking golden retriever.

'There was an old car parked out front of my house,' she said, 'that's how I happened to notice it.'

She seemed unafraid of Shanahan, a stranger who knocked on her door. It was one of the benefits of growing old. He seemed harmless and sadly, he thought to himself, probably was.

'What did you notice?'

'It was an old luxury car. I'm not sure what kind,' she said. 'Big car. It was all dusty. Maybe that's why I paid attention.'

'Did you notice who was driving it?'

'No, I'm sorry.'

'Anything else about the car? The license plate?'

'Well, it was foreign,' she said, then laughed with embarrassment. 'I mean, it wasn't an Indiana plate. It had a bird on it. A stork or pelican. And I remember the word "paradise". I just glanced as I backed out of my drive.'

'When was that?'

'A couple of days ago, late morning.'

Maybe it was something.

At home, Maureen was seated comfortably in the kitchen. Her laptop, two poached eggs on toast, orange juice, and coffee.

'We should start packing up things we don't expect to use in the next thirty days,' she said.

'I need to find out what state has a license plate with a bird on it. And the word "paradise". Can you find it on that thing of yours?' He nodded toward the computer.

'Maybe. But I'll have to go on-line.'

She took her computer to the living room along with her coffee.

'Finish your breakfast.'

'I'll be back. It'll only take a minute.' She clicked in a telephone cord and waited while the computer made a sound not quite as ugly as fingers on a blackboard.

Shanahan poured himself a cup of coffee and went in to be with her.

'Just a shot,' he said. 'Check Louisiana first.'

He waited as she typed, waited, typed, clicked. This went on for about two minutes, until she said, 'Bingo.'

'I have to make a call,' he said.

She handed him her cell phone.

He dialed, waited, finally spoke. 'What's the number for the Marion County Jail?'

# Twenty-One

An appointment tomorrow at the earliest, said the woman on the phone from the jail. Being a private eye didn't carry much weight. Shananan called Kowalski.

'I need to see Cross,' Shanahan said.

'What do you have?'

'A car with a Louisiana license plate was seen near his house. Long shot, but it's an odd enough occurrence.'

'You watch the news conference?' Kowalski asked.

'They didn't identify Howie.'

'They didn't, did they? That means they aren't sure. They booked him to keep him off the streets and to give comfort to the citizens of Broad Ripple; but they have doubts. Any way you can talk to Swann?'

'I could, but he won't tell me anything. Worse, he might start questioning me. It wouldn't take much for me to give up Rafferty.'

There was a pause, and Shanahan was sure Kowalski was smiling.

'I'd give him up just for the hell of it,' Kowalksi said. 'The Louisiana car. Could that be Father O'Connor's?'

'He's been up here too long. He'd have an Indiana plate. The lady said the car was dusty. I'm thinking that means it's been ridden hard...'

'And put away dusty,' Kowalksi added. 'How far is New Orleans from Indianapolis?'

'About 800 miles.'

'A twelve-hour day if he drives with intent.'

'Pays cash for the gasoline, stays out of motels. Can't be traced,' Shanahan said.

'I can get you in this afternoon,' Kowalski said. 'We'll go together. Do we have a make on the car?'

'Something big and old.'

Cross was glad to see them. Not only did it get him out of the cell, but it was a tie to the outside world. He didn't want to get his hopes up, but he figured this had to be good news. Had to be a break.

'Nice of you to drop by, but I'm out of cookies and cake,' Cross said, seeing Kowalski and Shanahan at the same table as before.

'Car with Louisiana license plates seen in your neighborhood the day before Marissa was killed.'

It didn't make sense to Cross. Someone drove up here to kill her. Cross was banking on either Clarkson or O'Connor. That suggested either Mom or Billy Dean or someone he hadn't the privilege to meet during his brief stay in that exotic city. Mom had some boys willing to protect her. What motive would Billy Dean have? Moreover, that would mean Billy Dean would have to have driven up twice. He was in his shop after the LaSalle murder and before Marissa was killed.

'What kind of car?'

'Big, old and dusty,' Shanahan said. 'Ring any bells?'

'I didn't think to look around for cars when I was there. If one of Momma Manchette's boys did it, they probably would have had a better ride. But I have an idea. You said you picked up my bag at the airport?'

'I did,' Shanahan said.

'What's with the strange-looking dagger?' Kowalski asked.

'Get prints from the dagger,' Cross said, 'and for the hell of it, from the wine glass in my house, the one in the sack in the bed-room.'

'What?' Kowalski looked confused.

'Match them with prints taken from the house.'

'Rafferty said he sanitized the place,' Shan-ahan said.

'He sanitized every spot he touched. If you remember, he said he always came in through the garage. He wouldn't have wiped the front door or either side of the door from the garage to the back. If he knew he didn't touch them, he wouldn't need to wipe them off.'

'You know who did it?' Kowalski asked.

'Maybe. But I kind of hope I'm wrong.'

'You want to get out of here?' Kowalski asked.

'Yeah. I know.'

Kowalski looked at Shanahan.

'Maybe I can take the dagger to Swann,' Shanahan said. 'You have information on this friend of yours?'

'If you need it, I have it.'

The door to Swann's office was open. Inside was Swann, leaning forward on his desk. Rafferty sat in front of the desk, arms folded across his chest. He wasn't happy. Swann's eye caught Shanahan, and Rafferty followed Swann's gaze. There was a split second of panic that crossed Rafferty's face.

'What's up?' Swann said, standing up, walking toward Shanahan. He was coming out of his office. That meant he wasn't inviting Shanahan in.

'Prints off this,' Shanahan said, handing him the dagger still in the sock, 'might land your killer in the LaSalle case.'

Swann was quiet. He looked back into his office. Rafferty was looking at the floor. Swann shut the door.

'OK, I'll say it again. What's up?' This time there was a threat in his tone.

'You want to find the murderer, maybe this will help.'

Swann scratched his head. 'What do you think I'm going to find?'

'Match the prints on the dagger with the prints you got from the scene.'

'We didn't get any prints,' Swann said.

'You got a few.'

'You know way too much.'

'I don't know anything. Just checking out some angles.'

'Your little senior hobby, right?' Swann said.

'Another thing. You got the wrong guy on Mrs Clarkson, and you know it.'

Swann closed his eyes, took a deep breath. 'I want to think so, but I can't read between the lines here.' He let down his guard. 'I know cops who could murder someone. There's one sitting in my office. I also knew

306

Cross when he was on the force. He's not one of them. That was part of his problem. You can have a little too much heart sometimes.'

'What are you going to do about it?'

'They're connected, aren't they?' Swann asked.

'There's a Louisiana connection,' Shanahan said. 'With the victims. They knew each other.'

'You're going to have to talk. You know that.'

'No I don't. I don't mean to tell you your business...'

'But you're going to, aren't you?'

'Get the prints off the knife,' Shanahan said. 'Let's see where they take us.'

'You're walking a tightrope, aren't you?' Swann almost grinned. 'I can't believe you two are on the same side.'

'I don't know what you are talking about.'

Swann opened the door to his office. Rafferty looked up.

'Swann,' Shanahan called him sharply. 'Do what you always do. Do right.'

The day had heated up. Another in a steady stream of steamy August afternoons. Shanahan could feel the heat rise from the sidewalk as he approached his car. The door handle was too hot to touch. He left the car door open as he sat inside and started the car. The interior heat could melt glass. For the first few moments the air-conditioning seemed to add to the inferno, but after a few moments he felt the air turn. He was about to shut the door when he noticed Rafferty huffing and puffing toward him.

Out of breath, face covered with perspiration, he leaned in. 'What's going on?' Rafferty said.

'Don't know.'

'You know something and I have a right to know,' he said.

'You don't have a right to anything, Rafferty. I'm not on your payroll. The guy who is helping you is behind bars for a murder he didn't commit.'

'I know,' Rafferty said, pulling a bright white handkerchief from his back pocket. He wiped his forehead, then the rest of his face.

'What are you going to do about it?'

'I talked to Swann,' Rafferty said. 'In confidence. He said he'd hold on to the information for a while. Not a long while, though. The murders are connected, Shanahan. Swann believes that. And that means Cross didn't do it. Just need some time. I need some help.'

'Something's in the works. Let's see what happens,' Shanahan said.

'What did you tell Swann?'

'Gotta go,' Shanahan said. He pulled the door closed. He didn't have to go. He had no place to go, except home or to Harry's. No trails to follow. No suspects to interview. Dead end. If the fingerprints didn't open up something, he couldn't see how he could help.

Rafferty never looked so sad and lonely. He had nowhere to go either, except down, Shanahan thought. He repressed an urge to help the beleaguered cop.

The day passed. Shanahan mowed the front lawn with his hand mower, temporarily pulling up the 'For Sale' sign. It was a small patch of grass, as was the back lawn, now that more than half of it was taken up with ferns, iris, and hydrangea. He'd have to get a power mower for the new place. He nursed a bottle of Miller High Life, stopping every couple of passes to sip. Fact was there wasn't much to mow. The grass gave up growing in August, like everything else. Just too much trouble.

Shanahan mulled over everything – Rafferty, Clarkson, O'Connor, Cross – as he worked.

By late afternoon, Shanahan had returned to his earlier view. He had no idea who was involved, why, or where to go next.

He called Swann. Swann was out.

He didn't remember whether it was his turn to fix dinner or not, but Maureen was having a long day and Shanahan had nothing else to do. He needed something to keep him busy.

He drove toward town, picked up some swordfish at O'Malia's. He wanted a firm fish because he wanted to grill it. Fish, some rice, some salad. He tried to work up a little excitement. He picked up a Chardonnay he knew Maureen liked. It was California Chardonnay. Maureen said it was buttery. He'd take her word for it. He hadn't thought much about wine tasting like butter.

At home he put the wine in the refrigerator and took a shower. He heard the phone ring, but by the time he heard it, it was too late to answer it.

He slipped on some lightweight khakis and loose-fitting shirt, grabbed another beer, and hit the button on the answer machine.

'The bad news is that the fingerprint matches nothing on file,' Swann said. 'The good news, the prints on the fancy knife match some prints found at Bay Colony. Where in the hell did you get the knife? You can't keep holding out. Call me!'

Instead of dialling Swann, he called Kowalski. No answer at the office. He called Kowalski at home.

'Kowalski,' came the abrupt answer.

'Cross knows who did it. The prints on the knife match the prints on the back door of LaSalle's place. Unless Cross was carrying the knife with him when he went to New

Orleans, he picked it up there. Our killer has New Orleans connections.'

Kowalski was quiet.

'The car was from New Orleans,' Shanahan reminded Kowalski and himself.

That took the spotlight off Clarkson, Shanahan thought. And probably Rafferty. It also eliminated another possibility that Shanahan had entertained. It was that Marissa killed LaSalle and then someone, perhaps in revenge, killed Marissa. Rafferty? It was a thought. It made sense. But when you think about something for a long time, a lot of things make sense.

'Let's get to Cross,' Kowalski said. 'It's late, but I think I can get in. I'll call you.'

Rafferty was in first class. How the police lieutenant could afford such luxury, especially with a same-day ticket, Shanahan could not understand. But the old detective was glad he wasn't sitting with the corpulent cop on the early-morning flight to New Orleans.

A taxi took them to the hotel Cross recommended. They weren't sure they were going to be in the Crescent City overnight; but they needed a place to use as a base. And it would come in handy if they had to stay over.

Rafferty placed a call to the New Orleans Police Department, was transferred to something called 'Homicide Investigators Support Unit', and then to some cop at the First

District headquarters on Rampart Street.

'We can go now,' Rafferty said, hanging up, and heading for the bathroom to wash his face in cool water. He'd already ramped up the air-conditioning.

Outside, Shanahan realized he'd left unbearable heat and humidity for death-causing heat and humidity. They caught a taxi, went less than half a mile and were there – First District Headquarters. They could have walked. On the other hand, Rafferty, in his suit and tie, was no doubt glad for the three minutes of air-conditioning.

Just a few blocks from the hotel, the police station was nonetheless in another world. Rampart separated a flat any-city-anywhere kind of neighborhood from the cozy European nature of the French Quarter.

A tall, thin cop in a light suit, but with telltale shoes, took them into a conference room that didn't look much different from a room in Indianapolis' police department. Another policeman, McCavity, who looked like whatever he did, he did the hard way, joined them. Barbeaux, who looked bored and simply nodded as Rafferty unfolded the tale, was the thin one.

'Thought we should check in,' Rafferty said.

'Good idea,' said McCavity without feeling.

'We need to talk to this Billy Dean. Not sure he's gonna want to be talked to.'

McCavity nodded. The cop named Barbeaux said nothing. His face said nothing.

'We'll go with you,' McCavity said after a long, awkward silence. 'Barbeaux, check his record. Billy Dean you say?'

'Yep,' Rafferty said. Rafferty followed Barbeaux, leaving Shanahan with McCavity.

Shanahan stayed out of the conversation. Police generally disapprove of private eyes meddling in anything but domestic unrest, maybe not even then.

'You're private, huh?' McCavity asked, cocking his head, suggesting that he was about to give Shanahan a little test.

'Yeah.'

'How'd you get into that?'

'Retired from the Army. Intelligence.'

'See action?'

'Too much,' Shanahan said.

'OK,' McCavity said, nodding. 'So what's with your friend Rafferty?'

'He's not a friend. He's just on the case.'

'Pretty much of a dandy, isn't he?'

'He likes fine things,' Shanahan said.

McCavity smiled. 'The victim was Michael LaSalle, you said?'

Shanahan nodded.

'He hung around the Manchettes. Questionable character. LaSalle, I mean.'

'When we talk with this Billy character,' McCavity said, 'you guys might want to let us do most of the talking.'

'This is too easy,' Barbeaux said as he rummaged through the big 1980s Lincoln.

Litter occupied front and back seats as well as the floor. Barbeaux had found charge slips for food and gas purchases.

'All the way up to Indianapolis and back,' he said, tossing them back and rummaging through a few more papers.

He backed out of the front seat, examining more charge slips.

'Twice,' he said. He looked at McCavity, who looked at Shanahan.

'There are two murders,' Shanahan said.

'Two different times?' McCavity asked.

'Yep.'

'This evidence going to hold up?' Rafferty asked.

Barbeaux put the receipts back in the front seat. 'We'll call and get a warrant. Meanwhile, let's talk to Mr Dean.'

Barbeaux went in through the back door. McCavity went around to the front.

Rafferty just stood there. 'I don't know if I can talk to that motherfucker,' he said finally.

Shanahan could see Rafferty's chest rising and falling in slow, exaggerated movements.

'You don't have to,' Shanahan said.

Rafferty shook his head. 'Why do I feel this way? Why the fuck do I care?'

'I'm going in,' Shanahan said.

# Twenty-Two

Shanahan stood by the door. Rafferty sat on the desk, shoving the shop's computer to one corner of it, making room for his large frame. He glared at the floor. The tall guy in the light suit stood behind Billy Dean, a phone in his hand ordering a warrant to search the car. McCavity faced the suspect up close and personal.

'Mr Dean,' McCavity said softly, so softly Shanahan had to move closer to hear what he was saying. 'These fine gentlemen from the state of Indiana have brought us some disturbing news. They say they have your prints on the back door of a house in which a Mr Michael LaSalle was slain in the very prime of his life.'

Billy Dean looked like he hadn't slept for a few days or was worrying a great deal about something, or both. Shanahan noticed a zombie-like look on his face. Nothing would phase him.

'I see that you might not be understanding the gravity of the situation,' McCavity continued. 'My guess is, Mr Dean, that we can place you in Indianapolis at the time of Mr

315

LaSalle's demise.'

McCavity looked up at Rafferty, then back to Billy Dean.

'You knew him – Mr LaSalle, I mean – didn't you?'

The young man nodded slowly. 'Yes, I did.' The tone was polite, deferential.

'And you killed him?' McCavity said, without a threat in his voice.

The young man again nodded slowly. 'Yes, I did.'

Rafferty got up, moved toward Shanahan and motioned for Shanahan to get involved. Rafferty took Shanahan's place at the door.

'This boy, LaSalle, did something to you, didn't he?' McCavity said.

Billy Dean stared blankly ahead.

'I see. He betrayed you, didn't he?' McCavity asked that so gently, he made it seem like it was only he and Billy Dean in the room.

Billy Dean didn't answer.

'Mr Barbeaux here is going to read you your rights,' McCavity said. 'It's a formality. We want to make sure you're being treated fairly.'

Barbeaux read them. Billy Dean was quiet while the words were spoken, but it was doubtful he was hearing anything at all. His mind had gone inside.

'You went up to Indianapolis twice,' Shanahan said.

316

McCavity shrugged.

Billy Dean didn't answer. He was gone.

Rafferty stayed in New Orleans as bureaucrats from the two cities worked out extradition. The search warrant had been executed and Shanahan was allowed to bring copies of all of Billy Dean's travel receipts with him when he flew out the next morning. They corresponded to the dates of the murders of both LaSalle and Clarkson.

Though he hadn't confessed to the murder of Clarkson – nor was it clear what motive Billy Dean had to do either of them – it seemed to Shanahan that the whole affair was nearly over. He was eager to get back. Unfortunately by late afternoon, Shanahan couldn't get a flight back unless he was willing to buy the plane, so he took another room at the hotel for the evening with a flight out the next morning. In the lobby, Rafferty invited Shanahan to dinner. Shanahan declined.

'Don't get to New Orleans that often. The food is great,' Rafferty said. 'Please? I owe you. Let me make a down payment.'

'Don't go soft on me, Rafferty.'

Rafferty grinned. 'I'll knock on your door at seven,' Rafferty said. He started to leave. 'Oh, I'll call Swann, see what we can do about Cross. I don't think he can do much until we get Dean up there.'

In his room, Shanahan turned on the television, searched for a ball game. The Cincinnati Reds were playing the Texas Rangers. How could he watch a game in which he hoped both teams would lose? He flicked to CNN. Two silver-headed men in gray suits were talking about the Middle East. Seems the turmoil had been on television news since they invented television. The discussion of more failed peace talks faded into background noise. He clicked off the TV, sat on the edge of the bed, spreading out the copies Barbeaux had made of Billy Dean's receipts and the list of other items found in the car.

The reason Billy Dean kept the receipts was the same as the reason he kept empty Burger King bags, candy bar wrappers and Budweiser cans. He was too lazy to throw them away. It was a stupid thing for him to be so lazy, especially in light of the danger they held for him. The trail was tracked by all of the computer-printed receipts with dates and times and addresses. The whole trip, from Indianapolis to New Orleans and back and then again, was virtually time-stamped thanks to the new information society. They had him.

Shanahan had no doubt poor Billy Dean committed both murders. Why was a different question and more difficult to answer. Could be one of those mystifying motives like love or something more base like revenge. Perhaps Cross could shed some light on motive. He had a broader picture of the players and their relationships.

Shanahan showered, got into some fresh clothes, realized he was impatient to leave. He checked his watch. He had dinner with Rafferty, a night in a strange hotel, away from Maureen, and a long ride with a change of planes before he could get back and wrap things up. He wasn't happy.

They had dinner in the hotel restaurant, an elegant if not ostentatious room. Tables also spilled outside, though no one was out there. Not only was it earlier than the chic meet to eat, he thought, but it was also damned hot out there. Actually, there were only a few dining inside.

Rafferty ordered the soft-shell crab and crayfish. Shanahan, who despite his world travels in the military remained singularly unadventurous in the food department, ordered steak.

'You'll get him out right away?' Shanahan said.

'I've made the call. Swann is working on it,' Rafferty said, perusing the wine list to ensure he had made the right decision.

'You must be glad it's over,' Shanahan said.

Rafferty didn't respond. Shanahan didn't really think it was over. Despite what they knew, it didn't seem over.

'You must be relieved,' Shanahan said, needling Rafferty for a response to his first comment.

'Yeah, I guess,' Rafferty said.

'Did they ever trace LaSalle back to you?'

Rafferty looked up, unhappily it seemed. 'I think we can put all that behind us.'

'You mean you, behind you,' Shanahan said.

'Whatever,' Rafferty said.

'You just going to go back to the way things were?'

'What's changed, Shanahan? Back to the way it was. Only thing is that now you and Cross and Swann know something about me you didn't know before. As far as everybody else is concerned, I'm the same old asshole. What's with you? Suddenly you're awful talkative.'

'You invited me to dinner,' Shanahan said.

'I owe you something, don't I?' The waiter came with the wine for Rafferty – a bottle all of his own – and a bottle of beer for Shanahan. 'Thanks,' Rafferty said, without looking up.

If one drove, it was 800 miles from New Orleans to Indianapolis. By air, it was 700. For Shanahan, it was 700 miles too many and however many hours it took, it took too long. He never liked this idea of travelling, not being able to just step outside when he needed to stretch his legs and get some fresh air. He didn't like the idea of a layover, either, and the whole process of boarding all over again. He quickly exhausted the thin in-flight magazine so he returned to the bits of paper the New Orleans police had copied for him.

This time he found something more than a little curious. One receipt dated after the murder of Michael LaSalle and the other the morning of the murder of Marissa Man-chette was more than a little curious. The receipts came from the same gas station for a fill-up, some smokes, some chips, and a couple of bottles of Mountain Dew. What surprised Shanahan, though only for one sickening moment, was the gas station's location.

Michael LaSalle was murdered in his house on the city's far northwest side. Maris-sa Clarkson lived in Carmel, Indiana, pretty far due north of the city. Broad Ripple, the scene of the second murder, was also on the north side, quite a distance from each other. The problem was that the gas station was on the far northeast side, close to an address Shanahan had visited a couple of times.

Shanahan was glad that Maureen was wait-ing on the other side of the security gate. There she was among those who were waiting to pick up family and friends, or, in some cases, unknown business visitors. There were signs that said 'Thompson', and 'Matsumoto'. He wasn't nearly as thrilled to see his beloved, once he saw, her holding a sign that said 'Poopsie'.

Behind her was Howie Cross, giving Shanahan a big, intentionally goofy grin. Shanahan's mood lightened considerably, not for the embarrassing display of humour, but that Cross was out.

'While you were *enroute*,' Cross said, as Shanahan kissed Maureen, 'the New Orleans police were able to extract a complete confession. Billy Dean killed both Michael LaSalle and Marissa.'

'Why?' Shanahan asked.

'They're still working on that,' Cross said. 'They tell me he keeps saying "it's personal".'

'Deeply personal,' Maureen said.

'My question is how did he find them?' Howie asked as they walked through the garage toward the car.

'Young Billy didn't know where LaSalle was?' Shanahan asked.

'No. He claimed he was devastated when his friend disappeared and took it hard that Mr LaSalle might be in hiding. And Marissa? She was about as undercover as anyone could get. Changed cities a couple of times. Changed her name. Changed sex.'

'Somebody told him,' Shanahan said, knowing pretty well who it was.

Shanahan opened the car door for Maureen in front. Cross climbed in the back seat. Shanahan got behind the wheel.

Cross was relieved. Life was back to normal or predictably abnormal. He had renewed affection for his little home tucked away on a residential street. September was coming; it would be cooler. October would follow and there would be leaves to rake and gutters to clean. The air would be brisk and breathable.

Shanahan dropped Maureen at the new house near Pleasant Run Parkway and he swung by the Butler Tarkington area to take Cross home.

'Your friend, Rafferty,' Shanahan said. 'Maybe he'll drop by to thank you.'

'I'll settle for what he owes me,' Cross said.

'Your time in jail? Billable hours?'

'I think time in the shower is time and a half. Where are you headed?'

'I promised someone I'd pay them a visit, depending on how things turned out. And that's the way they turned out.'

# Twenty-Three

'You're going somewhere?' Shanahan said to Father O'Connor when the priest opened the door of the rectory. Behind him, in the entryway, were four pieces of mismatched luggage.

'I thought I made myself clear,' the priest said.

'You did. So did I.'

The priest looked at Shanahan warily. But his deep breaths showed rising anger.

'You probably want to know,' Shanahan continued, 'that Billy Dean confessed to killing both Michael LaSalle and Marissa Clarkson.'

The priest wasn't shocked, but his eyes moved, seemingly searching for some meaning in the news.

'You knew Billy Dean, right?' Shanahan continued.

The priest thought too long, then finally said, 'Sure. Of course I did. One of the boys in my parish.'

'Yes, along with Michael LaSalle and Mark Manchette. Sensitive little boys, all of them.'

'I'm very sorry to hear that. I guess that

puts an end to a sad and unfortunate affair.'

'I doubt it,' Shanahan said, nodding toward the inside. 'Why don't you and I have a little talk?'

'I don't think so. I'm busy. Very busy right now. And we have nothing to talk about, do we?' He backed into the room and started to close the door.

'No,' Shanahan said, forcing the door open, surprising the priest. Shanahan moved in, pushed the priest back against the wall. 'We're going to talk.'

'Listen,' the priest said. He was younger and clearly stronger than Shanahan, but he seemed frightened.

'No,' Shanahan said. 'I'll talk and then you'll talk.' He pushed the door shut and nudged Father O'Connor into the living area. 'Sit down.'

'I'm going to call the police...'

Shanahan didn't wait for him to finish, he pushed him back so that the priest fell into the upholstered chair.

'Here's my take,' Shanahan said. 'When I'm done you can correct me. You got a hold of Billy Dean and told him how LaSalle used him, screwed him out of his money for the business they were in, how LaSalle laughed at him, made fun of him and then you told him where LaSalle lived.'

'A motive for murder? Come on?'

'You knew Billy Dean well. He was one of

the sensitive little boys you controlled and molested. You knew what buttons to push, didn't you?'

'You're being absurd.'

'You played up the fact that LaSalle deserted him. Michael LaSalle was the only person Billy Dean loved and had faith in.'

'I don't have to listen to this nonsense.'

'Other than you. Billy Dean had faith in you, didn't he? You two kept in touch. And when the time was right you told him about LaSalle.'

'Goodbye, Mr Shanahan.'

'Billy stayed here,' Shanahan said, 'didn't he?'

The priest said nothing.

'Both times,' Shanahan said. 'And when you called him again, you tied Marissa into all this. What did you do? Did you tell him it was her idea for LaSalle to leave New Orleans? That they were in this together in some way?'

'You don't make an ounce of sense.'

'What did Marissa do? Did she change her mind about testifying against you for molestation once she figured out you were responsible for Michael LaSalle's death? What did you tell Billy Dean?'

Father O'Connor started to get up; Shanahan nudged him back in his seat.

'You told him something. What? What did you tell him that caused him to drive back up here again – 800 miles each way?'

'I cared for those kids,' Father O'Connor said.

'You did, didn't you?' Shanahan understood. 'Young Michael was in love with you. Marissa wasn't going to turn you in until she found out you had Michael killed. And Billy Dean? He'd do anything for you. You were all he had left. You manipulated him into killing and he thought he did it. Or is he taking the blame because he's loyal to you?'

Father O'Connor looked away, then down at the floor.

'Was it your idea to set up Cross for the crime?'

The priest looked up slowly. 'You've underestimated Billy Dean. He's quite creative, all on his own.'

'I don't know what kind of silly-ass justification you use for your conscience. But you killed them. Both of them.'

'I killed no one,' he said.

'Yes, you did. Poor Billy Dean was only the gun. You aimed and fired.'

'There you go,' the priest said as if to confirm, in a kindly way, Shanahan's accusations or just that he wasn't going to argue anymore. 'But what you think doesn't matter.' He stood up. 'It doesn't matter what anyone thinks.' He straightened his jacket. 'I'm catching a plane in a couple of hours, Mr Shanahan. I'm going to Italy, called to

Rome, as they say. Vatican City, to be even more specific. A kind of diplomatic immunity comes with the new job.'

Shanahan felt like the air was sucked from his lungs.

Father O'Connor smiled, walked to the door. 'You couldn't prove it, anyway,' he said, opening it, nodding toward the sunny exit.

'Tomorrow or the next day you put on the robes,' Shanahan said, 'and you're a representative of the Lord.'

'Yeah well, some people say "clothes make the man", Mr Shanahan.'

'There are days when I really want to believe eternal hell exists,' Shanahan said, starting toward the door. 'But in case there isn't,' Shanahan said before catching Father O'Connor against one side of his nose with a punch.

The priest went down, looked up angrily, but made no attempt to get up.

'Too little, too late,' Shanahan said, 'I'm afraid.'

# Twenty-Four

Sunday morning, Shanahan and Maureen sat in the kitchen. Shanahan sipped his coffee, and scanned half of the thick Sunday paper. Maureen sorted through the other half.

It was awkward. The only things not packed away in boxes were the toaster and coffee maker. Einstein wandered around the disarray perturbed. Such things didn't bother Casey, who found a sunny spot on the kitchen linoleum to sleep. Why was it, Shanahan wondered, that animals of advanced years slept more and humans, like himself, slept less?

'Take a look at this,' Maureen said, folding a section of the newspaper to highlight the story she wanted him to read.

The headline read: 'Clarkson Resigns Family Values Post'.

It was a long story on the front of the second section. A picture of Clarkson with his kids accompanied a narrative about the man's life and loss and the importance of raising his children without his wife.

One quote struck Shanahan:

The Lord giveth and the Lord taketh away. I have been given a new direction. There are greater concerns for Christians, I believe, than defining what is family and what is not. We all belong to the human family. And there are desperate needs around the world. Famine, war, floods, slavery are all too present on this earth. The time I have left, I plan to devote to these issues.

'Why is it we all have to learn the hard way?' Maureen said.

'Father O'Connor and H. Ray Clarkson. Two men of God going in different directions.'

'Kind of an odd, sad balance in that,' Maureen said.

The heavy pounding on the door wouldn't stop. Try as he did, Cross was unable to muffle the sound with the pillow. He got up, slipped on his jeans and walked barefoot to the door.

'Christ, Rafferty. Why in the hell aren't you in bed? Or in church?'

'It's eleven, Cross. When are you going to grow up?'

Rafferty brushed by Cross, uninvited.

It was then that Cross noticed the dog. A boxer. Still young, probably not quite a year.

'Who's your friend?'

'I got custody,' Rafferty said. 'My kid now, I guess.'

'Good thing he takes after his mother,' Cross said.

'You have some coffee?' Rafferty asked.

Cross rubbed his dry eyes. 'Coming up, sir. How would you like your eggs?'

'Over easy.'

'Fat chance. Are you on duty?'

'No.'

'Day off?'

'Yeah,' Rafferty said, following Cross into the kitchen.

'Then why are you wearing a suit and tie?'

'I always wear a suit and tie.'

'What do you wear to bed, a cardigan?'

'I came to pay you for your work,' Rafferty said. 'You could be more civil.'

He pulled a thick roll of green from his inside breast pocket. Hundreds, it appeared to Cross.

'Cash, I hope you don't mind.'

'Not a problem.' Cross put the water on to boil. Given the situation and how long he wanted it to last, he'd make instant coffee.

The dog, after sniffing around, came back into the kitchen. Cross put down a bowl of water.

'Ten thousand. Submit your expenses. I'll pick up those as well.'

'That's pretty generous,' Cross said.

'Not really. Give some to Shanahan. And...'

Whatever he was going to say wasn't easy.

'And you want to buy my silence?' Cross asked.

'Yeah. That too.'

'You don't need to pay for that. That's your business.'

'Still,' Rafferty said, putting the stack of bills on the counter top.

'How will I pay my income tax?' Cross said, smiling. He put a teaspoon full of freeze-dried coffee in each cup.

'Your problem.'

'So how long you going to stay in the closet?'

'It's not so bad in there,' Rafferty said. He shook his head. 'Unlucky at love anyway. So what would I do? You know? The love of my life, turns out that he...'

He didn't need to finish the sentence. Cross understood.

'Been there. More than once. Anyway, you got the dog.'

'I got the dog,' Rafferty said. He smiled. 'I think this relationship will work out.'

Sunday afternoon, Cross brought two bottles of champagne and enough glasses for the four of them. Harry brought a case of Miller High Life beer in the clear bottles. The tablecloth was spread out on the dark hardwood floor of the living room.

'To your new home!' Cross said, pouring the bubbly into the glasses.

Cross's voice echoed.

Casey's steps sounded like a couple of tap dancers as he moved about on the rugless floor and empty space. Einstein, moving about on his old, creaky bones, investigated the kitchen while Maureen dipped up some baked beans and potato salad to go with the fried chicken.

Shanahan looked around for something to sit on. Sitting on the floor promised to be at best uncomfortable if not downright painful. He found a three-legged footstool and a fairly sturdy wooden box in the garage. He was sure Harry, and his bony butt, wouldn't be able to maneuvre a floor seat either.

'He victimized them twice,' Cross said to Shanahan who balanced himself on the stool and politely sipped the champagne before switching to beer.

'Get them while their young and destroy them when they get old enough to threaten him,' Shanahan said.

Life was unfair, Shanahan thought. He knew that. And there are always loose ends. Nothing ever really ends; certainly nothing ends with everything all tied up neatly in a bow.

'How did Billy Dean get into Bay Colony without his car showing up on the video camera?'

'He didn't come by car,' Shanahan said. 'He came by boat.'

'What?' Harry asked.

'There's a little dock across the street. He pulled his kayak up on dry land late that night, crossed the street, went in through the back. It's a gated community, not a fenced-in community.'

'How did he know to do that?' Cross asked.

'Same way he found out LaSalle was in Indianapolis. Billy Dean was comfortable on the water. And Father O'Connor knew all about rowboats, kayaks, sail boats. Probably knew where to find them at Eagle Creek Park on the reservoir.'

Maureen came in with two of the plates, handed one to Harry and one to Cross and went back for the other two.

'Nice place,' Harry said. 'Feels good, you know. You two will be happy here, I know it.'

Life had been good to Shanahan lately. He had made his peace with the memory of his late wife, Elaine. He had gotten to know his son and his grandson. Maureen was incredible and now they had this fine home the two of them could work on. He felt a little guilty thinking that things had been going so well for him. A little guilt. A little seed of Catholic guilt remained, didn't it?

Not that he thought a lot about it, but death was never far from his mind either. He could die now and feel as if there was very little left to make right – at least of those things he could make right.

The thought of his brother flickered across his brain.

Almost.

# ACKNOWLEDGEMENTS

Writing is a lonely job, people say. And unlike a filmmaker or a playwright, novelists require little assistance as they create. But for many, me included, there are others who contribute mightily to the process all along the way. My brothers, Richard, Robbin and Ryan, have all read early drafts and offered valuable insights. I also thank friends who have done the same or helped in other ways – among them David Anderson, Terri Crane, John Fleener, Douglas Varchol, Karen Watt, and Bud and Fran Johns. Thanks to Ruth Cavin at St. Martins Press for first publishing the Deets Shanahan series and to Edwin Buckhalter at Severn House for publishing Shanahan's most recent adventures.